The Macken Charm

D0873303

OTHER BOOKS BY JACK HODGINS

Spit Delaney's Island
The Invention of the World
The Resurrection of Joseph Bourne
The Barclay Family Theatre
The Honorary Patron
Left Behind in Squabble Bay
Innocent Cities
Over Forty in Broken Hill
A Passion for Narrative

The Macken Charm

• a   n o v e l   b y •

JACK HODGINS

M&S

For various types of assistance, the author wishes to thank
William Bell, Doris Child, Allan Cram, Heidi Hodgins, and
Bob Wakulich, as well as his parents, Stan and Reta Hodgins.

Canadian Cataloguing in Publication Data

Hodgins, Jack, 1938–
The Macken charm
ISBN 0-7710-4185-3
I. Title.

PS8565.03M33 1995   C813'.54   C95-931723-6
PR9199.3.H63M3 1995

Typesetting by M&S, Toronto
Printed and bound in Canada on acid-free paper

The publishers acknowledge the support of the Canada Council and the
Ontario Arts Council for their publishing program.

A Douglas Gibson Book

McClelland & Stewart Inc.
The Canadian Publishers
481 University Avenue
Toronto, Ontario
M5G 2E9

1 2 3 4 5   99 98 97 96 95

for Brent and Joy

I

By Macken standards, Glory's funeral was meant to be plain – the usual day-long reunion on the site of the vanished hotel. But anyone who knows the Mackens knows they couldn't manage a simple funeral without letting it jump the tracks and head for somewhere new. Sooner or later, things would get out of hand.

Mackens have always had their own approach to the special occasions in life. Tom Macken's retirement party put seven people in hospital, but not before an inconvenient creek had been slightly rerouted and a baseball diamond built where an abandoned shingle mill had stood the day before. When Billy's Leila was married in the great white lacy dress that cost her two months' salary at the Moonlight Café, Billy delivered her to the church in the back of the same Ford truck he used to take his Holsteins up to Coleman's bull – wooden side rails up and all. Some laughed, some didn't, but no one was surprised. It may even have been the bride's idea, to suggest what she thought of the groom. She laughed loudest, standing with her fistful of flowers behind the cab.

This sort of good-natured excess goes down a whole lot better at a wedding than at a funeral. People went to Glory's funeral braced. Mackens had never known what to make of that city-bred beauty, with her long fingers and dreamy walk and Rita Hayworth looks. She'd descended upon them from another world and they had never grown relaxed enough around her to be themselves. You hardly dared to guess what might happen now she was gone.

Of course she hadn't just descended. She'd been brought to the Island by Toby, the youngest brother. Glory was Toby's bride, breathtakingly frail and pretty, mysterious as a star. For ten years Toby stood back and grinned. He'd brought them in a prize.

He was a prize himself. A favourite. Not just the family's but the district's too – a hero in his youth. He'd rescued Swampy Aalto off the railroad tracks minutes before the logging train came clanging through town, and tied the famous boozer to the main-street river bridge so he'd be sure to know where he was when he sobered up. He'd been expelled from high school for breaking the arm of a teacher who liked to jab his pointer into distracted students. He'd been captain of the baseball team that defeated Victoria's all-stars and sent them limping home from the brawl that followed the game. When the pitcher with the 30:30 bullet wound in his leg persuaded the police to drop charges, in exchange for an apology and a donation to charity, Toby's photo appeared in the local paper beside an interview. He regretted violence in general but doubted he could shed his natural high spirits. Donations poured in for the cause.

He'd been tree-climbing champion of the Island for a while as well. Toby Macken went to the top of things as naturally as a bubble. You could come upon him sitting on the ridgepole of his little shack at dusk, smoking a hand-rolled cigarette and gazing off through the trees or across the Strait. You might see him stop his lumber truck in town and scale the squat square tower of the fire hall, to call down insults to the passersby. Up there he looked as though he might take flight. At loggers' sports he was always the fastest to scale the spar tree in his climbing gear, but he was never content to ring the bell and come down. Instead he climbed onto the sixteen-inch top, where he teetered, and swung his arms, and broke into a little dance. People whistled and cheered. They also shook their heads: who else but Toby Macken would risk his neck only to make you laugh?

What did he see up there when he danced? That's what people wondered when he stayed up too long, looking out across the world while he shuffled his feet: What does that crazy man see? He never told, he wouldn't tell. No point in asking him either – he'd only laugh in your face. It was impossible to know what he might do at Glory's funeral.

Since all Macken funerals gathered on the grounds of the vanished hotel, this meant that Glory's would take place outside her own front door. When Toby built that three-room tarpaper shack, he'd rested it upon the brick foundation of the burned-down dining-room wing. One door in the middle of the front, one on the side, one six-paned window in each wall – it wasn't much, compared to the handsome structure that stood there once, beneath the heavy boughs of the Douglas firs.

Tarpaper shacks were not so unusual then. Trailer homes hadn't found their way onto the Island in any great numbers yet, to rust like cookie tins beneath the firs while their corrugated-plastic porch roofs collected needles to rot in the rain. Geodesic domes and double-wides hadn't been invented. At least a tarpaper shack, though it was small and might never be finished, was a *house*.

The Island Highway was still a strip of pleasant tarmac in the year of Glory's funeral – 1956. A whole half hour might pass between cars. More than three hours of driving and two hours of steamship away, Vancouver could have been in a foreign country. You expected to see it two or maybe three times in your life: optometrist appointments, the Exhibition. Ferries hadn't yet been built to haul tourists by the thousands every hour across the Strait and set them racing up our roads, trucks and Winnebagos nose to tail from dawn till night. Developers hadn't yet begun to replace stands of timber with cement-walled shopping centres and mini-golf theme parks and rows of shiny Lego houses with treeless yards. Hollywood had not yet even dreamed of taking over our fields and houses for weeks on end in order to film stories pretending to be set in Oregon or Maine. We knew the world went on out there – papers told us. Egypt had seized the Suez Canal, China was gobbling Burma, some sort of trouble was brewing in Hungary, the RCMP were keeping an eye on Russian scientists who worked on floating chunks of ice in the Arctic. But these events had little to do with us. Not much had yet got in. Some of us longed to get out.

I speak of "the Mackens" as though they were a breed apart, but the fact of the matter is that I am a Macken myself. Eddie's eldest, Frieda's. In a family crowd I stood as tall as my father and uncles, but I was the one with hair the colour of iron rust blazing away up top. A speckled nose as well, usually burnt and peeling. They said I'd had a burnt and hungry look about me all my life, dropped in the wrong place by mistake and desperate for a way out.

Well, I hadn't got out yet. I was so anxious to leave I was already more or less packed, but university didn't start until fall. This was only July. Rusty Macken would belong to the family for a few weeks yet. I was, as my father put it, expected to pull my weight.

The morning of Glory's funeral, my mother shook me out

of an uneasy sleep to drive her up to Toby's shack and help her get things started. My dad would not be far behind, once he'd loaded the family car with folding chairs and coffee pots and slabs of plywood meant for makeshift tables.

I wasn't ready for this. No one could be. I'd resisted this particular morning even in my sleep. Awake, I burrowed under blankets as though to escape my own body, electrified with dread. On top of the confusion and grief I'd felt since hearing of Glory's death, there was now the horror of facing Toby. Looking him in the eye. Wondering what he knew.

"I've decided I don't want to go," I announced at the foot of the stairs.

My mother laughed. "I'd rather not go myself." She stacked dishes in a cardboard box. "What makes you any different than the rest of us?"

"I don't feel so hot this morning."

"Just so long as you're strong enough to gather wood and set up picnic tables. Wear jeans for now – something old."

"Suppose I help for a while and leave?"

"Where's the firing squad!" She threw up her hands – mock-exasperation – and searched the kitchen for help. "We've got a traitor here!" She grabbed the broom and aimed from the hip.

"Okay! Okay!" I raised my hands above my head and started back up the stairs.

Tide was out when we got there. My mother lifted her face to breathe in what a soft breeze carried: the salty odour off the beach, of sun-baked kelp and crustacean shells and glittering tide-scrubbed stones. Low sunlight winked off the Strait, and glared from the bone-white heap of driftwood above the high-tide line. Thick fir trunks laid shadow stripes across the coarse pale grass all down the length of the neglected golf course property – larger than some famous battlefields, my father liked to say, and with far more peculiar ghosts.

A narrow tea towel swelled and fluttered from the clothesline by the kitchen door. Glory's battered pickup sat beneath the boughs of a Douglas fir, but not the MACKEN LUMBER three-ton flatbed truck. Uncle Toby was nowhere in sight.

He was not in the shack, not on the beach, he was not on the peak of his roof – which was where I'd expected to find him. He was not on the top of his practice climbing-pole either, which stood near the shack, splintered and shaggy from his spurs. My mother called. Only the seagulls answered.

I knew better than to trust the relief that rushed to fill me. Sooner or later he was bound to show up. All I had gained was some time. I could do what I had to do and then get out, though there'd be an uproar amongst the Mackens when I did.

All around Toby's shack, half-buried in the grass and broom and overgrown roses, were stacks of discoloured lumber sawn at Uncle Toby's mill but never used. Lengths of rusted pipe lay everywhere, a collection of porcelain plumbing fixtures, a bathtub green with slime to the overflow pipe, and rolls of mouldy carpet scavenged for the repairs he'd never got around to doing.

My mother waded in through weeds and amongst the rotting floor joists of the vanished hotel kitchen, and tossed scraps of three-ply off an enormous cast-iron stove. Still connected by a rotted pipe to what was left of the chimney, this tilted relic was crusted with flaky blisters and scabs. With two ovens, a reservoir, and a giant firebox, it was as long as my '50 Meteor sedan. "My gosh, this is worse than I thought," she said. She drew on her gardening gloves and wriggled her fingers like an eager surgeon. "Dirt and fir needles and – look at this – bones! You'd think a mouse could find a better place to die."

"What if nobody comes?" I said.

"They'll come," my mother said. They'd better, she meant.

And lit into the stove with a strip of emery-cloth. "Get out there and bring me some wood."

Broken limbs and chunks of bark were scattered across the yellow stubble – orchard grass and canary grass too starved to form any sod. Brittle fir cones were the size of hand grenades. I wouldn't have to go far for something to burn.

My mother looked at her own reflection in Glory's kitchen window. She turned a little, to check herself in the glass. She'd lost weight – in the spring she'd had a bout with jaundice, scaring us half to death. Her cheeks were hollow still, her skin too pale. She was wearing a flowered cotton housedress until it was time to put on the navy-blue tailored outfit that hung with my graduation suit in the car. Her flat round hat might have been a dyed-blue cow-pie sitting above her Jane Wyman bangs. "I've been too heavy all my life, I might as well enjoy being skinny while it lasts. Some man whistled yesterday, in town – what do you think of that?"

"What man?" I said.

I rolled down my sleeve; bark would leave tiny irritating slivers in your arm. For the morning I'd put on jeans and a white T-shirt, with a tartan shirt hanging loose.

"You think I ought to get sick more often, just to stay slim? I'd forgotten what it's like to have a waist."

"Sonny's coming by to get me," I said, gathering up a few chunks of wood from the grass. "Track-and-field team's going up to the Lower Campbell, to see if anything's biting."

She set her jaw in a way that defied the world to be anything but what she declared it to be. "It wouldn't be like you to let people down."

"I'm busy not letting you down right now. Later I'm getting out." To take the sting from my words, I bonked her lightly on the head with a stick of wood.

Mackens were never much for the usual signs of affection.

Few hugs were given, brief kisses exchanged only at serious departures. Love was never mentioned. And yet occasionally I would grab my mother in a hammerlock and pretend to twist off her head. She would squeal and complain, "Careful, careful, stop it, you know how I bruise!" Laughing all the while. My father would growl: "What're ya doin' there, you stupes?" My mother would soon break free and grab the back of my neck, and shove my head down into the kitchen sink. Then she would turn on the tap.

So she understood the rap to the head. She grabbed my wrist, and twisted my arm up my back. "A traitor *and* a bully! You think I want to be picking slivers out of my head at the funeral?"

"They'll just think your skull sprung a leak," I said, trying to wrench my arm free.

All at once she went glum, and released me, and turned away to brush sad fingers across the top of the stove. She opened the warming-oven door, and then closed it. She rested against the stove and looked up, frowning. Was she surprised to find the rest of the hotel not there?

"You want me to do that for you?" I said. "Maybe you're still too weak."

"I'm not weak at all," she said, getting back to work. "I've got the constitution of a horse. I *know* this great old beast, I learned to cook on it, don't forget."

She'd learned to cook on that old stove when it stood inside the kitchen of Great-Uncle Jim's hotel. The building used to sit beneath the firs, looking across the bay, its cedar shakes painted green, its shutters white, its verandah posts entwined with roses that climbed to the dormer windows. A times I was half-obsessed by this tangle of thorny branches and heavy red blooms, like the mysterious homes of wild and beautiful creatures out of stories.

It was a landmark – horse-and-buggy travellers used to stop for the night on their way to Campbell River. It had even prospered for a while. On tables covered with linen cloths, the uncle had served meals prepared by his widowed sister, until his sister moved away. When horses were replaced by family cars and the government paved the highway, travellers no longer needed to stop. The uncle closed the business and drank. He offered my parents free rent if they'd move in after their wedding and keep him sober. When my father was not at work in the woods, he repaired the roof, mowed the golf course hay, and cut firewood for that stove. It was a peculiar sort of freedom they enjoyed, an exaggerated sense of playing house in an abandoned world. A perfect way to start a marriage, or so they later claimed.

I'd seen the giant woodstove gleaming in its narrow kitchen before the hotel burned down. As a boy I'd wandered through the dining room where tables stood before the row of tall French doors, looking past the driftwood to the breaking waves. Across the bay was the old sailing ship that had been hauled in and sunk for a breakwater, its surviving mast a tilted cross, its weedy barnacle-crusted hull not yet rotted enough for the wind to sing in its ribs, as it was doing now, in the rise and fall of the tides.

Upstairs, I'd explored the thirteen empty bedrooms stripped of everything but bedsteads and sagging mattresses. Movie magazines could sometimes be found in the walls, and the occasional bottle of pills. In pale green light from windows overgrown with briers and leaves, cousins and I had played cowboys-and-Indians in one room, Emergency Ward in another, movie studios in a third and fourth – various sorts of fantasy down the hall.

I was probably conceived in one of the empty bedrooms of that old hotel. I would like to believe I'd been conceived in all of them – the honeymoon had lasted more than a year.

Each room had its own dimensions, each its windowed angle to the world, each its separate volume of possibilities for a life begun there. Why should I have to be just one person all the length of my life?

Nothing was left of that hotel by the time of Glory's funeral, of course. There'd been nothing left of that old thing for years – it burned to the ground in '47. The sea had gone on crashing against the shore as though nothing had changed, but the sheds and stables leaned and sagged and started to fall, and the gate fell off its hinges while Toby lived in his shack with his pretty bride. Nothing remained of the hotel itself but a few rotted floor joists and a heap of fallen rafters, charred and bent, and that enormous cast-iron stove resting at an angle amongst the weeds.

Before I'd brought in any more firewood, Uncle Buddy's pale green Mercury turned in off the highway and came whining down the potholed drive. Buddy seldom got out of second gear. Grace jumped from the car before it had stopped, pulling a flowery cotton smock over her blue silk dress. A dozen sewing needles glistened at the left-hand shoulder, dangling threads of every colour from her heavy bust. While Uncle Buddy parked, she waded through weeds, her great round magnified eyes bulging behind her fishbowl glasses. "I know we promised to bring a rake to clean up this mess but you won't believe me – the bloody thing's been stolen!" She bent over with her hands around a match to light her cigarette.

"By somebody's hog!" Buddy cried this in his thin, excited voice. He slammed his door and came hurrying up behind her, elbows high. "Woke us at three in the morning, rootin' around in the cabbages." He was the family worrier. His bottle of nerve pills bulged in his red-plaid shirt. "Hey, Rusty!" he said, and shook my hand. He shook my hand every time we met, looking pleased and surprised to see me, as though he'd forgotten I lived a mile up the road from his farm.

"Right outside our bedroom window," said Grace. Smoke came shredding out between the words. Under the stove lid went the blown out match. "So I pulled my fur coat over my nightie and –" She paused to remove a speck of tobacco from her tongue. "– grabbed the rake off the porch. That damn pig snatched the handle in his teeth and ran into the bush!"

She doubled up to laugh, a long, steady, nearly soundless wheeze. Then she slipped into a coughing fit she couldn't seem to get out of – *horrack, horrack, horrack!* She stomped one foot on the ground. She flailed her arms above her head like someone drowning. The rest of us waited – this was common.

"Not that I slept a wink," Grace eventually said. "I laid there feeling awful about Glory. That poor sweet beautiful girl!"

I'd rather not even *think* of Glory in public until it was safer to do so – days from now. But how would this be possible where people would be talking of little else? I stacked slabs of bark and branches up my arm to my chin and kept on stacking until I could barely see.

"You'll trip and break your neck," said Uncle Buddy, taking three pieces of bark from the top. He walked beside me, carrying those, his free hand clutched to his chest. "My heart's been floppin' around like a headless chicken since I chased that goldarn pig."

"Last week you were dying of a stomach ulcer," my mother said. "Make up your mind." She resumed her work with the emery-cloth. "While you're waiting to see what kills you, find something to put under these legs – level this stove if you can. Let's get a *move-on* here."

"Wait!" Grace threw out both arms as though to stop events from bowling her over. "Why don't I see Toby anywhere?"

For a moment we looked out at the Strait as though Toby might be bobbing with the gulls on the gentle waves. Purple vetch bloomed amongst the dunegrass between the logs. "He'll show up sooner or later," my mother said.

"I'll bust his kneecaps if he don't," said Grace. She blew cigarette smoke as though exterminating bees in a hollow stump. "I'm kidding! Can you imagine us turning on Toby?"

"Brace yourself," my mother said. She'd shifted her gaze at the sound of an approaching truck. "Here comes Reg's tribe!"

A movie of Glory's funeral (in CinemaScope and Technicolor) would not begin with a mother, son, and ancient stove in the seaside morning breeze. It would open with a series of scenes, all brief, as members of the family awoke in their homes all over the district. Every Macken farm was crossed by one or another of the many nameless, weedy streams that drained into Portuguese Creek, a narrow watercourse that began in a swamp behind the original Macken place and eventually emptied into the river on the outskirts of town. The camera could follow those creeks to make connections: Buddy and Grace already bickering in their canary-yellow house, down near the General Store; Aunt Kitty and Uncle Reg in their ranch-house kitchen (Reg played by fat Burl Ives) with cowboy music wailing from their radio; Avery milking his docile Jersey; Aunt Nora in her four-poster up at the old home place, angry and disapproving even before she remembered what day it was. I couldn't guess where Toby had spent the night. Not in his shack. Maybe the titles could be superimposed upon a shot of his empty bed.

But my Bell & Howell 200 stayed in the glove compartment where it had been for a year – I couldn't afford to replace the motor. Uncle Reg's arrival was not recorded. The pickup came sputtering and honking down the road, three kids standing behind the cab and waving their arms as though they were desperate for help. Mike, Mark, and Jack weren't happy unless your heart was in your mouth. As soon as they'd come to a stop, the boys went screaming off towards the beach. Nothing alive would be safe. Their own black spaniel ran off to hide in the trees.

I gathered up more bark and broken limbs. For a few minutes, Reg and Kitty sat in the cab of the truck, with Aunt Nora between them, while Reg finished singing "The Tennessee Waltz" along with the radio. When the old friend had stolen the sweetheart and the song had come to its end, Kitty and Reg grinned for a moment in silence, then *yahooed*. Not even a funeral could dampen their natural energy. Relatives would not object, though strangers might.

Fat Reg got out from behind the steering wheel – a tight squeeze. Puffing and red-faced from the effort, he rested against the front fender, crossed his arms, and leaned back so far his cowboy hat dangled free while he contemplated the sky. He drew to everyone's attention that it was blue and unbroken by clouds. Reg Macken could look at a sky and tell you whether your lunch would agree with you. "Not a day for selling a horse, but good enough for a funeral."

He rolled his head around to contemplate the direction the boys had gone. "You boys keep a lookout for one another now," he said, though hardly loud enough for the boys to hear as they went screeching over the pile of logs. Seagulls would be caught and mangled, crabs smashed underfoot. Limbs would be torn from starfish to see if they'd really grow back.

In his leather vest, his bandanna, and his blue silk shirt with the flowered yoke, Reg looked like a giant child in a catalogue cowboy outfit – everything but guns. His shiny high-heeled boots had pointed toes, and fancy patterns tooled into the leather.

"You think he'll go to the funeral dressed like that?" my mother asked. For questions like this she didn't move her lips.

"Let's hope he doesn't decide to warble some Wilf Carter song at the grave," I said.

My mother laughed. "Kitty'd kill him first. At least I'd like to think so."

"Kitty's just as liable to do it herself," said Uncle Buddy. "Goodness gracious, I bet they've got their guitars in the back. Russ – you get a chance, go hide them."

Aunt Kitty opened her door and executed one of her expert yodels, by way of saying hello. *Yodel-lay-ay-deeyo!* Beneath her white cowgirl hat, her little pointed face was always so thickly painted that you could never guess what sort of mood she was in. She stood outside the truck, all the fringes and fancy bead-work shivering and shimmering on her leather jacket, and checked her enormous eyelashes in the side-view mirror. "I still can't get it into my head that Glory's gone!" she bellowed. No bigger than a minute, as my mother put it, Kitty had voice enough for a giant, and might break into song or yodel at any moment, causing heads to turn and jaws to drop and dogs to go into fits of barking. "Reg has written her a song that'll break your heart." Her white cowgirl boots had "Kitty" written on the sides, in letters painted to look like the lariat coiled at her hip.

"Steve Bonner phoned," said Uncle Reg. "Says he saw Toby roar through Nanaimo yesterday, ninety miles an hour – heading south." His bottom lip dropped open, shaped like a milk-jug spout.

"Sounds like Toby," Grace said. Sadly, I thought.

"Corky McDougall phoned last night from Victoria," Aunt Kitty said. Her lips were painted to look much larger than nature had meant. She'd also plucked out every hair of her eyebrows and painted dark thin lines higher up her forehead.

She looked permanently surprised. "Says he seen Toby downtown, drunk as a skunk. Some woman on his arm."

"Oh dear," my mother said.

"We'll just have to hope he sobered up before he started home," said Uncle Reg.

What would Toby do? was on everyone's mind. Toby tended to overreact, especially when he was disappointed by life. When a fellow who'd worked for him lost his legs in a car accident, Toby drove the car over a cliff to get rid of it, and was badly hurt himself. When a buddy drowned in the river, Toby stole dynamite and a Public Works grader and started to punish the river by filling it in. It took police and several hours of talking to stop him. Naturally he would not let the death of his wife go unmarked.

I had my own reasons for fearing what Toby might do. I knew how quick he was to place blame. I'd been with him when he stole the dynamite, and helped him hijack the grader, though he'd sent me home before he punished the river. This time I would just as soon put a good safe distance between us, since I was already more than halfway convinced of my own awful share in the guilt. Toby could make things worse.

Aunt Nora had stayed rooted to the truck seat all this time, looking as stern and stubborn as the Dowager Queen while she fingered her pearls and waited for someone to help her get out. Why should she do anything for herself?

Kitty helped. "Come outa there." She stuck her thin sharp elbow in for Aunt Nora to hold, and winked at the rest of us.

Aunt Nora was the oldest surviving Macken and the only sister. She lived alone on the farm their parents had carved out of the bush, and took a certain amount of deference and pampering from the family as her due. She expected deference from everyone else as well, of course, which was why the world was such a disappointment. Non-Mackens didn't know what she expected.

Uncle Buddy knew. While Nora stood by the truck, he went over to kiss her cheek. As usual, she looked surprised and flattered, as though she couldn't understand why she was the object of this masculine attention, even as she peered around for more. I knew what was expected too, but hung back long enough to give her a chance to pretend I wasn't there. "Where's Martin and Avery?" she said. "Where's Eddie?"

"It's early yet," my mother said. "Eddie will be here any minute."

"Don't expect Dennis," Nora said, pulling her dark cardigan down around her hips. We knew what she meant. Dennis didn't go to things. He'd been known as the family loner all his life. He hated crowds. Though he hadn't exactly courted my mother, it was said that he'd made cow eyes at her for a while when he was young. Nora had put a stop to that. "The boy was born to be a bachelor, like Uncle Ottawa-Clive."

Uncle Buddy hoisted cases of Lucky Lager and Phoenix Export out of the bed of Reg's truck, and hurried across to the icebox on the front porch.

"No sign of Toby, either, but he'll be here," said Uncle Reg. "You won't see him miss a chance to play to a crowd."

"Poor boy," Aunt Nora said. Toby was twenty years younger than she was. "He must feel awful."

From her brothers' wives Nora expected little, since she thought none of them was up to much, looking as hard as she did for their flaws. "Naturally Frieda was the first one here!" Frieda didn't want anyone to look more generous than herself, she meant. This was said loud enough for my mother to hear, but in Nora's manner of disguising her contempt with a jolly sort of teasing. No one was ever fooled.

She advanced upon the stove. "You sure you can make this

old wreck do the job?" She chuckled throatily in that Macken way, as though to suggest: Here I am, being my awful self!

My mother turned and stood her ground, pulling off her gloves. She'd been deflecting this sort of thing since my father had started taking her for horseback rides – grade four. She'd learned to smile when she might have snapped off Nora's head. "Oh, I should know what I'm doing by now!" She had a way of almost singing these things, all too familiar with the words of this old tune. Everyone knew that Frieda Macken could cast a spell over the most decrepit stove.

"Your weapon loaded, Rusty?" my mother said. "This thing is ready to light."

Nora pulled her cardigan about her shoulders and turned her frown on me, while I stuffed newspaper into the firebox. "I thought he'd be over there conducting panty raids by now."

"Yelling 'Eureka!' over test-tubes – isn't that what they do?" Grace said, dropping her cigarette stub to the ground and grinding it in with her foot. "Professors droning on about nothin'." She shuddered. "I'm glad it's him that's goin', not me, it gives me the creeps."

She looked out across the Strait as though the university might have shifted north to where we could see it. Nothing but blue-treed mountains. The far side was less than thirty miles away, and probably as ragged-edged as this side was, but the Strait had its own horizon out there beyond the halfway point – a line as straight and hard as the far side of a kitchen table.

"Already gone!" my mother sang out. "He just forgot to take his body; it stays at home and eats!" She handed me a box of matches. "Even so, it claims it would rather go somewhere else than stay for my pancakes."

"To do what?" Nora was clearly shocked. "Exams are over. You can't practise high jump all day long."

25

Pole vault was what she meant, though she'd never come out to see me compete.

"He wants to go off and fish," my mother said.

"Nonsense," said Nora, watching Uncle Buddy puff by with cases of Canada Dry and Coke from Reg's truck. "No true Macken would let us down today."

Of course Nora did not believe that I was what you'd call a "true" Macken anyway. "We'll make a Macken out of this one yet," she used to claim. Though she never explained how this transformation was to take place, she knew her father could have managed it. "If Father were still alive he'd whip him into shape. There's plenty rocks need pickin' out in that field." But she'd long ago given up. "City's the place for this one," she liked to say. She meant that I would never be good for much around here.

Still, when I stood up from lighting the stove she offered her cheek. "Come give your old auntie a kiss." Putting my lips to her powdery face, I tried not to inhale her scent, which was a little like the apple and sprouted-potato smell of the root cellar behind her house.

"I bet he don't stay over there," Grace said. "He won't be able to live without the rest of us, he'll come wailing home. Like Reg."

The story was that Reg ran away at seventeen. Because he'd dreamed all his life of singing on the radio, he set off for the Grand Ole Opry in Nashville, Tennessee. But by the time he'd hitchhiked down to Nanaimo he'd missed that day's last sailing and had to stay overnight. Overwhelmed by the two-storey buildings and noisy crowds in that city of six thousand people, he was afraid to leave the hotel. Every sound was a thief creeping down the hallway to slit his throat. He couldn't sleep. The next morning he caught the first bus home.

Uncle Buddy had also run away – had even got off the Island

for a few months – but he never told anyone where he'd been. Grace said he carried on long conversations in his sleep in a language that sounded Chinese. But he claimed that, goodness gracious, he couldn't remember his dreams. He never again set foot on a boat that might take him away from home.

No Mackens had gone to the war, though Toby had tried. Flat feet and trick knees kept them home. None had ever complained.

Aunt Nora agreed with Grace that I'd be no more successful at staying away than the others, but she wasn't surprised that I'd try. She couldn't imagine what I might do if I stayed. "Anyway, don't stand here yacking like an old woman," she said, pushing the heel of her hand against my shoulder. "There's plenty you could do to help. Take a mower to some of that grass – stubble's hard to walk on." She set out towards the circle of folding chairs beneath the largest firs. "First you could bring me a beer." She chose the highest ground, of course, and sat to wait for others to come to her, a network of wild strawberry plants at her feet. "Lucky Lager," she said.

"No, I've changed my mind," she called after me. "I'll wait till somebody brings some Old Vienna."

"Don't say it," my mother said.

"Don't say what?" I said.

"Don't say what you're thinking."

"How would you know what I'm thinking?"

"Because I'm thinking the same myself. I've been thinking it most of my life." She laid plates on the wooden table, and didn't need to look up at the sound of another approaching car. "Here comes your dad. Let's hope he didn't forget the coffee, I'm panting for something to drink."

2

Of course my father hadn't forgotten the coffee pots. Or the tin-lined plywood icebox he'd made for these family events. He was probably the most reliable person in the district, if not the world. Not only had he remembered everything he'd been asked to bring, he'd also hammered together more sawhorses to hold up the sheets of plywood for the tables, and knocked together a few rough milking stools in case there were not enough chairs for people too old to sit on the ground.

He'd brought my sister, Meg, with him as well – who ran off to play on the beach – but of course he hadn't brought my brother. As soon as Gerry got wind of the funeral arrangements he decided to drive to Cowichan Lake with a friend. He wasn't old enough to have his licence but he'd been secretly driving the cars of friends for more than a year, since turning thirteen. While we were getting things ready here, Gerry would still be in his sleeping bag, amongst the beer bottles and overturned furniture on some cabin floor. If he hadn't drowned in a leaky rowboat during the night.

He ought to have been here. He ought to have *wanted* to be here. Gerry stirred up nearly as much laughter and admiration as Toby did. Another family hellion. "A real Macken, that one," they said. "Reminds me of Old Uncle Ron." Old Uncle Ron had gone to jail at the age of seventy-three for burning down a church for a lark, somewhere far to the north. For a Macken to be dubbed black sheep of the family was a major achievement, the sign of their greatest approval. Only one was allowed in each generation. Toby was the one for his. Gerry would likely be next. Even his staying away would somehow become a mark in his favour – "A mind of his own, that one!"

For a moment my father stood by the Ford to watch my mother stir pancake batter, the bowl in the crook of her arm. "You'd have to tie that woman up with wire rope before she'd take it easy."

While my mother was in the hospital we could hear him pacing the house at night. He ate his meals, but only so that he wouldn't hurt my feelings. "Is this liver or somebody's boot?" he'd say, but he'd force it down. Now that she was back on her feet he had trouble letting her out of his sight. Those two had not been apart for any length of time since they'd married. They hadn't been apart before that either, very much – inseparable since they were children.

He could see that old hotel, I imagined, looking just as it had looked when he'd come home from a day of setting chokers. His bride would have his supper ready on the giant stove. (A movie would show the bride's face at the window, then pull back to show the '35 Model T coming to a stop near the door.

"Here, I wouldn't mind if you give me a hand," he said.

I hadn't yet dragged the picnic tables out from behind the shed but I took the time to help him unload an axle he'd rigged up to the gas motor from my mother's washing machine – a barbecue spit to turn the side of beef. Uncle Buddy came over to help. "Reg's playin' cowboys with the kids," he said.

"Big kid himself," my father said, grinning. You could hear

their gunfights amongst the shoreline logs, cap guns answering the *pows* from those who shot with their fingers.

"Anybody else'd just *buy* one of these things," said Buddy. His thin voice rattled from his rapid thudding walk. He wasn't taking much of the weight – afraid for his ticker.

"Good thing some of us don't throw everything out," said my father, who thought buying was a waste of money if you could build a thing yourself. There wasn't much he couldn't build himself, there wasn't much he didn't have the parts for. An aeroplane might have stumped him, but probably not for long.

We set about gathering up fallen bricks from beneath a drooping bush of ocean spray. "Toby could've fixed this thing in ten minutes," my father said, "but of course he don't even see."

Uncle Buddy put a hand to his chest. "Goldarn, I think I've gone and overdone it." He set off for his car to stretch out for a while, probably until there was food. My father looked at me aslant from under the brim of his hat. He never pulled faces or rolled his eyes like my mother, he just looked and you knew what he meant.

"I don't suppose that would work for me," I said.

"I don't suppose it would."

He was wearing his suit pants and braces and his white shirt, and even though he wore silver arm bands he'd rolled up the sleeves. He hadn't yet put on his tie. He wore his best brimmed hat; he never left the house without something on his head. My mother said this would eventually make him bald.

"I don't see why we have to make a whole day of this," I said. "We'll have to listen to the same old stories again." I knew what they would be. How Grandpa Macken used a manure fork to rescue little Toby from a cougar's jaws. How Grandma Macken refused to live in a house after three burned down around her, struck by lightning. How Great-Uncle Fred was nearly killed in the Donnelly massacre before he left

30

Ontario and ran for the Pacific coast. "Who wants to hear them again?"

My father took off his hat and ran a finger around inside and put it back on his head. He gave a little tug on the brim, to settle the hat at an angle. "Who wants to hear them?" He looked like Gary Cooper when he frowned. (Women sometimes called him Gary Cooper, for his quiet ways as well as his looks.) "I never thought about it. Maybe they need to *tell* them."

"Why?"

"At a funeral?" He raised a hand to the Home Oil truck roaring past on the highway. It tooted twice – Roy Holland making deliveries to Campbell River. "Maybe it makes them feel safe for a while. It's kind of like gathering the tribe around, to prove that it still exists." My father looked down at his dress shoes for a moment. Elastic garters kept his socks from sagging like mine. "Lynette must think it's funny you didn't bring her."

The scent of sun-warmed pitch was strong here, bleeding from the gashed root of a fir. "She wouldn't be interested in the funeral," I said. "She says when Mackens get together they're too loud."

My father laughed. "Mackens are always too loud," he said, and went back to the bricks.

Of course my father didn't usually encourage my interest in Lynette Macleod. "We don't have to tell you what a shotgun marriage would do to your plans," he'd said more than once. "You'd spend your life back there in the bush with that outfit, stripping wrecked cars for their parts. Nobody's got the money to send a married man with a family off to school."

Sonny Aalto pulled up outside the gate in his old man's wartime Jeep, handpainted an egg-yolk yellow over the wrinkles and dimples and other souvenirs of countless mishaps encountered in midnight ditches. He tapped his horn, then got out to stand inside his opened door.

"Why don't he come in?" my father said.

"He's waiting for me to go out. They're going fishing above the dam. They want me to go along."

I couldn't tell him why I was in such a hurry to get away. I wasn't sure myself. I was afraid that staying here would make me ill. If Toby came, I wouldn't be able to stand it.

My father looked a little surprised, smiling as though he were waiting for more. "Today?" He waved for Sonny to come on in and join us. Sonny shook his head and looked down, running a hand over his gleaming ducktail.

My father jabbed his chin in the direction of Toby's shack. "This thing has got your mother all tore up," he said. "It wouldn't hurt to keep an eye on her, just in case."

"That means 'Stay'?"

"It wouldn't hurt if you hung around and helped out."

He would not say anything straight out if he could help it. This was the Irish in him, my mother said. Dodging confrontations unless he got good and mad, something that seldom happened.

"I don't think I can," I said. I knew that even though my father would not insist, he'd be disappointed. As a man who instinctively did what was right for others, he never seemed to think that I mightn't do the same.

"You could ask him in instead," he said.

Sonny gave me the hurry-up signal. Of course he did it in his offhand Marlon Brando manner, as though he didn't want me to think he cared.

"Why would he want to come in?"

"Because you asked him to. Because he knows this is where you belong."

"Nobody'd miss me," I said, conscious of the note of petulance that had crept into my voice. *Self-centred and spoiled,* Aunt Nora would say. *No sense of family pride.*

32

My father turned and regarded me for a moment with amusement. "Nobody'd miss you?" Self-pity was never allowed to pass without comment. "I think you have to stick around for Toby, when he finally comes. You might be the one he needs." He pushed back his hat with the back of his hand and once again smiled. "Do I have to speak plainer than that?" Amused, this time, at himself: laying down the law.

"You'd think I was six years old, the way I get bossed around! With seventy million other Mackens showing up, what difference would it make if I wasn't here?"

My father's grin broadened, his usual way of responding to indignation – he couldn't believe you'd take yourself so seriously. "Well, poor you!" Somehow he could mimic your expression without losing his grin. "What a terrible life we force you to lead. Some of the rest of us aren't exactly thrilled to be here either – I don't suppose you ever thought of that."

His mockery was so exaggerated that you had to laugh. "Forget it!" It wasn't possible to live in this family without knowing when you looked so foolish that you ought to be ashamed.

"Maybe after the cemetery," I offered Sonny.

He slammed one hand on the hood of the Jeep. "Jesus, Macken," he said. "You're letting them drag you to a bloody *graveyard?*"

Its crumpled surface made the Jeep look as though it had been crushed in giant hands and then plucked and pried back into shape, like a letter rescued from the wastepaper basket.

"It's family, Aalto! They count heads! Anyone missing is the next one they put in a hole."

Despite his Tab Hunter face, Sonny thought of himself as more of a Brando type. He frowned a lot. He kept the back of his collar up to meet the ducktail of his boogey cut, sheered off flat as carpet on top. Even on a sunny day like this he wore a black leather jacket and black denim jeans. We'd seen *The Wild One* twice.

"You gotta be crazy, y'know that? My ol' man couldn't make me go to no funeral."

"Your old man can't make you do anything," I said.

Sonny laughed. "Sometimes he tries, but only when he's sober." Which wasn't often, he meant. Sonny was sure he was widely envied, and maybe he was – no mother, a father who was usually too drunk to care what he did. "Shit, you got chains on you so thick I'm surprised you can walk." He said this with genuine pity. "Lynette not here?"

I showed him my empty palms. "Haven't seen her since Tuesday night."

"Since your *fight*?" Again he slammed that hand on the Jeep. "Holy Jesus, Macken, get a brain! Get over there and talk to her, willya? That's three days – she's gonna forget who you are!"

I shrugged. "She's gonna forget who I am ten minutes after I leave for Vancouver anyway."

"Her crazy old man'll come after you with his twelve-gauge, for hurting her feelings."

"Old bugger tried that once, did I tell you? Met me at the door and stuck both barrels in my face – trying to be funny. I offered to arm-wrestle instead. He beat me easy but he's liked me ever since."

"Then he'd rather kill you than lose you. Go talk to her. Bring her. Beth's coming. Everybody's bringing a girl."

This was not the day to think of Lynette. "You want to come in for a while? They're making pancakes."

Sonny levelled a look of deep suspicion in the direction of everything and everyone behind me. "Your bloody relatives might put a spell on me like they done to you, I'd never get

34

away." He started to slide into the Jeep, but straightened again. "Your cousin here?" Despite his look of indifference, there was a tremor in his voice.

I knew why. I knew which cousin he meant. "If she was, do you think she'd let you stand here this long without hanging herself on your neck? She'd have your shirt undone by now, maybe your belt as well." Caro had been after Sonny since grade three. If her parents hadn't moved down-Island she might have got over him long ago. As it was, she mentioned him every time she came up. "She ought to be here any minute though," I said. "You could stay and tell her in person how much you've missed her."

Sonny lowered his head and spoke into the yellow paint job. "I never think about her – except when I remember how she likes to rub her boobs against your arm."

"Not my arm, she doesn't," I said. "Maybe she likes the way she can make you drool."

Caro once demanded that I arrange a date for the two of them, which I did but would never do again. I didn't like the way Sonny talked about it later: "Shoot, Macken, I can hardly walk! Your cousin's some kind of animal, you know that? She thinks I oughta quit school and look for work down there – whaddaya think?"

"You can tell Uncle Martin how much you miss his daughter too, when he gets here," I said. "He might break your arm to show you how pleased he is." Just shaking Uncle Martin's hand could drive you to your knees, checking your fingers for broken bones.

This drove Sonny back into the Jeep. "I'll tell him sweet bugger-all!"

"I'll tell him for you," I said. "Leave a trout or two in the lake, in case I pull off an escape."

"Go talk to Lynette!" He swung a wide arc to go back the

35

way he'd come, and accelerated ahead of a cloud of blue smoke – the Jeep burned more oil than gas. He tapped the horn twice, put the pedal to the floor, and fishtailed a few times before he got settled into a steady course down the centre line.

Go talk to Lynette! It was taken for granted that I was in love with Lynette Macleod. We'd dated through this whole past year, going to movies in town and dances in Union Bay. Afterwards we parked until two or three in the morning amongst the rusted car bodies in the alder thickets on her father's land. She wore my signet ring on her middle finger, but planned to date other fellows as soon as I left. She didn't intend to sit home on Saturday nights while I had fun in the city. A pretty girl like her. A passionate girl as well. Just keeping her options open, was how she put it.

Lynette could not understand why I thought so much of Toby. "He's a lunatic." This was not easy to take. Uncle Toby had been my hero all my life. I'd wanted to *be* him once; I still wanted to be someone Toby could admire. Yet if I mentioned his reputation as a man who liked to make people happy, Lynette reminded me of his reputation as a Saturday-night brawler. "Billy Stevens still has a cauliflower ear. The Finnegan twin's a cripple, can't even work." If I brought up Toby's status as a former hero, she brought up his history as a public nuisance: piglets had appeared in the middle of sermons, school-bus shelters had burned to the ground. Worse, she believed that he was a thief – her father was taking Toby to court for stealing a white-face steer. When I reminded her that Toby employed me so I could save money for university, working at the little sawmill where Toby liked to think he was making people's dreams come true, she pointed out the shack that Toby's own wife had to put up with. "You don't think *she's* got any dreams?"

Not that Lynette thought so highly of Glory. "To put it

36

mildly, she's a little *odd*. Everyone knows why she disappears for periods on the mainland – don't tell me you don't know that! It isn't to visit her folks."

The day I learned of Glory's death, this sort of talk eventually led to words that should not have been said. I hadn't made any effort to get in touch since then. She could stay in the bush with her crazy old man and her brothers and all her runny-nosed sisters and barking dogs. If she showed up here, I would pretend we'd never met.

My father was still working on the barbecue spit. He'd known I wouldn't leave. The maddening part was that I couldn't even curse him properly and mean it.

Life would be so much easier if I'd been blessed like Sonny with a falling-down drunk for an old man, or a stupid bullheaded father like everyone else. Someone who got red in the face and yelled that you better do what you're bloody-well told, you little shit, or I'll kick your arse. You could get red in the face yourself and yell back, and hate his guts with a passion, and do what you wanted anyway, pleased to be another justified rebel. That would never work for me. I wouldn't be just a rebel without a cause, I'd look like a total fool. Other kids had been telling me all my life that they wished my dad were their own.

Especially my cousin Gordon, who'd worshipped his Uncle Eddie. In the days when he used to play with me and Sonny, he hated his own dad, Uncle Martin. Poor old Gordie would have traded fathers with me in a minute.

It wasn't hard to imagine Gordie here right now. I missed him. I could see him sitting on the lowest branch of a nearby fir. He was exactly as I'd last seen him in life: eleven years old, with gaps between his teeth, dirt in his ears, his laces undone, and his hair mangled by one of Uncle Martin's haircuts. "You just got your chance to get outa here, dummy. Tell him you're going to get Lynette, don't bother coming back."

37

"You never had to live with him," I said. "It isn't as easy as that."

Gordie made no response. He pulled himself into the higher boughs and disappeared, except for his unlaced shoes.

Soon more than thirty cars were parked on the golf course grass. Relatives who hadn't come to help had gathered for something to eat before starting off together for the funeral chapel. Kids joined the shoreline cowboys-and-Indians shoot-out. Uncle Reg appeared at the top of a tangled heap of driftwood, red and puffing, holding a handkerchief aloft like a flag. He beckoned his troops to follow. They did – dozens of children warbling war cries. They swarmed up the heap behind him and leapt onto the enemy, who went screaming off down the beach. Those who were caught by Mike, Mark, and Jack were scalped.

Most people stayed on the grass and drank steaming coffee, sitting wherever they could. Aunt Helen recalled her first Macken funeral, soon after she'd married Uncle Avery, where the whole front pew packed tight with Alberta relatives keeled over in a faint to the floor. "Dropped at the preacher's feet." She had a way of laughing shyly, while her wandering eye checked everyone else to see if what she had said was accepted.

"They didn't faint," cried Kitty. "They'd dozed off, leaning on one another. There wasn't a sober person in that row. When one of them slipped, the rest fell off right after him, like shingles off an old roof. Preacher's mouth just *dropped*. I saw cavities deep as wells!"

I helped myself to a stack of pancakes and drowned them in syrup, then joined my sister at a picnic table. I was hungry. Nothing had reached my stomach today but a glass of orange juice. I'd even skipped the compulsory spoonful of foul-smelling Neo Chemical Food, since no one had thought to remind me, and I'd forgotten the daily Halibut Liver Oil ampoule from the slide-out box: my mother's double-whammy fortification against germs with designs on her children.

Meg was pouting because at ten years old she wouldn't be allowed to attend the service. One of the aunts would stay to look after the kids.

"It isn't fair, y'know." Holding her fork like a dagger, she stabbed repeatedly into the pale gooseberry jam she'd heaped on her pancakes, piercing the little berries that looked, as our father put it, like eyeballs boiled in goo. "Will you tell me what it's like?"

"What *what's* like?"

She lowered her voice. "To look at a dead person, stupid. You better tell me what it's like, Rusty. You *better*."

There were purple bird stains on the table. I should have washed them off.

"Nobody's going to see a dead person," I said. "There'll just be a coffin. There'll be boring speeches and prayers."

"It isn't fair. I don't get in on anything!"

Again and again the door of Glory's little icebox was opened and closed on the porch, for milk and beer and fruit juice and pop. More supplies went in for later. Kik Cola. Orange Crush. Cream soda. Canada Dry. Old Vienna. Pilsener. Capilano Old Style. Uncle Avery's homemade wine. Avery made wine from blackberries, from cherries, from rhubarb, from dandelions, he even made wine from the flowers of Scotch broom, though he was the only one who didn't believe it was poison. "Since we can't seem to root the goddam stuff out of the ground, nor shoot the sonofabitch that brought it onto the Island, we might as well pour it down our throats."

My mother carried a pot of boiled potatoes to the end of our

39

table, and stood cutting them up into little cubes. Grace and Aunt Kitty joined her, to chop green onions and tear up lettuce, getting things ready for the picnic supper later. Kitty complained of aching legs. "I'll just park my little fanny on this bench if nobody minds."

My mother said, "If your legs give out that easy, how'll you stand on that Nashville stage when your chance finally comes? You hear Kitty Wells complaining about her legs?"

"Don't say Kitty Wells!" Kitty gasped. "Reg hears you, he'll fall apart. He's crazy about that girl."

"So long's he don't start singin' about it," Grace said.

"He'll sing his brand new song for Glory tonight," Kitty said. "I bawled my eyes out when I heard it." Again she gasped. "Oh my God, I just thought of something. What if her parents show up? That awful mother will want to sing something from *Mozart!*" She trilled three high notes, "*La, la, la!*" and dropped her head like somebody shot.

"Don't worry," my mother said. "I called Vancouver. Well, I *had* to! Madam Soprano's off somewhere croaking out Lady Macbeth. Pittsburgh! The old fellow said they'd have their own service, thank you very much. He meant they don't want any part of ours."

"He meant that ours don't count," said Grace.

If I had to hang around I might as well be useful. As soon as I'd eaten, I hoisted a case of Phoenix under one arm, grabbed up a coffee pot, and went out to see what I could do for people's thirsts. Meg followed with cream and sugar. Coffee went faster than beer this close to the time of the service.

Uncle Buddy had recovered enough to help my father assemble the improvised spit. When Macken brothers worked together it was as if they shared a brain. They didn't speak, they didn't have to. They knew when a tool was needed, they always seemed to know what the other wanted. A grunt or a held-out hand was the most that was ever needed. This came from a lifetime of helping one another, knowing each other's ways.

Uncle Buddy jumped up and threw a pebble into the limbs of a fir. "Git!"

A crow squawked and flew up to a higher branch where it hunched its gleaming black shoulders, shifted its weight from one foot to the other a few times, and glared at Buddy out of its glittering eye. "Get one at a funeral and you'll soon have a thousand of them goldarn things. They'll come from all over the blasted country to steal food right out of your mouth, drive you off your own land." He crouched on his heels to hand a crescent wrench to my dad. "Toby darn-well better get here soon."

A shiny blue truck with a high plywood hut behind the cab turned in off the road and snaked its way amongst parked cars and people. When it had come to a stop by Toby's practice pole, Uncle Martin stepped out.

"Marty Macken, you're going bald!" Nora stood up to shout this across the tops of heads.

Uncle Martin worked his way towards Nora, shaking hands, kissing turned-up faces. Because he kept his sleeves rolled right to his armpits, he walked with arms out from his side like a gangster ready to go for his guns. When I set the coffee pot down and put out my hand he made as though to take it but ducked to grab my thigh instead and squeezed so hard it brought tears to my eyes. As usual, I pretended I didn't mind. Uncle Martin did this to all his nephews, used to do it to Gordie as well to see if Gordie would cry. "Hey there, how's Mr. Longlegs?" he said.

As he was kissing Nora, she said, "This is what happens when you let them move south. They lose their hair."

"Look what Martin went and parked!" said Uncle Buddy. "You gonna leave that GMC where people can see it?"

Mackens were strictly Ford people. At least those who still lived in the district were. Those who'd moved down-Island had converted to Chevs and GMCs. Those who'd moved down-Island had also been known to vote for Social Credit, which showed just how far they had strayed from their roots.

"I parked 'er there to add some class to this outfit," said Martin. "All them Fords make the place look like a bloody junkyard."

"Damn fool," said my dad. "What kind of mileage will you get on a rig like that?"

"At least I won't spend my life replacing fuel pumps."

Aunt Nora made Martin sit beside her. "You oughta be shot, buyin' that piece of tin!"

Edna had stayed inside the GMC, repairing her lipstick. Now she stepped down with a grunt, chewing gum with her mouth open and snapping it smartly. Her loud harsh voice stopped a dozen conversations dead. "We got to put a stop to this dying, it's too goddam expensive! You know how much they're charging these days for gas?" She had never cared what she said. She looked my mother over a minute before adding, "Jesus Christ, you're skin and bones – you planning to be next?" These two school friends threw arms around one another and laughed. Then "shhhhhhhed" in each other's face – this was a funeral after all – and laughed quieter.

Then blunt Edna said, "Now look, I'm the kind of person that says what I think – frankly, you look like hell. You must be feeling terrible, you were closer than anyone."

My mother's face went grim, as though she'd just remembered why we were here. "I'm not exactly kicking up my heels."

Edna never bothered to close her mouth; whenever she wasn't talking she was waiting for a chance to say what she planned to say next. "I always thought there was something about her," she said. "So delicate and dreamy, like she hardly belonged in this world with the rest of us beasts. A bloody sprite or something. An angel. And I'm not the kind of person that usually notices such things."

When she saw me she threw her fleshy arms out wide and closed her eyes, waiting for something to happen. I kissed her forehead. "My God, Frieda, don't you feed this boy?" Loud. Loud. She grabbed at my ribs with both hands and pinched at the meagre flesh. "Jesus, Rusty, I figured you'd be lost in the big bad city by now. Drowning in that goddam Vancouver rain. Now tell me one more time – what is it you're going there for?" She clamped her eyes shut, as though this would be something that needed concentration.

"Depends when you ask," my mother said. "I've heard diplomat, architect, it was archaeologist for a while. A movie director's what he's wanted to be all his life – you knew that."

"Big dreamer!" Edna said.

"I'm taking forestry," I said.

Edna's head shot up so that her eye could drill a scowl right into me. "I didn't think you could tell one tree from another."

"He won a scholarship," my mother said.

"It's the logging company gives it," I said. "You have to go into forestry – no choice."

Edna shrugged. "If all you want is not to get your hands dirty you could get a job in their office, writing paycheques for people that aren't afraid of work." She dug her elbow into my arm to make sure I thought she was joking. "Next time we see this kid he won't talk to us, he'll be one of them goddam city bohemians."

She could have been right. The life I was going towards was so alien that I couldn't guess how much of myself I'd be taking with me. Rusty Macken could become a bookie for the races at Exhibition Park for all I knew, or an office worker at the top of a skyscraper, or a dope addict begging in the rainy streets

43

below. One more sinner in the fleshpots of Babylon. Since the beginning of the summer I'd felt like a paratrooper perched in an open doorway, eager to discover human flight but at the same time afraid the parachute wouldn't open.

Who was I going to be?

Caro would never think to ask that sort of question. "You leave someone behind?" I asked Edna. "Or toss her into the ditch?"

Edna puffed out her cheeks and blew. "I should've! Me 'n bloody Caroline got into a screamin' match this side of Nanaimo so I made the mouthy bitch ride in the back. She's in there now, sulking. Go tackle the wildcat if you dare."

No Macken ever stayed in a hotel, or even an auto-court. Those were meant for people who had no relatives, and folks without the brains to build a bedroom on the back of their truck. Uncle Martin's camper was a high, square homemade plywood box with a window on each side and a stovepipe sticking through the roof.

I half expected to find Gordie waiting for me at the back of the truck. But of course he wasn't there, he couldn't be. His sister, Caro, sat in the open doorway, sucking a cigarette. "Where's Toby?" she said, by way of greeting. She might have been suggesting that I'd kept him from her.

"He hasn't shown up. We don't even know if he will."

She was a few months younger than I was, but looked older. She'd matured early, they said – the south-Island sun. By the time she was fifteen she had been, as she put it herself, "unofficially engaged" three times. Today, for Glory's funeral, she wore high heels and tight blue shorts and a white blouse with buttons undone. She sucked at her cigarette and yanked it away from her mouth in a jerky motion, then stepped down to the ground and leaned back against the rough surface of Toby's pole, gouged with holes from his climbing spikes. You could hear her false eyelashes swish down and up again when she blinked.

"Thank God *you're* here – one person that isn't ninety years old. Where's the rest of our generation – died out?"

"Just scared of a little work."

Her hair was still as white-blonde and curly as when I set a match to it and watched while it burned to her scalp. She was three years old at the time, still living down the road near Uncle Buddy's. She'd been given so much attention for those curls that I thought being bald might do her some good. Being Caro, however, she'd got mileage even out of that. She told everyone I'd tied her up and taken a blowtorch to her head. "The damn old bugger ought to be fed to the hogs!" This sort of talk would have earned the rest of us a few licks of the belt, but because she was Caro people laughed. "That girl has got a tongue in her head like a sailor."

She held out her package of Player's. "You see her?"

I borrowed her silver lighter. "See who?"

She rolled up her eyes. "Glory, of course. How long before she died did you see her?"

Was she hoping for gruesome details? "Just hours. She'd come back from Vancouver a few days before."

Caro blew smoke down her nostrils like a comic-strip bull. "Another one of her little 'trips' away. So how'd she look?"

"Same as usual," I said. "Glory always looked good."

"Poor broad," Caro said, looking at all the relatives under the trees. She tore what was left of her cigarette from her mouth and dropped it to the ground. "I hope you've got your car where you can get *out*. I'm not hanging around with these old fogies all day."

Nora came out of Toby's shack. "Someone's in there hogging the toilet – must be Grace." She headed towards the privy with her black dress over her arm. Toby's shack and the outdoor

45

toilet would be the ladies' change rooms; men would change behind trees.

True to form, Caro yelled the first thing that came to mind. "Plug your nose and grab the Airwick, Nora. Someone ate a crate of prunes and dumped everything but their lungs."

"Oh, you!" Nora waved the words aside. Caro was just being what Nora expected. "Your mother ought to've washed your mouth out years ago."

"She'd have to wash her own out first. Who taught me how to talk?"

People were starting to get into cars. "Who's ready?" my father shouted. "We might as well get the first loads outa the way."

"Without Toby?" said Reg.

"Toby's deserted us," my father said. "We can't wait around for ever."

"See you in church!" someone called. Everyone laughed: it was what Mackens often hollered as they parted company, knowing very well that church was the last place in the world they were likely to meet. This time, for a change, it happened to be true.

Men put jackets on over their shirts and tightened up ties at their throats. Women put on hats with veils, kicked off flat-heeled shoes and slipped on higher heels for the chapel.

"Damned if I'm goin' to their stupid service," Caro said. She ran her long nails down the length of her left thigh to her knee, then slid them back up. She looked like a tap-dancer in some chorus line. "What about you?"

I watched my father encouraging people to make the effort. Like my mother, he'd assume I would do what was right. "I'd rather not," I admitted.

"We'll take the wrong turn somewhere and forget to show up," Caro said. "If I have to listen to some Bible-puncher flingin' horseshit, I'll tell him to stuff it where the sun don't shine." She pouted her dark red lips and smiled. "Besides, I'd just embarrass you by puking down the back of somebody's neck."

"Reg is ready to go," my father said. "Where's Nora got to?"

"She's still in the crapper!" Caro said. Then she hollered, "Hey, Nora – you got yourself wedged in the hole?" Cackling wickedly, she looked at me. The lashes swept down, then up. "Move it, lady, or they'll go without you!" Then she lowered her voice. "Not that they got the guts to leave her behind."

3

ONLY now did Toby show up – time to leave. He didn't pull in off the road in his lumber truck as everyone had expected, bouncing and whining up the potholed drive. He was just there, all of a sudden, sitting on the roof of his shack.

I was the one who spotted him, but didn't let on. When his eye caught mine I pretended not to see. I left to change into my suit. I didn't want to go anywhere near him today.

But when I came back he was waiting for me – he knew I'd glance his way again. This time he put a finger to his lips and gestured for me to climb up and join him. I looked hard, hoping he'd change his mind. But he looked hard at me too, and clearly did not. I climbed the ladder against the kitchen wall, then went up the roof to sit beside him.

He had rolled a cigarette and now ran his tongue along the glue. "I could hear this goddam racket the far side of the Experimental Farm. Six hundred bawling cows couldn't drown it out."

He screwed up his eyes to look down on the crowd that hadn't noticed him yet. He needed a shave, but his checkered work shirt and denim pants didn't look any more than usual like clothes someone had slept in. His fine ginger hair was all raked up and going every way.

"How'd you get here?" I said. "You didn't wreck the truck?"

"Parked 'er down the road." He lit his cigarette and shook out the match. He offered me his Zig Zag makings but I shook my head. I couldn't have rolled a cigarette without dropping tobacco all down the roof. I couldn't have smoked without choking. "I didn't want them starin' at me when I drove in, so I parked 'er and walked along the beach. Stopped to give one of Reg's brats a piece of my mind – little shit was throwing rocks at his dog."

"But where've you been?" I said. I didn't mean it to sound like an accusation. "We figured you must be in Chile by now. Arizona at least."

"Arizona was too bloody hot."

"Sure."

"I wasn't off the plane an hour in Chile when this prick stuck a gun in my face and said he was going to blow my brains out. He would have shot me on the spot if I hadn't disarmed him and stood on his neck."

"How many of those people down there'd believe you?"

"Most," he said. "They're Mackens." He put his face in his hands, and for a few moments breathed heavily into them. Then he moved his hands. "I been drivin' around, visitin' friends. Tryin' to think. Down-Island, to visit Horny Hopper from school days. Spent the night and come back. Anything to put off dealing with *them*." He jabbed his cigarette at the air – he meant the family below.

From his roof you could see the plumes of smoke from the paper mill across the Strait, streaming up from behind a crease in the soft blue line of mountains. The world did look different from here. I could see why he liked to take on this added height. Except for the boughs of the firs, nothing got in the way of seeing whatever you wanted to see – the whole crowd of them down there at once, the cars going by on the road, the blue waves coming in off the Strait to break and spread out across the wide flat expanse of sand.

I could also see what was left of the old tilted sailing ship in the bay. Toby and his friends had been the first to play in it. When it was brought in for a breakwater, they discovered it was still partly furnished. Silver cutlery. Framed pictures. Chairs. They looted it. They hired me and Gordie to help them. We climbed a rope ladder up the side, then tossed down serving trays and velvet cushions. We lowered chandeliers and tables by rope. Some of the silver we buried in the sand, then drew maps we later lost. I never learned what happened to the rest. When Toby and his friends lost interest, we continued to play in the hull – Gerry and me and Gordie, sometimes Caro and other cousins. Toby told us tales of people trapped and drowned by tidal waves, of kidnapped children who'd died while rounding the Horn. Now its remaining planks were just the ribcage of some giant creature, crusted with barnacles and clusters of mussel shells, streaming with long green shreds of gleaming weed. I could almost smell the scent of it from the roof of the shack, and hear the singing of the breeze in its decaying ribs.

I'd once imagined using that hull in a movie. A beautiful woman is chained inside it while the tide comes in – tied to a post like Deborah Kerr in *Quo Vadis*. There'd be wonderful camera shots through those rotting planks, as the waves creep up her thighs and the sun appears from behind the mainland mountains. Then someone rescues her – a courageous young admirer who takes her away to live in a fabulous seaside hotel. Toby's shack would have to be moved and the hotel rebuilt with Hollywood money. I'd planned to give the building to Toby and Glory afterwards.

"All that down-Island lot got here?" Toby said.

I didn't want to talk about the down-Island relatives, I wanted to talk about Glory, but at the same time I was scared Toby might mention Glory himself. What else was there to think about today?

"Well, partner," Toby said. "I guess I screwed 'er up real good this time for sure – whaddaya think? You think I ever had a chance?"

"I don't know," I said. "I can't get any of it straight."

"Too bad you never went to Sunday School – you think I'm bein' punished?"

"I don't think so. No. It wouldn't make any sense." I'd been to Sunday School half a dozen times a few years back but Toby couldn't know that. Even my folks didn't know. They thought I'd gone to play with Sonny Aalto but Sonny and I'd decided to find out what was going on in his neighbour's living room – a Bible class run by an ancient lady in shawls. There'd been a lot of talk about loving your neighbour, and pictures of sheep to colour, but I couldn't remember anything about punishment.

"Last night I dreamt she come back and offered me one more chance. I woke up yellin' bloody murder – scared Horny Hopper's ol' lady half to death. You think I should've had another chance?"

"I don't know," I said. "Of course I do."

We sat without saying anything for a minute. A row of pulp barges moved slowly up the Strait behind a tugboat. The cable that joined them wasn't visible.

"Brought you something," he said, straightening a leg to root around in his pocket.

"What is it?" He'd been bringing me souvenirs since before I started school.

He shifted his weight to root around in the other pocket as well. "Damn, it's gone! Bottom's right outa this pocket, it

51

must've fell through. It was one of them little sprockets off a movie projector."

"Where'd you find it?"

"On a projector, what'd you think? Horny kept the guy talking while I fiddled around, to see what I could pry off without making too much noise."

"You thought I could build myself a projector to go with it?"

"I figured you could look at it now and then for inspiration, smart-ass. Anyhow it don't matter, the sonofabitch is gone."

"Too bad," I said. "If you'd only sew the hole in your pocket I'd eventually have a studio and movie lot and a theatre all of my own."

"I still feel like doin' something," Toby said, his tone shifting again to something darker. "What do you think I should do?"

"About what?" I said. "What good will anything do now?"

"Maybe I ought to burn down the chapel during the service – whaddaya think?"

"I don't think that'd make you feel any better."

"I don't want to feel better, for chrissake!" he said. "I want to burn things down, I want to roll things *back*." He thought about that for a moment. "You're not dumb – I want it to stop!" He almost smiled, caught up with another idea. "Maybe I'll nail myself on that bloody big cross over the preacher's head – greet them when they come in. That ought to make them happy."

"I don't know who would be happy," I said. "I don't know why you're talking like this, for God's sake. Do you know anybody that people like better than you?"

Toby didn't say anything to that. He looked at me as though I'd spoken a foreign language. Then he said, "It's bloody barbaric. I'd rather do just about anything than go through this goddam ordeal. I don't even know why I came."

I thought I knew, but I didn't say. When Toby glanced my way, I noticed a dark bruise high on his farther cheek. "Who'd you get into a fight with this time, besides yourself?"

He brought fingers up but didn't quite touch the bruise. "Horny Hopper's pals. Five of them piled on me."

"And you never did a thing to cause it."

He shrugged. "One was an eight-foot Limey with a face like a festered overshoe. They didn't like it when I told him so."

If Toby had really not wanted to be seen at all, or if he'd wanted to sneak in and let himself be discovered quietly by one person at a time, he would not have climbed up to sit on the roof of his shack. Even in that crowd of people all gobbling like a pen of turkeys someone was sooner or later bound to look up and see him.

Aunt Nora did. She glanced up as she was about to get into Reg's truck. Maybe she wondered where the racket was coming from – three crows trying to make more noise than Mackens. Instead she saw Toby and dropped her jaw. Of course she couldn't ignore him, she hooked up her arm and gave him a sharp scything signal to come on down.

How could this be explained? He *joked*! He shouted at her. I believe he hated knowing that he was expected to act the mourning long-faced widower in front of this crowd. He couldn't stand it that he was supposed to stop being Toby and start being someone else. He had to show them this. Besides, he knew Nora liked him to treat her in a way that was different from the other brothers. Even before she'd completed her gesture, he was shouting down at her: "Yer gonna catch flies with your mouth hangin' open like that! Come up and give us a kiss!"

Toby could turn the Dowager Queen into a blushing girl as fast as that. "Hew hew!" She laughed and swatted at air in front of her. Then she raised her whispery shout. "Toby Macken, you oughta be *shot*! Is this any way to behave? Get down from there before you break your neck."

It was not Aunt Nora but my mother who came to the foot of the ladder, looking solemn. "Toby, come down. It's time – we've got to go."

All that crowd looked up to the peak of Toby's roof. Silence fell. He was the sign they'd needed, to show this funeral was real. In the presence of the bereaved one, they wiped the smiles from their faces. This was more than just a family reunion. Grace put one hand to her mouth and reached out to rest the other on Aunt Kitty's shoulder. Men about to get into their trucks turned to look.

Not one of them would notice he wasn't alone on that roof. Toby filled every eye, always had. Even then, on that terrible day of his sorrow, I would have given anything to be him.

"Stick close to me, kid," Toby said, getting up to start down the roof. "I know I'm gonna do *something* before this day is through and I think you'd better be near."

"You want me to stop you?"

"You could try that, if you figure you're tough enough. Or you could help. Or you could just make sure you come back to tell this bunch about it afterwards. Whaddaya think?"

4

IF my mother could bring Toby down off that or any other roof it was because he respected her more than he did the others. He was wary of her as well. She was not like the women he bowled over with his charm, she was not the sort of woman he could understand. Yet he liked her, too, with the sort of amused affection a mischievous child might have for an eccentric aunt with a PhD in, say, astronomy – convinced she was a little unnatural but pleased that she'd noticed he was alive.

When my mother was in the hospital with her yellow jaundice, Toby had dropped by every day to ask, "How's Frieda doing?" He drove to the hospital every evening to visit her, sometimes with Glory, sometimes without. He couldn't stand it when people weren't happy. My mother would have to pretend she felt better than she did so that he wouldn't be too upset. It wasn't enough. He wanted to see her *laugh*. He wanted the old Frieda back, with the humorous snap in her eyes and the determined set to her jaw. Giving him hell.

He broke rules to make it happen. He nearly broke his neck as well. He climbed the hospital wall and stood in her window one sunny day, and surprised her with his face distorted against the glass, his eyes crossed, his tongue stuck out. Then he slipped and fell into lilac – broke several of the bush's limbs but none of his own. The next day he climbed the flagpole and unfurled a wallpaper roll beneath him: HEY LADY, CAN YOU MAKE A LIVING LIKE THAT ON YOUR BACK?

"My gosh," she said, while she packed to come home. "They'd kick me out even if I wasn't feeling better. That boy is crazy!"

Crazy or not, he spent that entire morning constructing a welcome-home archway over our gate, made of planks and poles but hung with old tires spilling flowers and draped with twisted lengths of toilet paper. Across the top, letters fret-sawed out of plywood stood up to spell BLOODY WELL ABOUT TIME!

Toby's respect for my mother had something to do with a relationship that had grown up between them while he was still a boy. He'd always liked the way she bossed him, he said. "That chin out, them eyes snapping, but always a little grin." He'd liked the way she didn't mind when he smart-mouthed her a little – she knew he would generally take her advice. For some reason her opinion mattered. Before Glory, he'd brought girls to our place for my mother's approval. Few got it, but he brought them anyway. She had a good head on her shoulders, he said. And one hell of a decent heart.

But mostly it had something to do with Glory. Glory trusted my mother. Right from the start, my mother had recognized something different about Toby's bride. She'd gone out of her way to treat Glory with special regard. Glory would drop in unexpectedly, sit over coffee at the kitchen table, and watch my mother do her housework while they chatted. She liked being in the midst of that cheerful bustle.

It was only natural, then, that when Glory returned from her latest visit to the mainland he brought her to our place first. She'd surprised him on a Saturday morning while he was reading the funnies, so naturally he didn't bring her until after he'd welcomed her back into the unmade bed for the rest of the morning. Then, singing loudly with his terrible voice, sure that everything was going to be fine forever this time, he drove Glory's pickup the six miles down the highway to our place with his foot to the floor. Then he roared too fast down our driveway, slammed on the brakes, and slid to a stop in the gravel just inches from the Ontario licence plate of a long grey Buick sedan.

The licence plate and the Buick belonged to an elderly couple Nora had spotted in town. The husband had "a Macken look about him" so she'd stopped him in the street. Because he turned out to be a descendant of Cider-Jim Macken from Ottawa, she'd brought them out to our farm to meet some of the local tribe. Stories could be swapped, she said, about Uncle Cider-Jim's adventures in the First World War, and the three separate families he'd later raised.

Reg and Kitty had come over to help put new siding on the house. Gerry helped for a while, but took off with friends to leave strips of rubber up and down the Campbell River streets. When Nora arrived with the Ottawa relatives, we went inside for a quick lunch, and discovered that Cider-Jim's offspring didn't share Nora's interest in family tales. He was a senior civil servant, and told us how he was trying to run the country. We were out of touch out here, so far away. We didn't know what was going on. We had no idea what Louis St. Laurent was trying to do for us all. Nora would later say the old coot was "no real Macken" at all, since he spoke nothing but figures and policies and boring literal facts.

The farmhouse my parents had bought when they left the hotel was a square two-storey structure, built by a man named Charlie Sullivan in an effort to win back his wife. A war bride like many of the other veterans' wives who settled here after the First World War, Mrs. Sullivan hadn't stayed long. After a year on the logged-off stump-land her husband had been allotted in the government draw, she fled to a wealthy aunt in London. News that her husband had finished the house did not bring her back. Everyone knew this, of course. We lived in "Mrs. Sullivan's house," though Mrs. Sullivan had never lived in the finished house herself. People said that the sadness of that poor man's broken heart had soaked right into the walls.

My father may have been trying to erase that sadness and make the house his own. Barely an inch of Mrs. Sullivan's house had escaped some alteration. He'd added a wraparound verandah, an inside bathroom, an extension to the living room, and bedrooms in the attic. The new siding followed new windows, new linoleum, new eavestroughs, new shakes on the roof, new wallpaper – all in the past few years. He'd also cleared the second growth surrounding the house and barn, and fenced in three new fields.

We stayed inside just long enough to be polite to the visitors, who admitted they felt uncomfortable on this island, so cut off from the world. They liked to be where things were going on. They wondered if there might be a bridge one day, to bring us into things. When we'd got outside and back to work, it was just in time to see Toby nearly smash into the Buick. "Whose limousine?" he said. Clearly he didn't care. He looked up at the rustling Lombardy poplars beside the house. High clouds flew past, turning sunlight off and on.

"Nora found more Mackens," said Reg.

"Where's Nora?" Toby hollered. "Where's that bossy old tart?"

Nora came out onto the step looking as pleased as she would like to have looked annoyed.

"By God, Nora," Toby said, "don't we have enough damn relatives already?"

"Hush," she said. "People aren't deaf. My word!"

"I hope you found some rich ones for a change. And old, ready to croak. Come see who's in the truck!"

Of course she wasn't still in the truck. Glory had got out on the far side and stood waiting. When she saw everyone turn to look, she stepped shyly out from behind the cab. Toby scooped her up, whooping like some kind of picture show cowboy: "Ya-hooooo!"

Just seeing Glory was enough to knock the breath right out of me. Maybe the others too. You never forgot for a minute that Toby had married a beautiful woman. You could not forget her long long legs and her dark, loosely waved hair and her laughing eyes. But seeing her again after not seeing her at all for a while could hit me like a blow to the chest. What if she hadn't come back?

She looked like Rita Hayworth – everyone said it. She said it herself. Salome. Miss Sadie Thompson. She spoke as if Rita Hayworth were her twin, off having the life she might have lived if Toby hadn't swept her off her feet. "Lord, did you see who Rita's keeping company with now? That girl can have anyone she wants – but why *him*?" She sometimes wore her hair swept up, she usually wore it down. She sometimes wore loose gabardine slacks that rustled around her legs. She wore red dresses and high-heeled shoes that showed off her ankles. She smiled a Rita Hayworth sort of smile that showed you all her perfect teeth, and laughed a husky laugh with some sort of challenge in it that for years had made this boy's neck tingle, and brought a racing breathlessness to my inexperienced chest.

Today her hair was down. She wore a sundress the dark green colour of moss, and green shoes with high spike heels. Fingers slid back and forth on a locket chain at her throat.

Aunt Nora had never considered Glory worth her attention, but my mother and Kitty came rushing out of the house, alerted by Toby's racket. "My gosh, it's Glory!" my mother cried, throwing up her hands. She mocked her own emotions so consistently that melodramatic gestures were second nature. As my father put it, she was in the habit of playing to the balcony.

"You musta heard my colour was growing out," was Kitty's way of breaking the ice. Aunt Kitty thought Glory exotic, a glamour puss. Glamour pusses made her nervous. For people who made her nervous she talked even louder than usual. "Get up here and give us a hug, kiddo. We *missed* you!"

My mother was less inclined to be boisterous. Glory remained a city girl to her, which meant she must be treated with a little reserve. "Nothing's changed around here – show up any day and you'll walk into a crowd. Now come in, it's not too late for some lunch."

But Toby held her from behind, digging his chin into her shoulder. "Isn't she a sight for sore eyes!" His face was all grin. He kissed her neck. He ran his hands down over both her hips. He was looking at me while he did this, with something more than joy in his face. "I'm never letting her outa my sight again. I'm a fool to let 'er outa my goddam bed!"

What did Glory do when she disappeared? No one seemed to know. Toby never said anything that helped. Kids had to make up their own explanations: another husband, a child from a teenage pregnancy, an operation – most of her insides removed. We were forced to guess.

It was known that she didn't stay with her parents. Her mother was seldom home. Her father had lost interest once she married Toby. If she saw them, it wasn't for long.

I suspected an institution – some kind of rest in the care of specialists, for her nerves. You could imagine Rita Hayworth doing this sort of thing. "She signs herself in somewhere, doesn't she?"

My mother would not deny this but her look suggested I was out of line. My father would shake his head. "It might be something to think about before you leave in September," he said. "A country hick in the city. He falls for the first real beauty that comes along and next thing he knows, she's miserable. Too bad that poor girl didn't interview his relatives before she said 'I will,' she might've had the sense to say 'No thanks' instead."

"Not that you're another Toby," my mother quickly added. "If you've got any sense you won't fall for anyone until your education's behind you. Otherwise, you might as well get a job in the woods and forget about everything else."

My mother believed there was no limit to the future awaiting her children if only we got off the Island in time. Ambassadors. Industrialists. Brilliant scientists. Anything that could be achieved with serious study and work. Giving up an education for a job in the woods was not what she had in mind. That's what my father had done. My father had been a good student at school but *his* father had noticed he was also good with his hands. If a boy was good with his hands, then school was a waste of time. The place for him was in the woods where he could earn a regular wage. My father started with the logging company when he was barely fifteen. "He might have been a doctor otherwise. Or a lawyer." I had heard this a thousand times.

It was the truth, of course. But still, I would look at my father's hands. The knuckles were large, the nails were cracked, his palms were thick with yellow calluses. Grease had worked itself permanently into the creases. It was hard to imagine those fingers thumbing through the law books my mother believed in, or holding a stethoscope against a lady's chest.

Toby stayed inside to entertain the relatives. Explosions of laughter rattled the windows. But Glory came out and started

61

towards the barn; someone must have told her about the new kittens. That lovely willowy woman never walked a straight line anywhere, she seemed to drift – brushing fingers across the faces of daisies, dragging her hands through the hay, stooping to pick herself a yellow cowslip from beside the spring. She paused to unclasp old quivering Sparks from his doghouse chain. He leapt and panted and ran barking circles around her, then raced in larger and larger circles until he suddenly veered off and nipped under a fence. We wouldn't see him now for three or four days.

When Glory reached the barnyard gate I dropped siding and hammer to run after her. Inside their high wire fence Rhode Island reds moaned in their dust baths (gravel grinding silently in their gizzards). As soon as we'd got out of earshot, she said, "You see all that stuff he brought home while I was away?" Glory had never taken up the family habit of saying everything loud enough for half the countryside to hear.

I nodded. I'd seen. More lumber, more salvaged plumbing, stacks of duroid shingles – all lying in the grass and rose bushes around the shack. Even our barnyard was tidier.

"He promised he'd have the kitchen fixed up like new. Surprise – he hasn't! Why didn't you make him do it?"

"You know I can't make Toby do anything."

"Nobody can. Did you remind him?"

"I reminded him."

"Good for you. He'll feel terrible for a while, he'll love me to pieces, but I still won't get my kitchen. Did you think of offering to do it for me yourself?"

"I thought of it. I've thought of it before. But you know what Toby would think of that."

She laughed. "I didn't really mean you should." Once she'd tried to do some repairs herself but had only made Toby mad.

"So here I am," she said, turning to face the buttercups and cow-pies of the barnyard, "back in beautiful downtown Mackenville."

She would never say "Waterville" if she could help it, she couldn't make her city tongue slur it like the rest of us: *Warrvull*. Warrvull General Store. Warrvull Hall. Sometimes she said "Portuguese Creek," to take in the whole wide area north of town where scattered Macken farms were linked by those nameless streams. Whatever she called it, her tone of voice suggested that none of it was real, at least that none of it was real for her.

"I'm glad you're back," I said.

She looked at me – I suppose she was wondering how much I knew. Glory had always treated me like an adult, even when she'd first arrived and I was seven years old. "I used to love dancing – did I tell you that? The Commodore Ballroom." She went in through the barn door and stood blinking into the dark. Motes of hay dust floated in the stripes of sunlight angling down from gaps in the wall. The air smelled of spilled milk and new hay. "A bunch of us used to dress up on Saturday nights. That's where I met Toby – you knew that." She crossed her arms and cupped her elbows in her hands. Toby had been in Vancouver to buy some machinery and decided to find out what city life was like. He'd been great at the polka then. Still was.

I scooped up one of the kittens from the hay in an unused stall and handed her over to Glory, who stroked the tiny head. The tomcat hadn't come back to kill this litter yet.

"You dig up any more names?"

She smiled. "The lawyer in *A Place in the Sun*? Born in New Westminster."

Every time Glory returned from the mainland she brought more names of Hollywood people who'd started life in this country. She had a friend at the Vancouver *Sun* who knew these things. This was meant to show me it wasn't impossible. Tugboat Annie, Glenn Ford, Deanna Durbin, Giselle Mackenzie, Norma Shearer, Fay Wray. Jack Warner was from Ontario. But she'd had to admit that most were taken south by their parents when they were children. And anyway, they were all from Back East. Glory had promised to find people from closer to home.

"Alexis Smith was born in the Okanagan." She shifted the jar of Vaseline around on the dusty two-by-four spacer between the studs, then rearranged the wire brush and the stiff greasy rag – tidying up.

"*Of Human Bondage.*" I hadn't seen the movie, but I'd seen pictures of Alexis Smith. "You think she and Yvonne De Carlo pal around?" Yvonne De Carlo's family lived just down the street from Glory's parents, I knew that. She and Glory might have waited at the same bus stop when they were girls.

Glory's gentle gaze was something I could almost feel, but after a moment she looked away.

It wasn't just that she treated me like an adult. The reason she could take away my ability to breathe was that she'd always treated me as though I was of some interest as a male. To the other aunts I was just a nephew – the memory strong of diapers and snotty nose. Glory made me feel that I already was what the others thought I might become only if I worked at it hard enough: a man.

Glory looked out the dusty window towards the house, where my father and Uncle Reg hammered siding. "Your mother's so lucky," she said. "She had it all from the start – your dad." Holding the kitten against her breast, she moved to the half-door at the end. "And she has you."

"Not much longer she hasn't."

She pushed open the half-door and stepped out, walking tiptoe on red clover and pineapple weed alongside the winding cow trail. The shape of last year's manure pile was stained into the unpainted wall of the barn.

"John Ireland was born in the Okanagan too," she said.

This was a surprise. "You sure of that?"

She nodded. "*Red River*."

Beyond a small patch of thistle, we entered the nearest pasture – a world where cows grazed amongst stumps left by loggers, and charred by a forest fire that had gone through before I was born. Most stumps were ten feet high, burned hollow – the forts and playhouses of our childhoods. Castles and dungeons. Cousins had come on weekends and summer holidays to act out bloody wars and tales of terror inside them. Fallen trees were pirate ships, with crow's nests up in the twisting snarl of roots. Toby had showed us how he used to play himself, before he'd got too old.

The trail passed between huckleberry bushes and skirted the craters of uprooted trees. Somewhere a meadowlark sang, then sang again.

"Jack Benny's wife grew up in Vancouver."

"You don't know anyone from the Island? You haven't dug up any directors?"

She sighed. "Oh, Rusty."

"But I can see in your face there's more."

She bent to peer in through the entrance gap to one large stump. In the first years of her marriage, she had sometimes joined in our games. She'd been our Sleeping Beauty while we fought our way through the vines. Now there was nothing inside that stump but powdery dirt on the floor and the lovely smell of ashes and charred wood. Red ants travelled up the wall from tiny holes, which spilled the paprika powder of interior decay.

Yet she ducked inside with a small cry, and came out with a strip of lacy curtain in her hand. "Look!" It was dirty, of course. And rotted away in places, but you could see the pattern of interlocking roses in it still. "This was draped over Sleeping Beauty's bed, remember? A flattened cardboard box!"

Laughing, she put the kitten into my arms and whirled away with the lace, tracing patterns in the air. Then she kicked off her shoes and leapt onto the log that had once been a pirate galleon, ploughing through the waves of buttercup and salal with plundered gold and kidnapped beauties on board. She ran up the slope of the tree's full length to the trellis-work of roots from which "Land ahoy!" and "Prepare to die!" had been shouted. She climbed the vertical network, the lacy curtain trailing down her back, and stood as high as she could with both arms flung out wide.

A cowbird alighted on a crabapple tree – male, green as oiled metal. Then flashed away.

"You never asked me to be your figurehead," she said. "I could have sung for you, while we sailed around the globe."

"You can be a figurehead now," I said.

She might not have heard. She dropped her arms to her side. "They can't see us from the house. The barn's in the way." She climbed down. It seemed that she may have been sad. She raised her arms out level and walked down the slope of the log as though it were a tightrope, one bare foot carefully in front of the other. Then she jumped to earth, and put on her shoes.

"You'll like it over there," she said.

"I hope so." In fact, the city world that awaited me was not yet as real as the invented world of these stumps. Though she had spoken often of Vancouver, I had little real idea of what to expect. Rain, skyscrapers, grey cement, crowds. Smart city students who would make me feel like a hillbilly. Maybe a glimpse of Yvonne De Carlo if she ever came to visit her childhood home. Movies at the Orpheum, with its giant chandelier. Thieves, dope addicts, prostitutes.

"You will. You're more like me than any of them." She touched her free hand to my cheek, then ran a finger along the line of my jaw. "It *is* a shame, isn't it?"

"What is?" I said. I had trouble saying it. Her finger moving along my jawline sent an electric charge directly down to my groin. She wasn't supposed to do this.

She looked at me as though she knew exactly how I felt and was sadder about it than anything had made her feel before. "You'll meet someone a little like me one day. I hope you do." She laughed like someone thinking of a sad joke. "But that won't do me any good, will it?"

I raised my hand to touch the curve of *her* jaw, but she moved away, shaking her head like someone who'd walked through spiderweb. "You better give me that kitten, I must have scared the poor thing half to death."

5

Whenever Glory returned from the mainland Toby shut down the mill, sometimes for most of a week. He couldn't stand to be apart from her another hour. Sometimes they went off to camp by an isolated mountain lake. Adam and Eve in a tent, my father said. Sometimes they stayed home and played like honeymooners on the beach – sunbathed, swam, ate picnics with salads and wine, made love beneath the driftwood – then went to movies at night, danced at the Union Bay Hall, or dropped in on parties up the Dove Creek Road. Glory wore a different corsage every day. Toby bought her dresses, underwear, bouquets of flowers. Whenever you saw them, they were laughing, they hardly noticed you were there. The night before Toby returned to work they threw a giant party for family and friends that lasted until the sun came up. Partyers gathered outside to see him off.

Nothing of the sort took place in July of 1956. Toby's joy did not last long. The next morning we were back at the mill, where scowling Toby pushed logs into the whirring saw as though he hoped to hear them scream for help.

At lunch we sat on the pier with our buckets beside us and our feet dangling into the water of Portuguese Creek. The heady scent of freshly cut yellow cedar dominated the smells from the golden sawdust mountain behind us. Bigleaf maples leaned out from the bank on either side, to lace a kind of canopy above us. "What an asshole I am!" Toby said. "She was gone for a month, you'd think I coulda done some of the things she wanted."

I knew what she had to put up with. Peeling wallpaper, a wide gap beside the kitchen window, cupboard doors hanging off rusted hinges, a little hotplate instead of a decent stove. She'd been asking for years. It was only because she was crazy about Toby that she came back at all.

"You got sidetracked," I said. It was what I was supposed to say.

It was also the truth. It happened every time Glory went away. Once, Toby had found a convertible two-door Thunderbird he wanted to buy her, but it had been in a few accidents and needed repair. He would paint it cherry red, her favourite colour. He would install twin exhausts, he would put in a radio, he would cover the torn seats with the skin of a leopard. Glory would be seen racing up and down the roads in the district's most glamorous car. Instead of working on repairs to the shack, he'd spent his evenings in the Riverside beer parlour arguing with Harry Crown about the price. Harry sold the Thunderbird to someone else the day before Glory came home. Parties, picnics, and new lingerie helped make up for the loss.

This time Toby had got it into his head that he wanted Cal Morgan's plane. He would take Glory up for joyrides over the Strait, up and down the Island. He and Glory would both learn to fly. Cal had been a pilot during the war, and ran a charter business with his Piper Super Cub, taking government officials and timber cruisers into the mountain lakes. Toby proposed a trade – the plane for a partnership in the mill. Cal only laughed. He wouldn't consider it, but he didn't mind sharing his beer. Toby went down to Cal's every evening and tried to change his mind, until it was again too late.

"She thinks I'm a shit," he said.

"I don't think so," I said. "You just think that yourself."

He looked as though I'd said something profound. "You're right. I've been thinkin' too much. Forget it. Glory knows I'm crazy about her – that's what matters." We watched a shy raccoon come out of the woods on the far side of the river. It stared at us for a minute, a masked bandit nervously curling and uncurling its fingers in the daylight. Then it decided not to trust us and returned to the woods with that awkward high-hipped walk my father called the dirty-diapers waddle.

"I hope ol' Miriam Lester don't go talking to her," Toby said.

"What's Miriam Lester got to do with it?"

He screwed up his face as though this were painful to think about, and drove his fingers through his hair. "Soon as Glory's gone she shows up and thinks we oughta be back where we were. Just try to get rid of her!" It seemed a terrific burden, having to fight off the Miriam Lesters of this world.

Don't fall in love with Toby Macken, people used to say, it could be fatal. Elvira Marsden threw herself in front of a truck when Toby announced he wanted a girl with daintier feet. When Toby got tired of Lindy Parkinson and started dating the Mitchell twins, Lindy ran off to Europe and was never heard from again. Of course, this sort of thing did not stop women from falling in love with Toby. It may even have made him more attractive. Though nearly every girl in the district had been crazy about him, he married a mainland beauty that nobody knew. Nobody had even *seen* her, until he came home and introduced his bride.

"It isn't fair," I said. "They chase you even when they know you're married. You better tell me your secret and leave them alone."

70

Toby raised his feet from the water and watched his toes wriggle. "Hold up your feet," he said. "Let's see."

I lifted my dripping feet and held them steady. They were bigger than his, and whiter.

"We know what they say about the size of a guy's feet," he said, "but that's a lot of bull. See that little patch of hair on my big toe? You don't have it. That's how you tell who's got sex appeal and who don't."

"Don't be stupid," I said. I dropped my feet into the creek and scooped sideways, splashing his corduroy pants.

"Okay! What you need advice about isn't how to get the girls, it's who you ought to go after. I wouldn't touch a Macleod. What's the matter with you anyway?"

"Lynette's pretty."

"There's lots better lookin' than her."

"Well, I like her, we're friends. And she'll park for hours."

He laughed. "She let you go all the way?"

"C'mon, Toby."

"Come on yourself. How far you get with that girl?"

"She isn't Nettie Rollins. She gets herself all in a lather and then she panics. She starts talking about some *husband* who'll be mad she never waited."

"Thank your lucky stars for that," Toby said. "Old Macleod'd have his shotgun up your arse in a minute, marching you down the aisle." We stared into the creek water for a few minutes in silence, and watched a pair of mallards nibble at grasses along the bank. Then Toby lay back on the uneven planks with his hands behind his head and looked through the maples at sky. "That her I saw you with the other night, going into the show?"

I nodded. "*Guys and Dolls*."

"Any good?"

"Marlon Brando's not bad. I'm not a Jean Simmons fan."

"She that long-legged broad in the posters?"

71

"That's Vivian Blaine. Singing and dancing's not my sort of thing either, but there's one good fight scene in a bar. Lots of bright colours. It's Goldwyn's sixty-ninth film, did you know that?" With Toby looking dreamily at the sky, it was easy to keep on talking. "They say it cost five and a half million dollars to make. He paid a million just for the rights – the highest price ever paid for a single property."

"Christ."

I couldn't tell if he was listening or if he was thinking about Glory again.

"That's because it was such a big success on the stage. Ran three years on Broadway. Toured sixty cities."

"Here I thought you bought them magazines to jack off at the pictures of movie stars. Sounds like you actually read them."

"*Battle Cry*'s coming next week. Tab Hunter. *The Creature with the Atom Brain* and *Apache Fury* are on now – double feature."

"*Apache Fury* sounds like something I'd like." Toby's voice was distant, his gaze somewhere beyond the tops of the maples. It didn't seem to occur to him that Glory would hate a movie called *Apache Fury*.

It was Toby who'd got me interested in movies. Before he was married, and even afterwards, he'd sometimes drive me in to town on Saturday afternoons, to meet with his pals at the picture show. Gene Autry. Roy Rogers. Horses, outlaws, and guns, sometimes a little singing. "Oh, that strawberry roan. . . ." At first I went to be seen with Toby Macken. Guys clustered around him outside the theatre. Girls made eyes as they passed, and giggled. Inside, I sat to one side of him, in the midst of his friends, but soon after the lights went down one girl or another would move in to sit against his other side. I never discovered how she knew she'd been chosen. Afterwards, if she knew what was good for her, she would make a fuss over me and the three of us would stop for a bottle of pop before they drove me home.

Toby never fell totally under the spell of the movies. He had trouble with being anonymous in the dark, he hated to share attention with the figures on the screen. He would make comments, holler out warnings, crack jokes – "Where the hell is the cavalry?" – just enough to get a few laughs, keep people aware that he was in the theatre, but not enough to get us kicked out. He commented upon the quality of the popcorn and made a great noise unwrapping chocolate bars. He threw wadded-up silver gum wrappings at the backs of people's ears. No one ever claimed that the movie had not been improved by his presence.

I wasn't much aware of Toby's alternative show – even later, when Glory was with him. Heart racing, I disappeared into the world on the screen. When the cone of projector light faded out at the end, I was sick with longing. I didn't want to live inside the movies, I wanted to make them. When I confessed this to Toby, he laughed. I laughed too, to show that I wasn't a fool. I said it myself: "Why not plan to be King?"

Yet, over the years, he showed interest in the "storyboards" I sometimes sketched out, for thrillers set in primitive jungles and murder mysteries starring cigarette-smoking beauties. Like the other aunts and uncles, he and Glory sat through calendar-photo travelogues and cartoon melodramas I'd pasted to the backs of wallpaper rolls and projected with my red tin lantern-slide on the bedroom wall.

Aunt Kitty said she could see it coming: a remake of *Gone With The Wind*, set right here on the Coast! "I'm putting in my order now – I want to be Evelyn Keyes and I want to *sing*."

Uncle Buddy could already see my name beneath the

roaring lion. "Metro-Goldwyn-Mayer-and-Macken, whaddaya wanna bet?"

Toby said little. Mostly he grinned. But it was Toby who stole showcards for me from the glass case outside the theatre. It was Toby who bought me a book about Hollywood. And when he found a 16 mm movie camera in the men's room of a Nanaimo beer parlour, he brought it home and handed it over. "Just remember, I expect to get in free whenever they're showing your stuff."

It was a single lens Bell & Howell magazine 200, with chrome edges and brown leather sides. I held it in the palm of one hand, hardly able to breathe. "Something's broken inside," Toby said, "but your old man should be able to fix it." It wasn't the giant four-lens sound-proof camera pictured on page 6605 of the *Book of Knowledge*, Volume 18, but it was a start. Holding it in my hand, I could see myself sitting where Sidney Franklin sat in the photograph. Beneath the mounted camera with his hands together in his lap, he strained forward to watch Fredric March and Norma Shearer record a scene from *The Barretts of Wimpole Street*. For a day or two I thought Toby had altered the course of my life.

But my father who could fix anything could not repair the spring motor for a Bell & Howell 200. A replacement, I learned from a shop in town, would be as expensive as buying a whole new camera.

"Where'd you plan to find the money for film?" my father said. "You think a projector is going to drop out of the sky? Where'll you learn what you'd need to do it right?" This movie business clearly worried him. "You'll end up like Stewie Foggitt, pouring his money into that homemade zoo that nobody ever goes near. He lives poorer than them ratty old beasts he feeds."

I shrugged, and made as though it didn't matter much one way or the other. But I understood what he meant. The woods had been closed for fire season last summer, and closed again in January for snow. There was no money lying around. When he could afford only a few dollars towards my education, how could I spend my savings on a camera?

Anyway, I knew that to make real movies you'd need a 35 mm Moviecam at least, not to mention an editing machine and an endless supply of film. When I'd saved enough summer wages to replace the motor, I bought the Meteor instead. My father had heard about it from a friend at work. Silver-blue. Sun visor. Lowered rear end. A radio. A sizable dent in one door. Five hundred dollars cash. I'd need something to drive at university, he said. Especially if I hoped to come home on holidays. I put the useless camera in the glove compartment with the intention of tossing it into the bush one day, or off a bridge, but hadn't yet got around to doing either.

Whenever Toby felt bad about disappointing Glory, he would shut down the mill and deliver overdue orders, pushing one guilt aside by taking care of another. "We gotta get that lumber down to Peterson." He used his socks to dry his feet, then pulled them on. "He's been bitchin' again. If we don't do it today I'll never hear the end."

Toby would often forget to deliver the lumber he'd cut. It was only the cutting and planing he cared about, reducing that pile of logs on one side of the mill while building up the tidy stacks of lumber on the other. He liked to see the stacks of two-by-fours and two-by-tens pile up. If he hadn't had to make a living he'd have kept it all – just piled it in beautiful uniform rows, like a city growing in his yard. He put off deliveries until people threatened to take their business elsewhere.

Because Toby's mill was ten miles south of his shack and only a short distance north of town, getting to Peterson's place should not have taken long. We had only to follow the Lower Road until it joined the highway, then cross the high lattice bridge and pass up the main street in the direction of the glacier. But Toby never drove through town without honking his horn at everyone he knew, drawing attention to his many-coloured truck – red left fender, blue passenger door, yellow hood, all salvaged from other people's wrecks. He hollered insults out the window at friends. When there was a pretty woman on the street, he went around the block for a second look. Eventually he would find a reason to stop: sometimes for coffee, sometimes for a beer in the Riverside, sometimes just to stand on the sidewalk and talk. Once, when we were forced to stop while a railway train of logs crossed the street, he got out and talked with the tailor outside his shop. I sat where I was and watched them go past – twenty, thirty, forty flatcars, a half hour's worth, loaded with bark-tattered, pitch-smelling, yard-thick logs. At the same time I could see, through the flashing gaps, people watching open-mouthed on the other side. Counting, some of them, and covering their ears against the slow, steady, thunderous clacking. Drinkers in the Riverside stood at the window with beer glasses halfway raised. If I hadn't already known it, I might have discovered the principle of the motion picture film.

While Toby and the tailor yelled into one another's face.

This time he got through the whole three blocks of the main street before pulling up by the United Church. "Look here, they've finished the roof." The timbers had come from Toby's mill. Within a minute he was up on that roof. He lassoed the steeple with a rope he'd taken from under the seat and went right up the cedar shakes to stand on the top. When he saw that a number of people had stopped to look, he started to dance, holding the cross with one hand.

"It's that Macken," somebody said. "Come down from there, you fool!"

Instead of coming down, Toby insisted I climb up and join him. He threw down the rope so that I would have to obey. Without it, he couldn't get down himself.

Someone said, "Don't do it, son – you wanna turn out like *him?*"

This was all it took to get me started. After three limp throws, I finally lassoed the sturdy corner where Toby had hung the rope. This didn't guarantee an easy climb. The new shakes of the lower slope were slippery. I had to hang onto that rope and scramble – my knees did as much of the work as my feet. Eventually I got to the base of the steeple, but couldn't go any farther. When I looked out at the crowd that had gathered – including a man with a clerical collar – the world lurched to one side and went spinning. I closed my eyes and hoped I wouldn't fall.

When I opened my eyes the world seemed to have settled a little. Main-street traffic had slowed to watch.

Watching from a block away was the large neon face above the entrance doors to the movie theatre. It may have been Winston Churchill, or it may have been the theatre's owner, who was nearly Churchill's double and smoked cigars. Inside, he sat at one end of a plush chesterfield every night to watch the patrons filing through the lobby, counting heads and multiplying by six bits, my father said, to see how much richer he was tonight than last. I'd never found the courage to ask him if I might visit the projection room. I wanted to handle the round metal cans that came in on the Coachlines bus, and to watch the film go clicking through the sprockets, and to see a movie through one of those elevated slits in the wall, above and behind the crowds.

I once applied for a job. Ticket seller, usher, janitor – I would have done anything to prolong the joy of walking through the furniture-polish smell of the carpeted foyer, the magic of stepping into the sloped theatre where the heavy red drapes concealed the silver screen. But jobs were already filled by the owner's family and high school students from town.

I recognized some of those students now, amongst the other watchers down on the street. Three girls in peasant blouses were walking towards us, their flowered skirts swinging about their legs. Job's Daughters – their pictures were always in the paper. Popular girls, pretty. One had been a runner-up in this year's Miss Glacier Valley contest. I had seen them at track meets as well. They would probably recognize me as the long-legged redhead their own pole vaulter had barely out-jumped. Country hicks, they would be thinking now. (They smiled at one another and rolled their eyes.) Don't know how to behave when they come to town. I cursed Toby for getting me into this.

"No room up here for the two of us anyway," Toby yelled down. "Just toss up the rope and we'll call it quits." He'd attached a red-and-yellow MACKEN LUMBER pennant to the foot of the little cross.

Most of the crowd had dispersed by the time we'd climbed down and returned to the truck, but the minister was still watching us from the sidewalk. When Toby raised a hand in greeting, he smiled and waggled his head.

"You know him?"

"We've had a few words."

A woman hurried across the street towards us. "Hey Tobe, where you think you're goin'?" This was a broad frizzy-haired woman in a pair of lime-coloured shorts, holding a bag of groceries in one arm.

"Hey, Ruby," he said, leaning on the open door.

"You were gonna meet me Saturday. Where you been?"

"Aw – somethin' come up."

"I know what come up, you bastard, but it didn't come up for me. I heard your old lady's back."

Toby looked off up the street towards the mountains. Directly ahead, the triangular envelope-flap of glacier was white as a movie screen in the afternoon sun. The Indians claimed it was a beached white whale up there, left stranded when the Big Flood waters receded. Wherever you were, it was something you could fix your gaze on if you needed time to think.

"I told you, Ruby. You knew this could happen." He kept his voice low, like someone talking to a child who might throw a tantrum in public.

She hoisted the bag of groceries into the crook of her arm. "Well, ain't that just lovely for you. How lovely do you think it is for me?"

Toby put one foot inside the truck. "Buzz off, Rube. I got this load of lumber to deliver." He slid in behind the wheel and tried to close the door, but she yanked it open again.

"What about a promise you went and made?"

He pulled the door out of her grip and slammed it shut. "Not in front of the kid."

She wrapped both arms around the groceries and peered through the open window. "That's no kid, that's another goddam lying Macken like yourself."

"See you, Ruby. We gotta go." The truck was already moving while he said this. The woman jumped back onto the sidewalk, showing her teeth in a sneer.

"We'll get our ice cream on the way back," Toby said. We seldom passed through town without buying a brick of neapolitan. Toby jackknifed it in two – one half for each of us, to eat with wooden dixie-cup spoons while we drove.

"Okay, how do you do it?" I said, as soon as we'd left both Ruby and the church behind us. The cab smelled of the 3-in-1 oil Toby used on his 30:30, which was slung in its rack across the back window.

"Climbing? It comes natural. I don't even have to think."

"I meant the women."

"Look," he said. "Your mother'd kill me. She don't believe I don't go looking for this sort of thing. I'm crazy about Glory, you know that."

"I'm not married yet," I said. "I just want to know why women are always after you. What do you do?"

Toby knew this was a serious matter and thought in silence for a while. Ahead, the glacier appeared to span the corridor cut by the road through the trees, resting each end upon the pointed tops of firs. It was not a moving glacier; chunks did not break off and fall away; it stayed more or less as it was, draining into rivers at about the same rate as new snow and rain replenished it. Even in summer it remained a stark white splash of winter above the town.

Toby's style of driving was to drop his left shoulder, with his arm outside the door, his right hand high on the wheel. "Women like to think they're living dangerous when they're with a guy. That's what they got with me."

He thought for a moment. "Now you, you're too sensible. There might be girls who like that sort of guy but I don't know any – not around here. Most girls, they like surprise. They want to think they're on this big adventure."

"No hope for me then, I guess."

He shrugged. "You just don't have the good ol' Macken charm." He let some time go by before he added, "Well, maybe you could learn a thing or two. But hell, what good'll it do you over there?"

"There'll be girls at university."

"Sure! Every four-eyed fatso in the province is packing her bags for that place."

"Be serious, Toby. You know what I mean."

"None of your friends are going?"

"None." Sonny hadn't even considered it. He would stay

here and work for Toby. Don Burrows already had a job at the paper mill. Of the nine people in my graduating class, two others had talked about going to Vancouver, but Tommy Martin had decided to train as a physical education teacher in Victoria, and Elvira Storch would start her nurse's training in Edmonton instead.

"Well, don't ask me about university girls. Those sorority dames want men with money." We drove a few minutes in silence. "They'd turn their noses up at us both if they saw this truck." He tapped his fingers on the outside of his door for a moment, then grinned. "But not for long. Give me a week, they wouldn't look at them college eggheads again."

"Not all girls will be sorority girls," I said. "City girls – you should know about those."

"Not me," he said. "I don't know nothin' about them."

Toby could not simply drive into the Petersons' yard and deliver the lumber as someone might deliver a load of hay. When he was forced to make a delivery Toby delivered dreams – or at least the means for making dreams come true. He might be carrying several board feet of two-by-fours and two-by-sixes to the Peterson's front yard, but to Toby we were conveying a dream house to a family that had lived in a shack for years – just as on other occasions we had delivered a perfect barn to a farmer who'd had to house his cattle under a canvas lean-to, and a spectacular little church to a congregation that had been meeting in someone's house.

Toby could not drive two miles down any road without pointing out buildings that had not been there before he'd cut the lumber for them. Solid houses that had been two-room shacks. Supermarkets that had been corner stores. He saw himself as a sort of Johnny Appleseed, making good things grow where there had been nothing before but bush.

We were still a hundred yards from the Petersons' gate when

he reached beneath the dashboard and pulled a lever. Bright red-and-white MACKEN LUMBER flags shot up out of each front fender. Horns beneath the hood played the fanfare associated with thoroughbred races. By the time we turned into the drive-way and started down between two mustard-ruined hayfields, the Peterson family had rushed out of their shack to greet us. Toby turned the ignition off and on again to make the engine backfire. Blue smoke surrounded the truck.

Children danced up and down, applauding, then ran around the truck. Barking dogs accompanied them. The arrival of a load of Toby's lumber resembled the entrance of a travelling troupe of actors into a medieval village. The cattle began to bawl.

I'd seen this many times. The grinning wife came up to take a whiff of the lumber. "That smells so good I could eat it." The husband ran his hand over the two-by-fours as though he could feel the life of his house stirring inside them. Neighbours started across the field to see what was up.

"Goldarn it, Mister Macken," Peterson said. "I was yoost about ready to take my business to Fields'."

"A good thing you didn't, you goddam Scandihoovian bohunk. Get your gloves on and give us a hand to unload it."

"In the Old Contry, I never having to wait so long for nothing." Peterson drew a stack of two-by-fours off the truck and onto his shoulder. "I got to hand it to you, though. Even when a fella he wants to strangle you, you got a way of turning it into a circus. Lookit those little poikas' faces."

"Lookit your own face, Lars," Toby said. "You know I brought you a damn-sight more than lumber."

When we were out on the road again, Toby pounded his fist on the steering wheel and said he'd thought of what he would do for Glory, to make up for being a shit. "I'm taking her to Paris. She's always wanted to travel. I've never been nowhere myself."

"You want to go to Paris?"

"Vienna, then. Where's Peterson from? It was talking to him that made me think of it."

"The Petersons come from some village in Sweden."

"I like the sound of Vienna better. Glory would like Vienna. Isn't that where they have the canals?"

"That's Venice."

"Hell, we'll go to both. She'll think she's royalty. Flowers every day. Servants bowing and scraping. Foreigners kye-eyeing in all them languages. I'll even let her drag me off to one of their operas if she wants, there wouldn't be anybody there that I know."

"Sounds expensive."

"We'll work double-time, catch up on the orders. I'll put the screws on some of the bums that haven't paid for lumber they built their houses with years ago. Morrisons went to Hawaii. Hansens live in a shack but that didn't stop them from goin' off to Norway when his old lady took sick. You and Sonny can keep the mill going and send money when we need it."

"How can I run a sawmill when I'm across the Strait?"

His face was flushed with excitement. "I don't suppose you'd want to put off school for a year?"

"For God's sake, Toby – you know how I want to get away!"

"Another year won't kill you. Anyway, maybe Reg'll come back and work for me. We'll iron out the wrinkles later."

"Glory'd like that," I said. "But you'll have to come home some day. And she'll have to put up with those springy floors again, and doors that don't fit."

"You've only heard the half of it. While we're off there guzzling Italian wine, Cal and Harry'll build her a goddam

83

castle. The lumber's there. When we come back the place'll be waiting. Whaddaya think she'll say?"

"You really mean a castle?"

"A mansion, then. While we're gone I'll have them tear down the shack – to hell with all the repairs that never got done. They'll put up a great big house on the same damn spot. Everything she ever wanted. Picture windows, fancy staircases, chandeliers. Now whaddaya think?" he said. "Is that a good idea or not?"

"I think it's a good idea," I said.

"But you don't think I'll do it."

"I think you'll do it."

"The hell you do. You think I'll never do it."

"Well, it's a bit 'grand.'"

"You don't think Glory deserves something grand?"

"I mean, all of a sudden you're taking her to Venice, and building a mansion? She'd be happy if you took her down to Seattle for a weekend once in a while. And built her a new set of cupboards."

"Good Christ! That's what I mean! You don't have any adventure in you. Seattle! You gotta learn to think bigger than that." He blasted his horn repeatedly at a Chev that was going too slow. "Just keep your eye on Toby Macken, because he's going to make a few changes. You think I don't know how to take off and bloody-well fly?"

6

I hadn't been to many funerals, but I'd witnessed dozens from a seat in a movie theatre. Gold miners buried their pals in the dusty soil of Nevada. Wealthy families gathered in an English churchyard, their stricken faces partly obscured by veils. John Wayne read from the Bible over the grave of someone he'd shot himself, trying – as one of the cowboys says – to make the Lord a partner in his crime. But rather than a predictable graveside scene, a film of Glory's funeral would need to pay attention to Mackens stepping out of cars before the little chapel in town, bracing themselves to enter a building that filled them with dread: Kitty and Reg removing their cowboy hats and eying the chapel as though it might reach out and swallow them; Uncle Buddy plucking at his flushed hot throat while waiting, with car door open, for Grace to finish her cigarette; Uncle Avery and Helen linking arms and waiting for their adult children to join them; Uncle Martin and Edna stepping down from either side of their truck with the homemade camper, eyes narrowed as though prepared to do battle. Crowds of friends and acquaintances waited outside the door, to see how things would turn out.

For all their sorrow you couldn't be sure they'd behave.

Mackens were uncomfortable inside anything resembling a church. If Mackens stayed uncomfortable long enough they began to act up, even if they didn't want to. They liked to remind themselves of the time Martin accidentally released a two-tone fart in the middle of a prayer, at Grace and Buddy's wedding. Edna was so shocked she yelped, and elbowed him. He snorted. Others snickered. Soon the entire family was hunched over and shaking, trying to keep their hilarity to themselves.

Solemn occasions made things worse. Mackens couldn't believe long faces weren't exaggerated. Of course they knew that to act up at Glory's funeral would be going too far, Toby would go off the deep end altogether. Not even other Mackens would find it amusing. But knowing this would only make it harder.

At least I wouldn't have to sit amongst them. As soon as my mother had got Toby down from that roof and bullied him into his wedding suit, he grabbed me by a sleeve and asked me to go in his truck. He wanted me with him in the chapel's little private back room. "If you don't do it, Nora will. I don't want her anywhere near me."

"I hope this fellow don't get started on sin," Uncle Buddy said, as we gathered outside the chapel door. He checked to see that his pills were still in his pocket. "Goodness knows I'll walk right out." He said this in the direction of the undertaker's assistant, an awkward lanky boy whose face appeared stiff with terror. "When they get their teeth into sin they make me want to puke."

"Don't look at me if you do!" Grace waved her arms about as though to fight off several attacking bees. "I only have to catch you looking my way and I'll snort! Otherwise I'll bawl."

"We'll have to try." My mother snapped a warning glance around. She brushed lint from my father's suit while he checked his pocket for peppermint Life Savers, for the tickle that would attack his throat the minute he was trapped in a pew. Then she did the same for me, and for Toby, who stood glum and flushed and resigned while he waited. This was the only suit he'd ever owned – narrow grey stripes, hardly worn since his wedding. In ten years the jacket had become too tight across the shoulders, pulling up the sleeves to expose the cuffs of his shirt.

Nora had moved on towards the door, pressing the hands of those who stood by. In her long black coat and veiled hat she looked more than ever like the sourpuss grandmother of the Queen. Accepting sympathy as though it were meant as homage.

"I didn't bring any collection!" Grace threw out her arms to stop herself from taking another step. "I better wait in the car."

"Oh no you don't!" Kitty snapped her compact shut and grabbed at Grace's arm. "They don't take collection at funerals. Don't you even know that?"

"They would if they thought they'd get away with it," said Uncle Buddy. "They have to keep the preacher's liquor cabinet stocked."

No one ever explained this easy contempt, or this uneasiness at setting foot inside a church. Preachers were greedy hypocrites, religion was superstitious guff, and people who believed in any of it were fools. What wasn't guff was even worse – hoodoo. Religious pictures gave you the creeps, religious speakers wanted your money, church buildings were erected on the backs of the poor. My parents did not say this themselves; they were fairly quiet on the subject of what my mother called the mysteries of the universe and my father called that hellfire-and-brimstone baloney. But when a gentleman came to the door inviting us to a children's Bible camp one summer, they declined on our behalf. "I'm afraid we're just a bunch of heathens in this house," my mother said as she turned him away, a little sadly I thought. She made it sound as though she were saving him from whatever her heathens might do if she let us out of our cage.

My mother's rebuff was gentle compared to what the black-clad gentleman met on other Macken doorsteps. Uncle Reg grabbed his shotgun and explained that his family were devil-worshippers who believed in human sacrifice, preferably trespassers who'd mistaken a private doorstep for the public road. Edna, on the other hand, told him the Bible camp was welcome to her brats, "so long as you never bring the goddam little bastards home."

They said these things so that they could report to one another later. Mackens didn't need the Bible stories – or so they thought, my mother said, who'd been sent to Sunday School as a girl and seemed to respect what she'd heard there. If you recited Exodus at the Mackens, my mother said, they'd interrupt the Red Sea parting to tell you about their cross-country move, with the youngest kids and all their furniture piled in the Overland, Nora and the canary riding up top. Refer to the anguish of poor Job and they'd tell you how their mother behaved when two of the boys were killed at work in the woods, Vic and Tommy. Mention Lazarus and they'd laugh themselves sick over the time they thought the Old Man had croaked but was only playing possum, to find out what they'd say about him when they figured he couldn't hear. They'd called him Father Lazarus after that, behind his back, until he was permanently dead. After his funeral they'd laughed until they cried, imagining the look on that preacher's face if the Old Man had been playing possum again. "I was waiting for that coffin to let out a roar," said Uncle Reg. "That old fellow'd piss his pants."

The Macken disdain for religious matters was enough to make you think you were missing something. When I met Sonny's neighbour outside the General Store, more ancient now than when we'd sat in on her Sunday School classes, I told her I would look into these things one day when I had the time. She wanted to know if I remembered anything I'd been taught. I remembered her story about the Good Samaritan well enough, I told her, since she'd made us act it out. And some of her explanation of the Twenty-third Psalm – one of her husband's sheep had been tied to the doorknob for the purpose of illustration, but chewed itself free by the time we'd got as far as the cup that runneth over. I told her I'd bought a secondhand Bible and started to read it. "I bogged down in Deuteronomy so I thought I'd try the New Testament," I said, "but I haven't got past Mark."

I thought she'd be pleased that I planned to take a philosophy course at university, to see what the great thinkers had to say. But she looked at the sky and said, "Ha! They'll make quick work of *you*." That was what universities were for, she said, to convince young people that everything folks believed was really a pile of steaming horse buns in the road. She said "horse buns" a second time and, with her face as red as geraniums, strode off.

This wouldn't be any great shock to me, I might have told her. I'd been surrounded all my life by people who thought religion was something you didn't want to step in. Most of them would not have thought to say "buns."

Before any of us had gone inside the funeral chapel, Lynette Macleod came jaywalking across the street in a white sweater with a blue fake blouse-collar to match her gathered skirt. She walked with a lilting step as though she were listening to some happy music, carrying a white rosebud in one hand and driving back the long blonde hair from her face with the fingers of the other.

"Oh-oh, Romeo's got a visitor," Kitty said. "We better make ourselves scarce."

"You going in?" I said.

Lynette shook her head. After only three days I'd forgotten how pretty her eyes were, when she crinkled up the edges in a smile. She drew the stem of the small white rosebud through the buttonhole of my lapel, and reached up to kiss my cheek. "I'm sorry."

"That's okay," I said.

"I should have known enough to keep my mouth shut the other night. I know how you felt about her."

"It doesn't matter now," I said. "Will you come out to the place?"

She shook her head. "I just wanted to catch you. To say that I'm sorry."

"I'll call you," I said.

She was already moving away. "No." She came back and stood looking down. Her hair slid down over her face. She pushed the spread fingers of one hand back through it until it was in place, and tilted up to look at me, keeping her hand on the top of her head. "How long before you leave?"

"Five weeks, six."

She looked towards Toby and my father, who were waiting. "We won't see you around here after that. Christmas, maybe."

"I'll be home for Thanksgiving," I said. "Anyway, six weeks is not tomorrow. I'll call you tonight."

"I don't know." She started away. "Maybe not tonight. Tonight isn't good. Wait."

Uncle Avery watched Lynette walk away. "Not a bad catch," he said. "For a brain." His surprise was genuine. If you hadn't failed at least one grade you must be repulsive to girls.

My mother put a hand on my arm. "Get over there with Toby. Imagine what it's like to be him on a day like this."

As soon as we were in the little room behind the pulpit, I removed the rose from my lapel. This wasn't a wedding. Toby loosened his tie and undid the top button of his shirt. He took off his jacket as well. His face was blotchy. His upper lip glistened. He sat in the soft, plush, beige chair across from me and leaned forward to stare at the floor. Beige carpet. "C'mon, let's get this over with," he said. It wasn't easy to sit cooped up in that too-small bland and airless back room and listen to the minister talk about Glory as though he knew her. He knew less than the people crowded into the pews, and they knew little enough. Glory was only a name to this man, and a collection of facts that someone had supplied. My mother, probably. Toby would not have done it. Born in, raised in, went to school at, worked for, married and moved to. A lovely singer. (True.) An accomplished pianist. (True.) Popular amongst the members of her huge family of in-laws. (Not true at all.) A visitor to the minister's office along with her husband, where they talked over matters to do with the purpose of life and her own future.

Now this was news! Toby's head jerked up. I dropped my jaw in his direction, expecting a loud denial, but he shrugged and looked away. I imagined heads snapping to attention all through that room beyond the curtains. Nobody in the Macken family went near a preacher if it could be helped. If one member of the family had been secretly visiting the clergy, might there not be others? Raised eyebrows would be asking this all around the room. This was the sort of thing he could say about you when you couldn't sit up and call him a liar to his face. If Toby had gone, it must have been under protest.

I placed an eye as near as I dared to the narrow gap between the curtains. The Ontario relatives sat jammed together in the back row. My cousin Colin (Avery's eldest) bounced his newborn baby on his shoulder, while his bride of six months made faces at it and looked around to see if others admired her child.

The pallbearers sat in the front row, facing the flower-heaped coffin. Reg had his wide red face turned down, examining the top of his cowboy hat, his mouth dropped open in a silent exhausted O, the jug spout moist at the bottom. Beside him, Uncle Buddy leaned back with his hand on his heart, examining the ceiling with eyes that suggested he and the ceiling both knew nonsense when they heard it. Avery's eyes were closed. Billy Macken looked pure glum. My father shifted his shoulders around inside his suit jacket, trying to loosen the grip his shirt collar had on his neck. They were behaving themselves so far.

The preacher was the elderly gentleman who'd watched Toby dance on the roof of the United Church.

"Too hot in here," Toby said, getting to his feet.

"Where you going?"

Toby took four steps to the far end of the little room and turned, then paced the length of it again with his hands in his pockets. His face was wet – he was thinking hard. The rims of his eyes were red. He leaned forward to place both hands against the wall, as though he would push it away. He pumped in and out, touching his forehead to the wallpaper stripes. Then he swung and did the same thing against the opposite wall. With his head to the wall, he withdrew an Eddy's match box from his pocket and opened it, and looked down at the wooden matches inside. As though he'd never seen matches before. Then he quickly ignited one with his thumbnail and, pushing back to stand upright again, held the flame to the curtains between us and the congregation. I grabbed the match from his hand and shook it out, and put it into my pocket. "You crazy?" I cursed the undertaker's assistant for leaving us alone in this sweaty cage.

92

It was obvious that he hadn't been entirely serious – he would never have let me stop him so easily. "Well, I can't just bloody sit here, can I?" While voices beyond the curtain weakly attempted a hymn, he withdrew a mickey of rye from inside his jacket and tilted it up. Down his throat went several gulps of Walker's Special Old Canadian. While he wiped his wrist across his mouth he offered the bottle to me. But before I could either take it or refuse, he changed his mind. "Your mother'd kill me." He looked at the bottle in his hand. "I should toss it into the crowd out there. Or smash it against the wall." Instead, he tipped it up and once more drank.

"Sure," I said. "You could club the preacher to death with it, too, if you thought it would make you feel better. That would look good in the papers."

He put the mickey away and looked down at his shoes, rubbing his hand over his jaw. Then he looked at me again, as though he might be considering what I'd suggested. I knew it was my job to stop him. "What good would it do?" I said. "You think they might not be sure you're feeling *sad* enough?"

"They're sitting there waiting for Toby Macken to start his chainsaw and carve up the walls. They're wondering when I'm gonna go in and kick over the bloody pews."

"You don't know that."

"I know *them*. They're wondering who the hell's got me hogtied and gagged back here." He turned away from me – the guilty one.

"They think you're sitting here remembering Glory, the way we're supposed to be doing."

"That's what I'm trying *not* to do! You think I want to remember? You think I can stand it?" He was on his feet again and pacing the room. "If you were made of anything at all you'd've took that match and helped me set this goddam building on fire!"

93

It was a terrible thing to see Toby like this. There was nothing here he could do. He recognized this. He had been reduced to nothing but threats – big talk. Empty Macken talk. Pacing back and forth inside this cage.

"Dammit, Toby, you drag me here to be the one to stop you and then you sneer at me when I try. Why do you do this to me anyway?"

"You're supposed to be the one with sense."

"What sense? You think I don't feel bad myself? You think I wouldn't like to tear a few things apart?"

"Yeah, well, you wouldn't do it."

"You don't know that."

"I'm not so sure you even know why I've got to do something."

"I know why you've got to do something! But I also know that it wouldn't help."

"Excuse me." The undertaker's lanky assistant stood in the doorway. "I'm afraid you can be heard inside." He rubbed his huge hands against the pockets of his suit jacket.

There was silence in the room beyond the curtains, except for coughs and the sound of noses being blown. The preacher must have decided to wait until we'd quieted down. Toby's face turned red. He said, "Who asked for your opinion, you streak of mildewed turd?" but dropped into his chair.

Now my father appeared behind the assistant's shoulder, wearing the half-smile he adopted whenever he hoped to handle a serious situation by making light of it. The Macken chuckle rumbled in his throat. "You fellas think you're shouting over sawmill racket in here?" When we didn't say anything, he added, "The man with the funny collar's having trouble getting through to the Man Upstairs. I figured I better come back and see how much blood's been spilled."

All at once voices on the far side of the curtain began to

94

sing, as though they wanted to drown out anything more we might say. "I need Thee every hour, Most gracious Lord; No tender voice like Thine Can peace afford."

Toby leapt to his feet, giving me a look that filled me with shame. "Screw this," he said, and pushed past the assistant and my father to go out through the door to the street.

I followed as far as the door. "What're you going to do?"

The assistant's face was twisted with anxiety. Was he expected to drag us inside?

"Get pissed." Toby said this with anger, as though he would be doing it against his will. "What else can I do? I'll go find Cal and Harry. When I'm tight enough, I'll come back and burn down this whole fuckin' town."

Of course everyone inside heard these parting words. Those who had been standing at the back of the room stepped out to see what was going on. The others told me later that most of the back row slid out and followed. The preacher didn't look too certain about going on. Nora said, "There he goes!" and clapped a hand to her mouth. All eyes slid to the solid wall that separated them from the street.

The preacher finished up what he was being paid for, though he talked faster than before and may even have skipped parts of his prepared talk. He lost a few of his congregation – both Reg and Buddy felt they ought to see if they could help. Martin jumped up to follow. So did Kitty, ignoring my mother's frown. Still, the reverend forced the others through the verses of a final hymn – "Abide with Me" – before releasing them.

Cal Morgan and Harry Crown were first out the door when Toby said their names. Now they acted as though they'd been hired to protect him from dangerous mobs. "Stand back!" Cal shouted, and went into a sort of a crouch between me and Toby, arms out like a sumo wrestler. Harry put a hand on Toby's arm, but when Toby flung it off and started towards his truck, Harry danced about in front of my dad, to stop him from following across the parking lot.

Even while doing this I could hardly believe it. I darted past Cal and leapt onto Toby's back, throwing both arms around his chest and pinning his arms. Staggering forward, Toby cursed, and bent to buck me off, tilting me up so that my feet were free of the ground. "What're you doing, you stupid shit?"

An elderly woman with two heavy shopping bags stopped with opened mouth to watch. Out of the corner of my eye I saw a green station wagon slow down, and a McGavin's Bread truck behind it. "He's crazy from grief," I heard Kitty say.

Toby twisted, tossed, flung me this way and that. "Get off!"

"You told me to stop you," I said. I could feel the heat from his red ear against my cheek.

"Idiot," he said. He backed up and rammed me against a post of the *porte-cochère*, jolting himself free of my grip. "I figured you'd want to come."

"Dammit," I said. "How am I supposed to know what you want?"

Buddy took firm hold of Toby's arm. "That's enough," he said. "Goodness gracious, you don't want to go making a scene." My father took hold of the other.

Cal grabbed at Uncle Buddy and swung him around, then gave him a push on the shoulder that sent him staggering back a few steps. But Uncle Martin caught Cal's arm and twisted it behind his back, while Buddy recovered his balance and ran forward to grasp Toby by the elbow again.

"I think we've had enough of this," my father said. "Let's just get you into that limousine. We'll be off to the cemetery in a minute."

"I bet that's done the trick," Kitty said. "He's got it out of his system now!"

Toby hissed, and jerked himself free. This time he ran for

his truck and locked the door behind him. While the starter took its time turning over, the others yanked at the handle and banged fists against the roof. When the motor fired, Toby started forward with a jerk and cut a sharp U-turn, narrowly missing a mouse-grey Austin Healey. Uncle Buddy and Harry Crown were both on the driver's-side running board, clinging to handle and rear-view mirror. Cal leapt onto the flatbed and scrambled forward to stand behind the cab, hammering his fists on the roof. Reg grabbed at a back corner as it turned past him, and went running down the street, but Toby stepped on the gas and left him behind, mopping his sweaty face.

We rushed to the movie theatre corner where he'd turned onto the main street. Three long blocks of one-storey buildings stretched downhill towards the river bridge, many of them with awnings out over the sidewalk. Toby's many-coloured three-ton weaved jerkily from side to side; he was trying to shake his passengers. Unfortunately, Rick Percy's stock truck came uphill off the bridge towards him, bringing home three Ayrshire heifers he'd bought from Uncle Buddy a week ago but had only just now got around to claiming. To avoid Toby, Percy sideswiped a lamppost in front of Woodland Drugs and swung so sharply to avoid going in through the display window that his tailgate flew off and clattered to the pavement. When he came to a stop against the tall clock pedestal in front of Crosby's Jewellers, the heifer who'd been riding backwards took advantage of the opportunity to escape. She leapt, but fell to her knees on the pavement. By the time she'd got up, the others had followed her lead. The three went trotting off in different directions, tails high, bawling their confusion and leaving dark thin runny pancakes spattered behind them. Beanpole Percy tried to chase all three at once, in his mucky gumboots and low-crotched pants. Pedestrians fled, or ducked into recessed doorways.

Of course Toby would not have noticed this. He drove on

97

through the highway intersection without hesitating, causing an RCMP patrol car to slam on the brakes. By the time he crossed the railroad tracks by the Riverside he was going so fast that the sudden irregularity in the road surface threw the truck out of control. Plunging down the final stretch, he ran up onto the sidewalk in front of the tailor's shop, scraped a red front fender against the wall of Lowe Brothers Grocery, then veered back in time to enter the high lattice bridge so close to one side that he peeled back the fender, punctured the tire, and set up a squeal of steel against steel so sharp that people all up the street slapped hands to their ears. When he stopped, the police were right behind him. Toby leapt free and jumped up on the roof of his cab.

Uncle Buddy, meanwhile, ran back off the bridge before turning to look. He was nervous of heights. He was nervous of water. He was also nervous of cops. Cal and Harry were less rushed – they seemed to be talking to Toby for a minute or so, then ambled back as though they'd been crossing the bridge on foot all along and hadn't noticed anything out of the way.

"At least he didn't go into the river," my father said. We'd started down the slope.

"Them bloody Mackens," someone said from the sidewalk in front of the bus depot. Since all traffic had stopped, we could pass down the middle of the street. There must have been thirty, thirty-five of us, walking fast but not wanting to break into a run. The heifer that had chosen an uphill escape wheeled and ran back into Percy's skinny arms, then found her neck in a rope.

Someone shouted from the doorway of Hobbie's Café. "Use your lasso on that lunatic in the truck!"

Toby's little dance on the roof of his cab might have been only to taunt the police. When they went after him, he leapt to one of the girders and let himself hang out over the river, holding on with one hand. His dress shirt had pulled free of his belt and gaped open, as though buttons had been torn off. I might have torn them off myself. His red tie flapped over one shoulder. The Mountie who had started to go up after him changed his mind and stepped down onto the deck of the bridge.

Colin walked beside me, holding his baby against his chest. "How come every time he decides to make a spectacle of himself he makes a spectacle out of the rest of us too?"

"Watch where you step," I said. We were passing through the scene of the cattle break-out. Percy had tied the one heifer to his truck while he chased a second down the sidewalk in the direction of Laver's Department Store. All Buddy's cattle tended to be endowed with independent spirits. When this one made a sudden detour through the open door of Ricksons' Men's Wear, Percy whooped and went after her. Shouts and curses greeted him.

I couldn't help imagining Gordie at the other side of me — laces undone — waiting to catch my eye so that we could have a good laugh at this. "Ma and Pa Kettle in Town."

Movie cameras loved advancing crowds. Giant dollies and cranes would be rolling down the slope ahead of us. Howard Hawks giving orders. Townsfolk arriving to lend Montgomery Clift their support against John Wayne, his adoptive father, who will ride into town any minute now to kill him for hijacking the cattle drive. "Take 'em tuh Muhssouri, Matt," was long behind them.

"Theresa's gonna throw a shit fit over this," Colin said. "Exposing the kid to public ridicule."

Sandy Kowalchuk stepped off the sidewalk. "If we're lucky he won't kill nobody but himself." He worked with my dad — second loader. "Something happen between you folks up there?"

My father said, "Toby's got a little steam to let off. He's taking it hard."

99

"Well sure," Kowalchuk said. "I don't blame him. Let's just hope that steam don't scald nobody else too bad."

I suppose there was some talk between Toby and the police. It didn't last long, though, because soon Toby was scrambling up the crisscrossed trusses to the top. By the time we reached Uncle Buddy, Toby was standing up, unsteadily, with his tilting arms out wide to steady himself, his open shirt flapping around his shoulders.

"Dammit," my father said. "If they make him feel trapped there's no telling what he might do. You fellas make sure you don't provoke him."

When the Mounties realized that my father was talking to them they stepped back, frowning. "Who the hell are you?" the shorter, thicker one said.

"That there acrobat's brother. His wife's funeral got him upset."

"It's got us upset too." The taller policeman looked from face to face in the crowd. "We got to close off the bridge. Are all these people his brothers?"

"Enough of us are," my father said.

"It might not be a good idea to make him mad," Reg said. "You better let us talk to him."

"You stay where you are," the thick policeman said. "And keep your mouth shut too – not a word."

A second patrol car pulled up. Uniforms leapt out from both doors. Road barriers were hastily set out, in case anyone was stupid enough to think of driving onto a bridge with an abandoned three-ton lumber truck on it and a man up top. One of the policemen started directing traffic. Since this was the only decent bridge across the river, highway traffic would have to be rerouted six miles through dairy country to a narrow bridge of planks. Cars on the far side would have to backtrack, if they cared about getting to town. It looked as though most had

100

elected to stay and wait for developments. People had got out to watch.

The heavyset policeman got a megaphone from one of the cars, walked over to the bridge, and hauled himself onto a truss. "Come on down, you're creating a public nuisance. Traffic's backed up to City Hall. Or is that what you want?"

"Look out! Look out!" Percy's third Ayrshire came dancing down through the crowd, tail high, bawling and kicking her heels and shaking her sawed-off horns. Percy wasn't far behind her, cursing. "Sonofabitch, sonofabitch!" She ran past barriers and policemen onto the bridge and right past Toby's truck. Percy went after her, gumboots thumping on planks. "Sonofabitchin' bitch!"

Buddy laughed. "If the goldarn fool had picked 'em up when he was supposed to, they'd be grazing away in his pasture by now!"

"You might as well come down," my father called up to Toby. "You don't wanna fall."

"You keep quiet," the policeman said. He swung the megaphone to his mouth again and shouted: "You got something to say, we'll find someone to listen. Just don't go being a hero. You want your relatives to see you break your neck?"

"Of course he does," Reg said. "What's the matter with that fella anyway?"

"He don't know Toby, that's for sure," my father said. "Where's Bert Corbett? This fella's new."

The tall Mountie climbed up the outside of the bridge, as Toby had. When he'd got to the top, he sat a few feet away with his legs dangling and said something we couldn't hear. Then Toby laughed, and shuffled the sort of dance he did on the tops of poles, looking off into space above and behind us. He could do it in a way that made you turn to see what he was looking at. This time there wasn't much. The main street aimed straight as a shotgun at the unchanging and familiar glacier that gave the blue mountain a sheared-off level top. It sat white and cold and brilliant above the town – above the whole valley – even in this summer heat. There was nothing above but unblemished sky.

"Asshole!" somebody called from the far side. A number of horns were honked. A small girl threw a rock, which clattered off the girders and clanged against the door of Toby's truck.

My father pushed past the road barrier and walked over to the heavyset policeman with the megaphone. "Corbett not on duty today? It might be worth calling him in, he's dealt with Toby before."

The policeman raised his chin while he looked at my father. "You better get back there, mister. We don't need any help."

"If you say so," my father said, retreating. "But you're making a mistake."

"Sonofabitchin' cow, yer gonna be hamburger now fer sure, you sonofabitchin' bitch." Rick Percy came back across the bridge, pulling his reluctant heifer at the end of a rope. He paused by Toby's truck just long enough to kick at a tire, and then came on towards us. The crowd divided to let him and his runaway through. "Bloody Macken cows're crazy as the lunatics that breed them."

Uncle Buddy and some of the others laughed. I suppose I laughed myself, though I felt all at once a little embarrassed. Were we here because we were concerned for Toby, or because we were part of a public demonstration of the Macken spirit? When Buddy and the others laughed, it was because they took pride in the insult. It might not have occurred to anyone else that Toby could be making fools of us all.

"We already know who can get him down," I said to my father. "Why didn't we think of this?"

"Frieda?" He went back into the crowd and brought my mother forward. "Think you can talk some sense into that thick head of his?"

My pale mother did not look at all as though she appreciated this responsibility. "I don't know," she said. "My gosh." She stepped forward just a step, to the barrier, one hand against her throat. "I suppose someone has to try." Then she raised her voice. "Toby? It's Frieda."

"He knows who you are," my father said, laughing. "Speak up."

"Toby?" she said again. The Mounties looked at her but didn't interrupt. "You've been up there long enough. Do you really want to cause us so much pain?"

So once again it was my mother who brought Toby down, though not in the way that she'd intended. He danced across to the downstream edge of the girders. Then he poised with arms outstretched for a moment before launching out to jack-knife and cut a clean arc down through air to the river. At least he has his suit jacket off, I thought, as his body and then his black shoes disappeared into a slit in the water. But he was never much of a swimmer.

Of course Toby remembered quite soon that he wasn't a swimmer. When the current's strong pull washed him close to the loading dock at Central Builders he thrashed out and grabbed at a sturdy piling. He held on with both arms until the police got there with poles and ropes to haul him to shore.

My father and Reg volunteered to go with Toby to the police station, so that the others could get on with the funeral. I went along, though there seemed to be little point in it. Toby was going to spend some time cooling off, one of the policemen said; there was nothing we could do to help. Toby had little to say about it himself. He sat on a bench in the office, wrapped in a blanket, and scowled at the floor between his bare feet.

"Look, I'm sorry," I said.

He shrugged. "Forget it."

"You want me to hang around?"

"What for? So you can try to break my neck again the minute my back is turned?" He looked up at me and grinned.

The hearse and the parade of cars had not yet started away from the funeral chapel when we returned, though motors were running and headlights turned on. Family members stood waiting outside the chapel door. When she heard that Toby would be staying at the police station for a while, Nora sucked in a long indignant breath. "Well, go back and get him out! My word, what must they think, a big family like ours and nobody cared enough to pay bail!"

"They weren't interested in bail," my father said. "They were only interested in having a talk with him, and in keeping him from doing himself some harm."

"Then go back and change their minds," Nora said. "Or do I have to do it myself?"

"Toby don't seem to mind," Reg said.

"You could've stayed," Nora said to me. "How does it look – just leaving him!"

"He didn't want me to stay," I said.

"I don't suppose he did," she said, turning away as though to dismiss me from the royal presence. "A fat lot of good you were. We thought you'd keep him from getting too worked up."

You oughta be shot, she would have said if she'd liked me.

"The cops didn't want us around," Reg said. "They said his family's not a good influence."

"Soon as the cemetery's behind us I'll take him some lunch," my mother said. "Then the rest of you can take turns dropping in. We can't just leave him there on his own."

We made some movement towards the waiting cars.

"Anyway, they won't be able to keep him," Nora announced. Kitty guided her by the arm to the opened door of Reg's truck, third in line. "Toby will stay in that place just as long as he wants to and not a minute longer."

"He'll be glad of the rest," suggested Kitty, who looked as though she could do with a rest herself.

"Rest!" Nora and Grace cried this together. Nora backed out from the truck to set Kitty straight. "How can he rest? He hasn't worked it out of his system yet. Them policemen only interrupted him, is all. Climbing to the top of a bridge isn't much – he's done that before."

To my surprise, I felt some relief at this. I hadn't realized that I'd been feeling much the same: climbing to the top of a bridge wasn't much. Not for Toby. I would hate to think that I was disappointed, and yet I admit that I was feeling a little let down. Toby had never been one to repeat himself. He had never needed to.

"The day isn't over yet," I said.

"That's what I mean," Nora said. "He'll still have to do *something* today if he's going to recover."

"You're right," said Grace. "Sitting in that cell'll give him a chance to think up what it might be."

7

M<small>ACKENS</small> liked to meet at Toby's shack because the place could make you feel that some things never changed. It might have been the stretched-out blue expanse of the Strait, or the ancient firs, it might have been the saltchuck-scented air. Once we'd returned from the cemetery, people kicked off their shoes and sighed. "We don't need nothin' more to happen, that's for sure," said Grace, putting on her smock again, over her blue silk dress. "Things can just stay put."

Of course there were signs of coming changes even then around the bay. New billboards invited you off the road to a nearby resort and camping ground. Grant Brothers no longer dumped logs behind the breakwater. The log pond had become a mire of rotting bark, its stink as thick and organic as something dead. Storms that battered the hull of the breakwater sailing ship would one day demolish it altogether, sending chunks of bolted planking up to lodge amongst the weeds at the high-tide line.

Change meant loss. I didn't need Glory's death to teach me that. What her funeral washed up was the sort of flotsam that would challenge us to name, if we dared, what we thought we had lost. Why did I think that someone ought to go howling down this beach, shirt flapping and hair upraised in the wind, while cameras watched from the trees? "We all got terrible crushes on Glory when she first arrived," my mother said. "You were hit the worst."

Uncle Martin stood on the beach to survey the Strait with his feet in last night's row of debris: broken boards, twisted kelp, a ladder with only three rungs, a one-legged chair, a long, thick fraying rope. You could build and furnish a house with what you found on the beach, my father had once suggested. He meant if you got up early enough, and were handy enough with repairs, and if you were crazy enough to spend your lifetime walking from one end of the Island to the other.

Caro lounged amongst the logs like flotsam herself in an Esther Williams bathing suit with tropical flowers on the bust. "The ghouls have returned," she said. She'd propped a magazine against a thigh. Photographs of movie stars: Sal Mineo, Susan Hayward. "I take it the deceased didn't change her mind."

"No, but Toby did." I tossed my jacket over a log and rolled up my sleeves. Hooking a finger behind the knot of my tie, I sawed back and forth until it was halfway down my chest and left it there. "He's cooling his heels in jail." Then I spread bare feet in sand and sat on a log, to look out at sea and mainland from the edge of the Macken world.

Tide had gone out farther. Down along the beach an overturned stump lay stranded on sand; roots that had stayed underground for hundreds of years now sunned themselves, like a dark giant flower. Driftwood scattered along the gravel slope mimicked every aspect of human life: here a side of beef, there a cannon, there a sea snake, an overturned canoe – a log so rotted out it was only a shell. Dragon faces, Medusa heads, circus performers with flung-out limbs, torpedoes.

Others joined us. Some crunched down across gravel to sit on their haunches near the water's edge. Others climbed from log to log up through the boneyard of heaped white driftwood — a giant beaver lodge of logs tossed up long ago by winter storms, resting solid as houses over sand and rocks. Here and there, like spectators on a deranged bleacher, people settled at different angles in the sun.

High above us all, Kitty rode sidesaddle on a slanted boom log, swinging one cowgirl boot back and forth. "Shoot me if you want but I can't keep it to myself no longer," she cried. "What was Old Man Stokes doing there?"

A name to make stomachs clench. Several people shouted at once: "Where!"

Kitty shouted louder. "In the graveyard!"

Everyone stared at Kitty for a moment. If Old Man Stokes had been at the funeral, there could be trouble ahead. But no one else had seen him. Some cried out against it: "Don't be ridiculous . . . You didn't see him . . . That old goat don't have the nerve!"

Kitty bristled. "Don't tell me what I seen!" The fringes on her jacket shuddered. "He was watching from behind Geoff Bull's ol' mossy headstone."

"Damn his hide," said Uncle Martin, still standing with his back to the rest of us. "Toby would've broke his neck if he'd been there."

"Toby could've broke his neck years ago if he wanted to," Aunt Helen said, stepping down to sit on the far end of my log. "But he didn't." Helen's left eye tended to wander about on its own — which was probably a good thing, my father said, since it would take a wandering eye to keep tabs on that husband of hers.

Everyone knew about Old Man Stokes: a giant who'd never

spoken to anyone if he could help it since the day he'd killed his own son. You saw him crammed into his ancient Model T going past and hoped he wouldn't look your way. No one could stand it that he'd edged himself into Glory's life.

"Was the bastard drunk?" Martin said to the waves.

"Probably never even shaved." Grace hauled embroidery out of her bag and set about clamping rings down over an unfinished flower.

"You shoulda told the men," said Em Madill. "They could've tossed him out on the road. He had no business there with family."

Em was not family herself, except by her own insistence. Her grandmother had been a Macken in Nova Scotia, she said, though no one had found a blood connection to this branch. No one at this end of the country had Em's sort of teeth, an overbite that my mother politely referred to as outdoor teeth but my father described as a cowcatcher locomotives would envy. Being postmistress at the General Store, she could declare herself a relative to anyone and get away with it.

Caro turned a page of her magazine. "I got boobs as good as Elizabeth Taylor," she said. "Of course, you probably still like Margaret O'Brien."

"I'm partial to Marilyn Monroe's myself," said Colin, who'd moved up to sit between me and his mother. He handed me an opened beer and tipped back his own, to gulp down half the contents. Aunt Helen reached out for her grandchild, whose name no one could remember, burbling and squirming against Colin's chest.

A yellow-and-brown butterfly visited the wild sweet peas amongst the dunegrass and yellow gumweed flowers at our feet, then flew up to alight on a bleached tangle of roots.

"Well, she had a good big turnout anyways," Grace said. She

held the embroidery ring up close to her face while the needle came stabbing up through. Out went one elbow, to pull gently on the blue threads. The tablecloth dragged its hems over ocean-washed stones.

"Everybody knows what a sweet girl she was," Kitty said, "even if she had a little trouble fitting in – she was shy." Kitty smiled down at Mrs. Korhonen, Colin's mother-in-law, who was shy herself. A sweet, plump woman whose English was very poor, Mrs. Korhonen relied upon her smiles and nods to do her speaking for her. And her famous baking as well, which people claimed they would kill for.

"Glory was refined," Grace said. "She never got used to living up here with us savages."

"You can blame her background for that," said my mother's sister, Lenora. "City people are brought up different than us."

"Let's not talk about those parents!" Grace shuddered.

"What are those little buggers up to now?" Kitty said. "Where's Reg?"

Her boys were a hundred yards down the beach. Mike and Mark sat on their spaniel while Jack dragged it into the water by its ears. Legs rigid, the dog refused to go any deeper than its knees.

"You leave that animal alone, you hear me?" Kitty yelled. "He's a hundred years old – you'll *drown* him!"

Mike and Mark kicked at the dog's sides, as they might a stubborn mule. Jack let go of the ears to drag him by the front legs into deeper water.

"Here comes your father!" Kitty threatened, though Reg was a good distance behind us, leaning on somebody's car. "Reg! Do something!" She spat on a Kleenex and rubbed at her boot. "Lookit that – pitch!"

Reg may not even have heard. Still, the boys raced off down

the beach to escape our attention. The liberated dog streaked for the trees. "Miserable little turds," Kitty said, though her eyes defied the rest of us to agree.

Behind us, cars continued to pour in through the gate. Most of Toby's brothers and their wives had arrived – all but shy Dennis, who'd been out in his garden picking peas when we passed his farm, and Uncle Curtis who must have run into trouble on his way up from Washington State. Cousins from the south of town had come – Bernice Macken and her brother Billy with their families, all thin as willow switches and swivelling their eyes for signs of food. Colin's fireman brother Warner had arrived, with his French-Canadian wife and little twin girls. Distant cousins had driven up from down-Island, some of them representing others who'd had to work, including the Mackens who pronounced their name with the accent last, as though their name had been Mackenzie, my father suggested, until somebody went and died halfway through signing a birth certificate. The Back East relatives had dropped Nora off and left for home in their Buick, convinced that if they stayed too long the Island could go adrift while they were on it, taking them out of the world.

Neighbours like the Korhonens and the Herberts and the Kruegers had brought loaves of bread and pots of hot foreign dishes wrapped in towels. Members of the community who were not exactly neighbours but who lived back in the bush – Prices and O'Mallys and the whole Svetich tribe – brought relatives of their own from out of town. The Winton brothers arrived in their twenty-foot plywood boat, Evinrude throbbing, and dragged it up onto gravel.

Friends of Toby showed up. People drove in who owed Toby

money for lumber aging on their barns, and three men who'd worked for Toby until he'd fired them for showing up drunk.

Outside Toby's shack the giant woodstove churned up smoke and steam like a furious locomotive mired in weeds and debris. Hot day or no, it kept several coffee pots perking, and heated casseroles in the ovens. Red steam rose from the reservoir – rainwater thick with rust. Smoke leaked out from hairline cracks in the firebox. Dark coils rolled out from the decimated chimney to engulf the lower boughs of the surrounding firs, where half a dozen crows rose up to fly with strokes like heavy panting to trees in cleaner air.

Ties were yanked off and stuffed into pockets, shirts unbuttoned. There wasn't a man who was comfortable in a suit, but most kept their jackets on for now. Mourners poured coffee from the pots on the stove, or opened a beer from the icebox. They found sandwiches and cake on the plywood tables, then drifted off past the firepit's turning beef to stand talking beneath the firs. Women walked on tiptoe, to keep spike heels from sinking into the sand. Some removed their hats. Reg ran with quick tiny steps to bombard the crows with pebbles until they decided to abandon the property altogether for a while. Some people came down to join us on the beach, to sit wherever seats could be found in the tangled logs, and hoisted pantlegs and skirts to expose white calves to the sun.

Kitty gave up on her boot. "Too bad old Millie Weston didn't grab him when she had her chance. She'd have kept him too busy to notice Glory."

"When did poor old Millie have a chance at anything?" Grace called. An arm stretched up into sunlight, pulling threads taut and giving a little jerk to set them. She narrowed her eyes against the smoke that drifted up from the cigarette clamped in her teeth.

"That day he drove onto her porch!" Kitty said. "Of course, even Millie didn't want him, she tossed him back."

"Tossed who back?" Edna said.

"Old Man Stokes," Kitty said.

"My God," Grace cried. "It was the earthquake sent him onto her porch. I forgot."

Em Madill jerked upright. "When did we have an earthquake here?" As postmistress she assumed she'd been told everything worth knowing. She wiped her teeth with a lace-edged hanky.

"This was before you moved down from up north," said Reg, who'd come over to stand above us. His beer bottle dangled by the neck between two fingers, twitching back and forth.

"Nineteen forty-six," Mr. Korhonen said. "Seven point six on the Richter. Centre was right under your store."

"The same day Toby brought Glory home," I said, in case anyone had forgotten.

No one said anything for a moment. Gulls squabbled over the edible life on the exposed ocean floor. Then Reg caught his breath. "By golly, Rusty's right!"

"That earthquake tossed us up a bride," Grace said.

"Well, no wonder I kept expecting something to happen in that chapel," Kitty told the sky. "A hurricane or something. I admit it – I'd forgot."

This was no small tremor they had just remembered. The chimney fell through the roof of the school and would have wiped out all of grade two if it hadn't been Sunday morning. The bells of the little church went chiming. Electric poles whipped back and forth like fly-fishermen's rods; wires hooped low like skipping ropes and snapped tight and clearly *sang*. The earth came rolling up in waves, and sent Stokes and his car right out of control and up onto Millie Weston's porch. He wasn't hurt. Neither was she. But the Model T would need a lot of repair.

"Buddy remembers that day," Reg said, the little motor in his throat already rumbling.

Uncle Buddy put both hands on top of his head and ducked. Mr. Korhonen, who'd lived next door to Buddy, sucked laughter between his snoose-stained teeth. "Khee-hee, he can't forget it!"

"Buddy was first in the district to put up an electric fence," Reg explained.

Not to be left out of his own story, Buddy started before Reg had finished. Being an excitable man, he held a hand before his mouth, to block saliva spray. "I, I, I spent most of an afternoon stringing that wire around my pasture. Then I went out in the morning to pull the switch, ready to laugh at the first cow stuck her nose in a field where she wasn't wanted." The tip of his tongue went back and forth, *flick*, *flick*, across his upper lip. He bugged out his eyes. "I pulled the switch and damn if the air didn't start to hum! The earth began to heave and roll. Trees started to dance around and try to fly! I saw two Guernseys drop to their knees; a third went staggering sideways down the slope and slammed into the wall of the barn. Chickens exploded right outa their pen, you'd think the juice had jumped a connection and zapped them! I figured I was to blame."

"But you couldn't make it stop by turning off the switch," my father said, who'd come with Jurgen Krueger to stand with Reg beside the little shore-pine.

"Poor Buddy was scared out of his wits," Grace said. She was his housekeeper then, marriage years away. He started to curse and blubber, she said. He hollered for her to come give him a hand. No more religious than the rest of the Mackens, he promised God he'd give up fooling with modern inventions right away. But God took far too long to think his offer over. "By the time the convulsions stopped, all his cattle had fallen and poor ol' Buddy was wrapped around a fence post starting to cry."

"I'm not the kind that likes to spoil a good tale," Edna said, "but dammit, I thought we were going to hear about Glory." Then she said to Caro, "You got lotion on?"

Caro might have had the beach to herself. She opened her package of cigarettes and ignored her mother.

"Burns in a minute, the moron – no more sense than that tree."

"We'll get to Glory soon," said Reg. He crouched down with his knees wide apart, to make room for his belly. "Me, I still owned the little sawmill up at Comox Lake. Remember that? Before Toby moved it down to the creek. He was off in Vancouver when the earthquake happened. I tell you, that whole lake emptied in front of my eyes."

Em Madill was the indignant unbeliever. "I never heard of this!"

"Right to the muddy bottom," Reg said. "I saw drowned trees and slime! Drained right down a crack that opened up, and must have gone right out to the ocean somewhere, because after a while it come back and flung seaweed and fish all up the trees and on to the sorting deck of the mill."

You only had to have walked along the lakeshore yourself to know that Reg was telling the truth. Things had dried in the sunlight that shouldn't be there: tangled knots of bull kelp and orange crabs and bouquets of purple anemones torn off the ocean floor.

Reg wouldn't go back to his mill after that, which was why Toby bought the business. Reg stayed home to raise horses and practise Hank Snow tunes on his ivory-inlaid guitar.

"I agree with Edna," Kitty said. "It's time we heard about Glory! It was Frieda's place he brought her to – I remember that."

"She had plenty of *fanfare*," my father said. "By the time she come into our yard we already knew this was something we wouldn't get over fast."

They told each other about it, then. Reminded themselves: the day that Glory arrived. Time – the future, even the rest of the day – was held at bay until the past had been put in its place. I could remember this myself. I was seven years old, nearly eight. Gerry was five. Meg was less than a year, and asleep in her crib when the earthquake began. My mother was kneading bread dough at the kitchen counter.

My dad had started back from the barn to run the milk through the verandah separator. The air began to hum around his ears. Something smelled, he later said, an odour of unfamiliar gas. Off across the nearer pasture the line of firs began to sway, as though from a burst of wind. The hayfield swelled up and moved in a series of ripples towards him. Tall pasture stumps rose and fell as though some monster beneath the ground were trying to heave them free. He braced his legs to keep from falling. Milk slopped over the rim of the pail. Before him, the chimney on the roof of our house bent as though it were made of rubber bricks, then swivelled a quarter-turn and toppled. Red bricks spilled down the slope of the roof and dropped to the roof of the verandah, then started to spill down the verandah roof directly above the door I was throwing open in order to rush out and join him.

Gerry hadn't wanted to leave the kitchen table. A fried egg danced on his plate. Cutlery chattered against the tablecloth. Milk tossed up bubbles from his glass and splashed on his nose. He laughed. He thought the world was acting up just for him.

My mother screamed. Cupboard doors flew open and spewed dishes onto her counter. Saucers crashed in the sink. Three china ducks dropped off the wall, downed in mid-flight. Above the stove, boiled underwear and shirts swished back and forth on the drying rack. My mother snatched the clothing down and tossed it across a chair. She went flying off to the bedroom where she grabbed up little Meg and cried, "Bring Gerry, quick!" But the outside front-room door was blocked by the dancing china cabinet, whose silver and heirloom china clanged behind the glass. "The other door!" But when we'd got as far as the verandah, we saw my father hollering something we couldn't hear above the clatter on the roof. He waved his arms. He might have meant hurry, he might have meant stay where you are. Then the bricks came crashing off the roof less than a step before us.

My father tried to run to us, but fell to one knee. We looked at one another with that thundering fall of red clay bricks between us. He might have been on the far side of an opening chasm. He might have been on shore while we drained down a hole. That's what my father was thinking. What sort of father could not halt a tumbling wall of bricks? I was thinking the same myself.

Had I believed the earth would stay steady beneath us forever? That fathers would be capable of heroic rescues, mothers keep calm, and houses stand solid and safe till the end of time? My father had encouraged this. Some things he didn't take as seriously as others did. One day he hadn't come home from work when he was supposed to, he didn't come home that night at all. He returned the next morning with his head wrapped in white bandages: two eyes, two nostrils, and a gaping hole for a mouth. A falling limb had nearly taken off one ear, had opened his nose. He laughed. I could take him to school for show-and-tell, he said. I could tell the kids I'd dug him up in the yard, where Egyptians had buried him thousands of years before. He would lie stiff as a mummy, he said, till everyone had made notes on the pleasures of archaeology, then he would sit up and groan, scaring them half to death. "This isn't funny," my mother said. "You could've been killed." But of course my father laughed in the teeth of anything that would try to kill him. The earth beneath our feet stayed firm.

Then this. The bricks stopped falling. The house settled. But something foul-smelling had been released to the air. The light was wrong. A rumble could be heard, going away beyond the trees.

Inside, one final piece of china crashed to the floor. Now could we laugh, to show that things were all right? Nobody laughed. Gerry began to cry. My father stood up and whipped off his cap to slap the dirt from his knees. He picked up the milk pail and looked into it: empty.

My father took the baby in one of his arms to hush her, and used his other arm to hold my mother against him. "You okay?" he asked me. I nodded. He didn't smile. He held my gaze with his to acknowledge what we now both knew. That the world could not be trusted after all? That a father and son must expect to view each other across a space of falling debris.

Minutes later Uncle Buddy and Grace were upon us in their car, to view the damage. Buddy was pale as paper. "My God, I thought I'd caused it!" he said. His eyes were wild.

"Me too," my father said. "I'd been thinking we shouldn't have moved into this old house before I'd finished renovations. Not with little kids. Too bad a person couldn't pick up a building like that and give 'er a shake, to see if she's safe. Then it started!"

"I was making bread," my mother said. "You know how they make fun of the way I punch down the dough like I'm mad. This time I thought, Well, now I've gone and done it, this dough's begun to fight back."

None of this was any comfort to Buddy. "I mean, I thought

I'd really started it!" he said. "I nearly peed my pants." So Uncle Buddy told how he'd pulled the switch and the earth heaved up, the cows fell, the chickens exploded out of their pen, and the fence posts shook themselves free of the ground. Naturally the rest of us laughed. He had to laugh himself. Then he said, "I guess I come over to see how far my damage spread. But that don't mean I'm fixin' up your chimney!" He stooped to remove a brick from the step, and then another, and stacked them on the verandah floor. "I'll tell you this for sure, I'm gonna dismantle that fence. Barbed wire is good enough for any cow, I'll just butcher the ones that ignore it."

Grace drew fiercely on her cigarette, and viewed the world sideways. "I'll never turn on another light without flinching."

My mother took the baby inside. The rest of us started collecting bricks. We'd got most of them gathered when Reg's truck came roaring in through the gate. Fat Reg was out of that truck before it had come to its usual stop against the walnut tree, and ran with his tiny steps across the yard, one hand holding his cowboy hat to his head. "You feel that?" he shouted.

"Feel what?" my father said. "We didn't feel nothing here." He put one hand on my shoulder. "You see anything here that's *changed?*"

"Maybe nothing much had changed for us," my mother said, back from her visit to jail. "But plenty had changed for Toby."

"How's our jailbird holding up?"

My mother dragged an imaginary ball and chain over to the scrawny shore-pine and became a prisoner looking through the bars of two scaly branches. "Pouting," she said, and pouted herself. "He took the lunch I gave him but wouldn't talk."

"No wonder," Grace said, "if you put on a show like that."

"It won't hurt him to stew in his own juice for a while," my mother said, releasing the pine. "You're talking about the earth-quake? Toby didn't even know there'd been one." She sat on a large flat stone and wrapped her arms beneath her legs, to keep her skirt from gaping.

"When his truck come down the driveway, he was grinning like he thought we'd come out to greet him," my father said. "He leapt up onto the hood and did this little dance."

"Sounds like Toby!" said Kitty. She shook her dyed-black curls from side to side, and grinned at the Strait. Her hat went pendulum swinging across her back. "I wonder what those boys are up to. Reg?"

"Then he jumps down on the other side. Opens the passenger door and someone else steps out –"

"Glory at last!" cried Em Madill, clapping her hands.

" – and stands looking at us like she's trying to figure out how we fit into what she's been told to expect."

"She was," my mother said. "She told me later he'd bragged about coming from a family of crazies. She was looking for signs of insanity. She thought she'd found it, too; she didn't know we'd all been stunned by an earthquake."

"She was pretty, I'll tell you that," my father said. "She had that shiny dark hair and big eyes, and she wore this yellow summer dress."

"You remember what size it was?" Em said. She winked at my mother.

"Anyway, Toby grabs her hand and drags her down the walk to meet us. 'Gloria,' he says. 'This is Eddie, this is Reg, that there is Buddy with his face hanging out, and Grace, and this here's my sidekick Rust.' Then, while Glory's shaking hands, Toby raises his voice and hollers: 'Get out here, Frieda, I got someone I want you to meet.'"

"Toby's soft spot for Frieda!" Kitty sang out, her eyes scanning the beach for her boys.

123

My father said, "I asked him did he enjoy the quake. He says he didn't feel a thing. 'Oh yes we did,' says the girl. 'You thought a wheel was loose.' 'That's right, I did,' Toby says. He looks at her like he was proud she was able to talk. 'The truck went out of control for a bit there, I had to fight the wheel to calm 'er down. Well, damn – so that was a quake?' "

"Then Frieda come out onto the porch with pieces of a broken plate in her hand," Reg said, starting to chuckle again.

"Grandma Barclay's dinner set," my mother said, as sad now as she'd been then. "Blue willow pattern, old as those mountains."

"She looks at Toby like he might've been there all along," Reg said. "Then she looks at Glory and puts the broken china on the railing. 'Who's this?' She puts on her Frieda smile – the one that looks like she's just waiting to be surprised."

"She's doing it this minute!" said Kitty.

"Well, pardon me for living!" my mother laughed. "I can't help the look on my face!"

Naturally, my mother took immediately to Toby's bride. She had a weakness for anyone refined. Since Toby told us Glory had come from the city, my mother assumed she had come from people with money and manners. An education. My mother could detect all this in the smallest gesture, perhaps in the way Glory smiled as she put out her hand. This caused her some confusion – unable to believe that the kind of girl she imagined this one to be would marry Toby. But she threw all her energy into making the newcomer welcome. "Now come in, everyone. I guess it's safe to make coffee."

"Not until that chimney's fixed it isn't," my father said. "I'll get the campstove out."

I had nothing to say for myself. This had come with the same surprise as the earthquake. Though I'd seen Toby all my life with girls on his arm, it had never occurred to me that he might marry one. Married men did not invite nephews on dates with pretty girls, or on down-Island trips with lumber. I waited for Uncle Toby to tell me what he had in mind. I waited for him to give me a bit of a shove to show we were pals, and say the kind of thing he always said when he turned up with a brand new girl. "Did you see the knockers on this one, kid!" or "Lord Almighty, Rusty, this girl is *hot*."

But he hardly looked at me, he was living in another world. When he stubbed his toe on the pile of bricks, he stood looking at them a moment, then peered all around and said, "What's been goin' on?" Hadn't he heard a thing? He stepped back and looked up at the roof where most of the exposed chimney had been broken off. Would he go racing up the roof for a closer look? That's what you'd expect of Toby – to go up and dance on the peak of the disaster.

But he didn't. He looked at me now. "She musta been something, eh? You see that chimney come down?"

I nodded.

"I should've stepped on the gas. I've always wanted to see an earthquake. Some people got all the luck."

After admiring Glory's ring, Buddy and Grace set off to check on others. Gerry went out to explain to the cows what had happened. Reg stood in the doorway and grinned at Gloria Macken, as though he'd never seen anything so pleasant to look at in his life. Maybe he hadn't. Maybe he was getting inspired for a song.

I felt much the same. Even in the midst of a house full of earthquake-shaken mess, this beautiful girl was all you wanted to look at. Toby knew it – you could see the satisfied look in his face: Now whaddaya think of *this*?

My father got out a bottle of rye and poured drinks all around. "To toast the new couple." Rye and ginger ale.

My mother said, "I still can't get it into my head what happened."

"Nobody's hurt," my father said, putting a hand on her shoulder. He held out a bottle of root beer for me, so that I could share in the toast.

A city girl! And prettier than the others Toby had brought around. Far prettier than the daughter of the logging company boss, or the tall stenographer from down-Island, or even the Campbell River Salmon Derby Queen. We'd been shown them all. He'd wanted my mother's approval. Few of them got it. This one obviously didn't need anyone's approval but we were being given a chance to grant it anyway.

To tell us how they'd met and married, the bride and groom sat at the kitchen table and interrupted one another. Toby leaned forward, resting his elbows on his wide-apart knees, laughing, driving his fingers back through his hair, shaking his head. Glory sat calm and steadily smiling, and occasionally slid a hand across the table to squeeze his arm.

"My mother's off on a singing tour. The surprise is still in her future. My father was putting together a business deal, but we told him afterwards. There was nothing much he could do about it then."

They'd met at a dance – the Commodore Ballroom. Toby was in the city to look over machinery for Reg's mill, and thought he'd have some fun while he was there. He'd danced with the sparkling beauty for three whole hours, then waltzed her down the stairs and into the night and right down Granville Street to the CPR docks. At four o'clock in the morning he proposed.

"All this happened in one night?" my mother said. You could

hear the shock in her voice though her face was lit up with pleasure.

"It took me a few more nights to think about it," Glory said. "But it was four o'clock in the morning of that first night that he climbed the side of the Marine Building – tallest in town – and proposed from the window ledge of someone's office."

Suddenly the moon moved out from behind a cloud and lit up the world, Glory said, turning everything silver. At the same time, a great white ship appeared at the foot of the street where there'd been only dark before, and blasted its horn so loud that it echoed up and down the streets. Then it slipped away from the dock, huge and shining with moonlight, and moved out into the harbour to sail for China! Seagulls flew up through silvered light.

"We laughed. Then he yelled it again, so I could hear him down on the sidewalk, with seagulls screaming and wind coming up off the water and that ocean liner blowing its horn. Who wouldn't want to live with a magician the rest of her life?"

Reg leaned forward from the doorway. "You mean to say that a week ago you hadn't met?"

Toby laughed. "You think I was gonna give her time to find out what I'm like?"

"I figure she must know by now," my father said. "It's five hours from Vancouver to here – more time than anyone needs to see a Macken's colours."

"You're making a mistake," Glory said. "All this happened months ago. I put him off. He came back this time for my answer."

Toby looked again at the rubble scattered across the kitchen linoleum. "We raced like hell to give you the news and you didn't even tidy up your house for the occasion. What kind of impression will Glory have now? No goddam earthquake happened here – Rusty, you say if I'm wrong. Frieda and Eddie had a big fight. Frieda threw dishes, Eddie threw bricks. Rusty tossed them socks and undershorts into the mess so his folks'd land on something soft when they fell."

"I hope Glory didn't believe him!" Grace cried. "I've never caught Frieda's house in a mess even once."

"You've tried!" my mother said.

"Frieda does her housework while the rest of us sleep," Grace said. "You can eat off her kitchen floor."

"Glory believed just about everything Toby told her," my father said, "but she knew he sometimes stretched the truth a little. Too bad she couldn't always tell the difference."

"Do you think it woulda changed things?" Kitty said. She hummed a note, as though to show she already had an answer she liked. Then she stood up suddenly on her log. "Reg! My God! What are they doing now?"

Mike, Mark, and Jack had come out onto the beach again, dragging a gunnysack behind them. Whatever was in the sack didn't want to be there. The boys sang "There's a Love Knot in My Lariat" as loud as three small boys could sing it, possibly to cover the struggling captive's yelps.

"Leave them," said Uncle Buddy, slipping a pill beneath his tongue. "Maybe they've captured Stokes. Found him sneaking around the trees and thought they'd drown him."

"That poor old dog!" Kitty cried. "Reg?"

Sighing, Uncle Reg heaved himself upright and started down the gravel. "I don't know why that mutt don't run away from home. I'm thinking about it myself."

By the time Reg got to the boys they had dragged the gunnysack a few feet into the water. Reg's threats fell on deaf ears so long as they came from shore. Only when he removed his boots and waded into the water did they relinquish their hold on the sack and run, laughing all the while. Rather than chase them, Reg dragged the sack onto gravel and bent to release the dog.

"By golly, it isn't the dog," said Uncle Buddy.

We were all standing now, to watch. Maybe Aunt Helen had had some premonition; she'd given Colin his baby and already started to run before we could see that it wasn't a dog crawling out of the gunnysack but one of her grandchildren, followed by the other – Warner's twins, both howling.

"I'm going to strangle them," Kitty said. "If I thought anyone'd take them, I'd give the buggers away."

"If they were horses, Reg'd have them shot," Grace said. She didn't look up from her embroidery to say it.

"You ought to have their goddam pointed little heads examined," Edna said. "There must be something wrong upstairs. Those poor little tikes coulda drowned!"

"They get carried away, is all," Kitty cried. "High spirits! A little water never hurt anybody – those twins are pampered, they overreact. Now look at Helen's face – she's going to try and blame *me*!"

8

EVEN if my Bell & Howell had not been broken I wouldn't have used it at Glory's funeral. I only imagined doing such things – it was a habit, a manner of thinking. It was a way of looking at the world: what if I made a movie of this? When I first began to dream of making movies I imagined jungles, lost explorers, and gruesome deaths at the hands of malicious spies. Or sagas in which natives were slaughtered by men in search of the holy grail – sailing up narrow inlets, riding on horse-back over logged-off slopes, climbing the treacherous glaciers of towering mountains, only to discover that by the time they find the grail they've already sacrificed their souls.

In later years, new elements crept in. Romantic entangle-ments. Murder mysteries. But always, sooner or later, the hero (Alan Ladd's young sidekick, bound by a vow to protect the older man's beloved after his death) must rescue the beautiful heroine (Rita Hayworth) from where she's been chained inside the hull of a sunken ship, left to die in the rising tide. After setting her free, the hero takes her to live in a deserted seaside hotel where they eat fish and wild berries, and wait for a passing ship to spot the smoke from their chimney.

In search of whatever secrets it might reveal, I pored over

my mother's copy of *Under the Crescent*, based on a 1915 "photo play" by Nell Shipman. This was a tattered hardcover stamped "Discarded" by the Vancouver Library on one page and "Compliments of the United Church Marine Mission" on another. A sticker inside the cover warned against malicious defacing of the kind my mother had long ago done with a schoolgirl's pencil, threatening up to two months in jail (Criminal Code, Section 539). It was written like a novel but illustrated with dozens of photographs from the silent film: Prince Touson and the American actress in the Khedival Gardens at Cairo, the new Princess bribing the keeper of the gates in order to escape from the harem, a spy reporting on the Princess's hiding place in a pyramid, the Prince threatening to feed his wife's lover to the leopards, Stanley Clyde summoning aid to rescue the Princess from her death cell.

Treating the book as a blueprint, I wrote a script based on the most dramatic scenes. Then I converted the woodshed to a movie studio in order to direct my own version. Bedspreads became tents. Cardboard boxes were piled in the shape of pyramids. Sand was spread about the floor. Sonny and I attached two tin pie-plates to the top of a vacuum cleaner and set the whole thing up on a tripod made from a lashed-together hoe, hay fork, and shovel – a movie camera in everything but fact.

My mother ransacked her closets and trunks for old dresses and jewellery to drape over the American actress who'd foolishly married an Egyptian prince. She got so caught up in the excitement that she wanted to play the Princess herself. Caro could have the part only on condition that I allow my mother to be all the murdered corpses and the makeup woman as well. She painted faces with lipstick, rouge, and eyebrow pencil. Sonny placed an overturned flowerpot on his head and allowed my mother to paint a thin moustache above his lip, transforming himself into the villainous Prince. Gordie was the Englishman who was supposed to become the Princess's lover, but in the end he refused to cooperate. He'd rather let her die than embrace her. Gerry was captain of the firing squad, but when the Princess tore the veil from her face to reveal her true identity, he refused to halt the execution as the story demanded and shot her several times in the heart.

As the director, I was as ineffectual as my phoney camera. Caro threw Gordie to the ground and punched him until he wept. She chased Gerry down the lane until she caught him by the barnyard gate where she twisted the flesh of his arm until he screamed. When my mother cautioned her to watch that temper of hers, Caro told my mother to drop dead twice and set off marching home. Gordie left soon afterwards, still crying. Sonny wrecked the scenery with his scimitar. And Gerry ran off with the tattered copy of *Under the Crescent* to hide it.

I found it months later, under an attic floorboard. Sometimes I would open it to the full-page photograph of the author, facing the title page. Nell Shipman. Dressed in a filmy low-cut dress, with a string of pearls in her dark hair, she was far more beautiful than the actress who played the Princess. This lovely woman knew secrets I wanted to learn. She knew how to write a screenplay, she'd seen moviemakers in Hollywood turn her story into a film.

Of course *Under the Crescent* was not a movie Glory would want to see. If I were to make a movie just for Glory I would make a sober drama in the manner of *The Country Girl* or *Track of the Cat*. Few of this type ever came to town but I'd been there for *Picnic* all three nights. I'd heard my parents talk about *Kitty Foyle* and *Mrs. Miniver*; I'd read the brief review of *East of Eden* in *Family Circle*, and made up my own plot – a movie I saw in my head.

Glory hoped I would make simple moving dramas with

humour and anguish and honest feeling. She sometimes suggested ideas: a city girl torn between a lumber baron's son and an uneducated boy from the sticks; an opera singer unable to face the inevitable end of her career.

Her suggestions did not appeal very much to me. I gave her a copy of a screenplay I'd sketched for Steinbeck's *Cannery Row*. A week later, at an after-school track and field practice, the coach asked me to stay behind. Mr. Collins, fresh from Normal. He was also my English teacher. When the equipment had been put away and the others had left, he said that my aunt had given him my screenplay to read. He leaned against the door of his '52 Chev, his face flushed – he was as uncomfortable as I was about this. My whole body jangled with the shock of this betrayal. I would never speak to Glory again, I promised myself, or trust her with anything I did.

"I assumed she had your permission," he said. He could see that she hadn't. "She was awfully excited, she thought I might have some suggestions."

I didn't ask for suggestions but he gave some anyway. My taste in story material was pretty good, he said, but I didn't seem to understand bums, prostitutes, or marine biology. If I wanted to make movies maybe I should start with something closer to home. Something I understood. Country life, for instance. Or school. I knew about going to school. He nodded towards the old cream-coloured two-storey box I'd attended since grade one. Two grades in each room, then you moved across the hall. Miss Carrothers' geraniums lay spilled from smashed pots beneath her windows – Ray Berry's revenge for humiliations in Spelling. Mr. Collins opened his car door and lifted a magazine from his front seat.

"*Ladies' Home Journal?*" No wonder he'd waited until the others had gone. Was this what he thought of my ambition?

He laughed at my horror, a little embarrassed I think. It wasn't all recipes and fashions, he said, there was a fine story in there, set in a school, which they were making into a movie. "To Break the Wall," it was called. It was a city school, he said, but I would recognize certain behaviour. A country school like this could be every bit as rough as a school in the poorer parts of the city. "Read it and sketch out how you would shoot it. Then, when it comes to town, you can compare. Do an oral report in English if you want, telling us what you learned."

Of course I didn't do any oral report. Movies were never mentioned between us again. I didn't tell him what I thought of the story. I didn't tell him when I'd seen *The Blackboard Jungle* either, so I didn't have to tell him my opinion of the movie's tacked-on happy ending, or the way it didn't seem to be about school at all but something else – holding on to authority. The use of sound was pretty good – trains, ticking clocks, type-writers, the noise from shop class, Bill Haley's music. Crowd shots of students hanging over bannisters and peeking through windows succeeded in making that school look like a prison. But I mentioned none of that to him.

How would Glenn Ford have handled Uncle Toby, if he'd shown up in his class? Or Sonny Aalto? Sonny got into more than one after-school fight with Mr. Brewer, the math teacher. They'd wrestled across the central hall, down the stairs, and right across the schoolyard to the door of the bus. Once, Brewer followed Sonny right onto the yellow bus and sat beside him, then marched him all the way up the long isolated gravel road to his door, ready to hand him over to his father with a demand that something be done about keeping his boy in line. But Swampy Aalto came to the door with a pitchfork in his hand, and ordered the teacher off his property, forcing Mr. Brewer to walk the five or six miles back to the highway, probably wondering why he'd ever gone into teaching. It was a nice story, Sonny and I had laughed about it often, but it didn't tempt me to plan movies about the battles that went on in our school.

Glory apologized for showing my screenplay to Mr. Collins. She would never do that again, she said, or anything like it. She'd thought a teacher might give me confidence, she hadn't imagined that we'd both be embarrassed. Only after some time had gone by did I go back to showing her what I'd done. She continued to give me ideas I didn't want.

She said, for instance, that I ought to think of a movie based on my father and mother's early romance and marriage. Glory never tired of hearing about their lives, their wedding, their year in the hotel. "Tell me about the time you thought Eddie'd been killed," she would ask my mother. "Tell me again how you met."

She couldn't hear these stories often enough. How my mother had sat up all night, just a week after their wedding, waiting to hear if my father had perished in the forest fire that was sweeping down across the mountain where he worked. How they celebrated their first anniversary by inviting enough close friends and relatives to fill every room in that hotel, for a party that lasted a week.

She'd begun to show this kind of interest in my parents from the day she arrived. This may have been because of the letters that fell from the chimney. When my father started to sort through the bricks that had spilled out of the wall behind the stove, he found more rubble than he'd expected: broken dishes, undershirts, a small wooden cigar box. "What's this?" He held it up. No one had seen it before. "Looks old." He slipped off a piece of twine and opened the lid. "Letters."

"Letters inside a chimney?" my mother said. "What kind of fool would do that?"

"Love letters," my father said. His gaze skimmed down one page, turned to another. He pulled in his chin and chuckled. "Letters from Charlie Sullivan to his wife in England. She must've sent them back."

"Oh, the poor man!" my mother said. She explained to Glory that Charlie Sullivan had built his wife this house but she wouldn't stay – ran off. Then she said to my father, "Why would he hide them in the chimney, for heaven's sake?"

"And look at this," my father said, standing up. "A snapshot. What're we gonna find next?"

"Who's in it?" Toby said.

My father frowned at the picture. Then his neck gave a little jerk, and he grinned. "By golly, Rusty, look here."

Three men sat on a steeply slanted roof amongst stacks of cedar shakes. You could tell the house was ours – Mount Washington's snowy nose was beyond the woods, the upper branches of the fence-line willow leaned to the side. The scowling man in the centre was Old Man Stokes – young still, before his tragedy. The fellow with one tooth missing from his grin was Charlie Sullivan, the man who'd built our house.

"Lookit this bugger here," my father said. He meant the third figure on the roof, a blond young man squinting into the sun. "He knows the whole damn country's looking for him, while he's helping put on a roof." He handed the snapshot to Glory. "You think you'd recognize the Prince of Wales if he sat on the top of your house?"

This was how they'd met, my father said. He and my mother, his first day in the district – he was hardly more than a kid. His family had arrived at their hundred acres of snags and second-growth fir during the night. In the morning, customers at the Store were so taken up with the coming royal visit that he was able to listen without anyone thinking to say: "Why isn't that child in school?"

It was the school the Prince of Wales was coming to open, on his cross-country tour. He would turn around here to start home. There was no more country to tour, he would have to go back or stay. Mrs. Flanagan (in the great red hat) had arranged to have her piano loaded onto her husband's hay wagon, which a team of Clydesdales would haul to the school-yard in the morning. She would play "God Save the King" in the open air.

It seemed ridiculous to everyone that this was happening now, my father said. Some families had barely moved from tents into their hastily thrown-up homes. Some fields had been cleared of trees, but wherever you looked heaps of roots and blackened stumps trailed scarves of smoke. Only the school was complete.

My father hadn't set foot in the school. He wasn't likely to do so, he knew, unless his Old Man relented. Home was a half-built shack in a stumpy clearing, anxious voices, hammering, shouted commands. Every pair of hands was needed. But while his father was sharpening a damaged axe, he'd saddled old Joe and ridden off to explore the gravel roads that twisted through the trees.

The school was emptying itself of children when he got there. Mostly girls. The building was small, with a door in the middle and four windows along the front wall.

"I've seen this horse before." A cluster of girls came up to stand before Joe – redheads mostly, my father said, with ribbons and rusty freckles. They squinted up at the boy as though he were bright as sun, or dangerous. The girl who'd spoken did not squint, but observed him out of a slightly turned-away face. She had thick dark hair. Two boys ride it – older than you."

"My brothers," he said. "They came ahead to build us a house, but didn't get much done."

"They're troublemakers," the girl said, and tightened her lips. "They milked Reynolds' cow in the field. They stole my father's hammer. They blew up the privy behind the school! They're not allowed on this property ever again."

The other girls giggled and poked at one another, but this one continued to look at him steadily, though askance. She had broad cheekbones, my father said. Pale blue adult eyes.

"They're not me," he said.

"Then who are you?"

"Edward."

"Same as the Prince!" This was one of the redheads, who slapped a hand over her mouth. All of them except the dark-haired girl burst into laughter.

"Ed." The boy, my father, corrected himself, feeling his face heat up.

"Is your dad a Returned Soldier?" said the dark-haired girl. He guessed she was ten, or maybe eleven. Younger than he was by three or four years.

"He was too old for the war. Too many kids," my father said. His father was a butcher, he said, who would carve a beef ranch out of land he'd bought from a Soldier who'd taken one look and hightailed it back to Quebec.

"Neither was mine. But you'd better watch out, they don't like anyone who isn't. They put poison down our well. We think so, anyway."

"How come you aren't dead?"

"I almost was. We were sick. They got used to us, though. Some of these are my sisters."

The sisters and the other girls started away, but the girl with the dark hair lingered. "Will you be coming to school?"

"Old Man thinks I oughta stay home and help – then look for work."

"I help in my father's dairy." This seemed to be in case he'd accused her of something. She lowered her voice. "After school, I sometimes sneak into the church," she said. The little church was next door, beyond low bushes, in its armour of cedar shakes – more like a doghouse, my father said, than your average cathedral. "To play around with the organ." For the first time she squinted, as the others had done, into the brightness of his face. "You can work the pedals if you want."

"I better get home," he said. "He'll take the boots to me when he finds out I've gone."

"Well, you better come tomorrow," she said. She looked off across the road to find a reason. "You see those stumps?"

The school stood on a small knoll, facing a clearing in the forest, torn-up dirt and rocks, a heaving brown battlefield of craters and jagged mounds. Heaps of roots and limbs were still to be burned. Thin ribbons of smoke trailed from smouldering fires. A number of high, charred stumps were still firmly rooted in ground.

My father said he had wondered what sort of people these were – uprooting trees so that they could root themselves. He wasn't so sure he wanted to stay amongst them.

"They're going to blow up those stumps for the Prince," the girl said. "They'll give him a twenty-one stump salute." She laughed, my father said, in a manner that was not at all like the others. This one saw a different side of things.

He laughed himself, to think of the King's son, who was used to palace balls and military parades, letting himself be saluted with exploding stumps.

"I might come," he said. "But you better tell him not to wait for me."

139

Prince or no Prince, his father wouldn't hear of a break from work. He roared his orders. Buddy and Martin hadn't finished the house, nor done a very good job of what they had built. A driveway hadn't been cleared – they'd had to come stumbling in through the bush in the dark, leaving the Overland and all their possessions out on the public road. They would have to deepen a poor excuse for a well. They needed a pen for the leghorns, which had made the journey in a crowded box. And there were all these acres of trees to be felled, and turned into logs, their roots blasted out and burned. Children were given tasks that made you think of the pyramids.

Only Nora went to school, where she was employed to help the teacher.

The boy, my father, waited until the Old Man had gone to town for building supplies. He arrived at the school in time to see the Prince step out of his car, brushing dust from his suit. Officials did the same. Men in uniforms strutted. Children spilled out the door of the school, and slammed themselves into terrified silent lines along the front of the building. Nora was amongst them. She was too taken up with the royal visitor to notice a rebel brother astride a horse on the shadow side of a stump.

The teacher was the last to come out of the building, my father said, a tall young woman in a white blouse and black skirt. She pulled the door closed behind her. Then she tested the handle to make sure she'd locked it, so that the Prince could open it later with the official key.

Mrs. Flanagan, resplendent in red and raised above the crowd on her husband's hay wagon, hammered a chord into the air before abandoning herself to a race through the anthem, with hanks of hair flapping about her cheeks. Residents stood at attention singing. Women clung to husbands' arms, amongst them a woman my father didn't yet know was Mrs. Charlie

Sullivan, dressed in yellow like dazzling sunlight in this world of dull brown dirt. Hers was not the only flushed complexion, he said. Children stood rigid. So did impatient Joe, though his horseflesh quivered.

When the anthem had come to an end and "The Maple Leaf Forever" had begun, my father noticed the teacher put both hands to her face. She slapped at her pockets. She bent to examine the dirt around her feet. She stepped back to try the door. Then she came along behind the rows of children to Edward Macken, one hand still pressed to her cheek. "I've locked the official key inside, and seem to have dropped the other in the dirt! Will you try a back window without drawing attention to yourself?"

His brothers would have laughed, my father said. *Get out of this one yourself, Missy.* They would have mocked the fear in her eyes, recognizing that she was only a girl herself, faced with the humiliation of her life. She put a hand on Joe's neck and looked up to the boy who regarded her from a man's height. There were girlish freckles on a pretty nose. Hair the colour of honeyed figs escaped in coils from the pinned-up nest of curls.

He swung Joe around, and cantered behind the school. He tried one window after another down the back wall – all locked. There was nothing to do but grab up a good thick rock and put it through, while singing camouflaged the crash. Then go after it.

"Edward, Prince of Wales," the blackboard announced in scratchy chalk lines, "will one day be King of this Dominion." Books were closed and stacked on desks. A wall chart listed characters and major plot events of the recent war: Kaiser Wilhelm and Passchendaele. Of course the map of the world that hung beside it contained no dot for this community, which had not yet earned that privilege.

The room smelled of chalk, and apples, and glue. He opened the front cover of a book like the lid to a box. A line drawing showed a gentleman in riding clothes, reading to a woman with ringlets pressed to a tree. "The world is more varied and wonderful than one might imagine," was printed below. No books had travelled in the Overland.

The key was easily found on the teacher's desk, while King George scowled from inside his frame, possibly for both the teacher's oversight and the boy's method of gaining entry.

The teacher would not have cared about the King's disapproval, my father said. She clasped the key against her blouse, and closed her eyes – joyous relief. Yesterday's dark-haired girl was risking a sore neck to watch him, while everyone else, including Nora, could not take their eyes off the future King.

So he watched from atop old Joe while a small girl welcomed His Highness with words that no one could understand, and received an answer in the same sort of language. "Theena is Welsh," one of the children whispered, too loud, and was hushed. More singing was blasted out. The Prince distributed silver cups, and planted two small trees in land where every effort was being made to get the trees out, my father said, and was finally given the key to do what he'd come here to do – insert it in its hole and turn. (The teacher glanced towards the boy on the horse and smiled.) The Prince was rewarded with applause, and then saluted by the first of the twenty-one stumps.

The explosion was dull, my father said, as though coming from beneath the earth. One giant stump hiccoughed, and cracked open down through its centre. A few rocks and some dirt and pieces of root sprayed out upon the clearing across the road. "This is how we've spent our lives since the war," explained a man with his hat in his hand. There was no time to admire the splintered rubble; a second explosion sprayed debris up into the surrounding trees, still waiting their turn to fall for the sake of the King's Dominion.

The Prince laughed, after the second explosion. And so did

the whole assembled crowd – schoolchildren, the teacher, gathered residents of the settlement (including the lady in yellow), as well as officials from town.

The twenty-first explosion was for the Prince himself to produce, my father said. Men showed him how. He said something that made them laugh, then did as he was told, to jolt another set of roots and tree trunk out of its place in the earth. More applause rewarded him, for doing what they did every day themselves. Now he was, so to speak, one of them.

Even a boy on a horse could see what it meant, my father said. Now that someone from Buckingham Palace had taken part in their life here, "here" had become more real. The Prince didn't say, "This is a stupid waste of your lives." Maybe it wasn't. A Returned Soldier explained: "We are doing our part, to open up another corner of the country." Once he was King, the Prince could remember this highlight of his youth.

When the Prince and the officials had driven away, and all the settlers had started to leave, the teacher ordered her pupils back into the school.

"You can come inside with us," said the dark-haired girl, who'd broken out of the line to say it.

"Only if I want my backside kicked," he said.

The teacher stood outside the doorway while the others filed past – her eyes, my father said, on him.

Nora might have gone in without noticing if it hadn't been for the teacher's interest. "Eddie!" she yelled, and broke away to come flapping cotton skirts across the dusty yard. "What're you doing here? Did Father say you could come?"

"Girls!" The teacher was coming this way, slapping her hands together. "Inside! The young man may come in if he wishes." She looked up at the boy on his horse. "But maybe he'd rather wait and attend tomorrow." Her face was still a little flushed, my father said, from the morning's adventure.

"He won't be here tomorrow," Nora said. The ferocity in her tone was directed towards the dark-haired girl. "Father will tan his hide when he hears about this."

"Don't exaggerate," the teacher said. She did not remove her eyes from Eddie Macken. "Perhaps your brother *wants* to come to school."

"And anyway," said the dark-haired girl, "why would your father know?"

Nora shouted into the face of the dark-haired girl. "He'll know! And he'll never let him! *I'm* the one that comes to school!"

"Then you can make sure that changes," sang the dark-haired girl, still smiling. "If he isn't here tomorrow no one'll speak to you again."

Rigid, red-faced Nora glared at my father. "You're a boy. Boys *work*! Why would he let you come to school like a girl?"

"That will be enough of that," the teacher said. "You can tell your father for me that I'm expecting his son tomorrow." She seemed a little surprised at herself, my father said. "And his other sons as well, of course, if they're the proper age. Tell him that if you don't arrive tomorrow I'll be up to ask him why."

Nora turned her furious gaze on the teacher and stomped off towards the school, where "Passchendaele" and books of poetry waited, and maps that didn't yet include them. The teacher stepped back, but showed no sign of leaving. The dark-haired girl started away as well, then turned to my father. "The church," she said. "If you come."

"That will be enough," the teacher said.

The boy leaned forward and stroked the horse's neck. "It made a mess," he said, "but the rock didn't hit nothing inside."

"I'm grateful," the teacher said. "That you happened to be here, I mean, and acted so quickly."

"You'll want that pane of glass replaced," my father said. "I'll come by tomorrow to do it."

She looked off across the road where dynamite had recently torn up the earth. Then she said, as though this mattered only as much as he wanted it to, "School begins at nine. A pane of glass could be replaced during lunch."

"Of course the bugger went missing right after he opened the school," my father told Glory. He looked at the snapshot in his hands. "Disappeared for a couple of weeks. This must've been him!"

"It was in the papers," my mother said. "Buckingham Palace was frantic."

"Something of a lady's man," my father added. "To put it mildly. I guess he spotted a lady in that schoolyard crowd that interested him. I guess she'd spotted him as well!"

Glory looked at the cracked and faded snapshot, where three men were nailing shakes on our roof. "You mean he might've stayed in this house?" she said. She looked at Uncle Toby as though he'd brought her straight from her wedding to a fairytale.

"He may have," my father said. "Even though it was no more than an outside shell. Sullivan never got around to finishing things until later."

"After his wife run off," my mother said.

Glory put a slim hand on the wallpaper. "The Prince of Wales slept here." Her other hand trailed fingers down her long, pale throat, then touched the neck of her dress.

"And that poor silly wife ran after him," my mother said, "only to disappear in London. That's something to keep in mind."

"And I accused Toby of bringing me to the back of beyond," Glory said. "I thought this was the end of the earth."

"That's exactly what it is," my mother said. "You notice the Prince didn't *stay*."

"So which of them was Frieda?" Glory asked my father. "Which of them did you marry?"

My father laughed. "It was because of the teacher I went to school. I could tell by the way she looked at me she had something on her mind besides adding fractions. But I must've looked more grown up on a horse than sitting in one of them desks. Once that window was fixed she barked at me the same as anyone: 'No-no-no-no-no, Edward Joseph Macken! *Think!*' Before long she was cracking my knuckles with her stick."

"It was Nora told on you every time," my mother said.

"Nora never forgave me for going to her school," my father said. "She never forgave Frieda, either, who had me buying ice cream before the week was out, up at the Store. And foolin' around in that church when I oughta be home building fence. She had two pairs of boxing gloves stashed in the organ, she'd already beaten them other boys and figured she'd try them on me."

"I knew I'd better grab the new boy fast," my mother said, and laughed. "Before someone else could get her claws into him."

"And I was fool enough to keep hangin' around no matter how often the Old Man took the boots to me." He looked my mother over, grinning. "You can see that *she* don't show much sign of runnin' off with the first damn foreign bigshot that comes and sits on her roof."

Toby did not find my parents' story as interesting as Glory did. If he and Glory had met when they were kids, he said, there might never have been an Elvira or a Lindy or the Mitchell twins. Not to mention dozens of others. He looked at my father with pity. "Stuck with the same ol' dame all your life!"

My father grinned.

Of course Toby had often said that if you were going to be stuck with just one woman you couldn't do better than Frieda. "Still, I wouldn't'a wanted to meet her until I turned thirty, make sure I'd got all my wild oats sowed. Because I sure as hell know Frieda'd take off my head if I sowed a single one of them after."

"You're only twenty-three now," Glory said. "Does that mean you think I wouldn't do the same?"

He didn't answer that. He stood up and went to the drain-board and took a carving knife out of the drawer. Then he tore open his shirt and cut an X into his chest. Not deep, not large, but blood welled up and spilled.

My mother and Glory cried out and leapt into action. Glory grabbed the hand that held the knife, my mother ran for a towel to soak up blood. My father shook his head in amuse-ment – Toby being Toby once again.

Would I ever have the courage to do a thing like that? Would I have the imagination? At seven years old, it wasn't possible to think that someone might inspire it. Still I knew, even then, that if I ever met someone with that kind of power I would have Toby's example to measure myself against.

A moving picture show of my parent's early life would be truly romantic, Glory said, but she didn't think all movies should be happy ones. Stories that broke your heart should also find their way to the screen. Whenever she was in one of her sad periods, Glory would bring up the history of Old Man Stokes. This would be an Oscar winner for sure. Gary Cooper. Deborah Kerr. She warned me that Hollywood would insist I change the ending.

She hadn't been in the family long before she heard about Stokes. Toby mentioned him. She saw him herself, sputtering by. Caro and Gordie and I had known about Stokes before she'd come into our lives. Sooner or later, every Saturday afternoon would be interrupted by the soft ticking of an approaching Model T. Gordie would hear it first. "Stokes! Get down!" We'd stop whatever we were playing in the pasture of fire-blackened stumps and watch for that ancient black tin box to come into view. Nobody breathed while it passed, the terrifying giant crammed over the steering wheel. His nose, his pipe, the bushy eyebrows beneath his jutting forehead, all pointed straight ahead.

"A good thing he didn't look," Gordie said. "We'd be dead."

Old Man Stokes was a silent man, he hadn't spoken to anyone for years. He looked at no one, either, if he could help it. He lived in terrible isolation because, as everyone knew, he possessed an impossible temper. We'd been warned – his fate was what awaited anyone who couldn't control his tantrums. Parents told us. Old Man Stokes had been a young man once, believe it or not. And even then his temper was legendary. Parents were vague about this, but Toby supplied the details: he'd tossed a disobedient spaniel into the upper branches of a cedar, he'd killed a workhorse with a fist to the head, he'd lifted loggers off the ground with one hand while breaking their noses with the other. He was taller than anyone. Nobody scared him. Nobody ever fought back. He lost his temper at the smallest thing, but – here adult voices would lower – lost it once too often.

He'd been married, Toby said – an English warbride. A quiet lovely woman with long pale hands. He brought her out after the Great War and together they started a farm, several miles back from the road. Another stump ranch like our own.

148

It wasn't long before they had a son. Stokes was so attached to that boy he could hardly bear for them to be apart. They dressed alike, in black wool pants and checkered shirts. The amazing thing was that fatherhood seemed to have changed the man entirely. In the Riverside Hotel he could not be provoked, even when they told him he knew nothing about farming and should have stayed in Nova Scotia where things were tame. He smiled and drank his beer.

They spoke little while they worked, father and son. A bit of a dreamer, the boy would help for a while but sooner or later would drift away. Like boys in later generations, he played amongst the blackened stumps that made a kind of city in the fields. But when the father barked, "Git over here! Whaddaya think this is?" the boy came running fast.

"One day they were out picking rocks in a new field," Toby said. "You know how stony it is up that road, every spring a whole new crop of boulders comes to the surface." After tossing a few small dusty rocks into the stoneboat, the boy drifted off to play in the stumps. This time, when Stokes hollered him back to work, the boy just didn't seem to hear. Stokes didn't curse, he didn't roar, he didn't drive a fist into the Percheron pulling the stoneboat. He started in the boy's direction, across the stony field, intending to get a few things straight between them. But the boy stood up from his play and made the mistake of laughing. Then he started to run. The man commanded him to stop, but the boy ran on. Worse, he screamed for his mother. The father tried to explain – don't worry, I only want to talk – but the boy's racket made it impossible. How do you stop a child from running who doesn't want to stop? He didn't know. Blood raced in his throat. He stooped and grabbed up the nearest thing – it could have been a twig, or a handful of dirt, but what he was only half aware of holding was a chunk of granite the size of your fist. He shouted: "Dammit, you stop where you are!" The boy ran on. Unable to cast a spell that would stop the boy in his tracks, the red-faced father reared back and threw. The rock was meant to land just in front of the child, he would later say, and startle him into halting. Instead, that flying piece of granite brought his entire world to its end.

At any rate, that was how the father told it when he answered the coroner's questions. The helplessness of a man in the face of a boy's loud terror. People shuddered, but could not pretend they'd forgotten the famous temper.

We shuddered, too, to think of it, so many years later. The boy himself didn't mean much to the others – Sonny Aalto, my brother Gerry, Gordie and Caro our cousins. He was only a story to them, a poor robin that had broken its neck at a window. They trembled when the Model T passed by because they thought the driver might one day turn on us the gaze of a man who had killed his own son. And maybe, out of his craziness, start throwing stones. The chill that invaded my organs had to do with something else. Had the boy believed that having a father who loved you meant you were safe?

The boy didn't die on the spot, but he was gone before they'd got him to town. The wife returned to England at the end of the month. Old Stokes continued to live on that farm, and seldom came off it, except when he went for supplies. Never talked to anyone. Never looked to one side or the other. Still drove that same Model T, his nose and that pipe straight ahead.

Glory said she could hardly stand to think of it. "How can he go on breathing, knowing what he's done?"

Still, it would do no good for us to brood about it, she added. If he kept to himself it must be because he wanted to. And so long as he continued to drive with his eyes straight ahead we needn't worry that his unhappy life would invade our world of play. "Time enough to worry about these things when you're older."

We played "Stokes" in an empty room of the old hotel. While our parents and the newlyweds slapped down hands of whist on the dining-room tables below, we took turns – Gordie and I – throwing spectacular temper tantrums and stoning my brother to death. Caro was the sobbing mother who threw herself upon her wounded son, then beat her fists against the father and packed her bags for England.

Other kinds of deaths took place as well. Behind the second door on the right, Grandpa Macken took forever to die, coughing and moaning on the striped mattress while the rest of us wept and looked at our watches and telephoned for the doctor who never came. Across the hall, cameras made from Corn Flakes boxes and toilet-paper rolls recorded Gene Autry shooting it out with seven hundred and fifty naked Indians. Sometimes Gerry was left in a darkened room to wait for the knock on his door that would mean the end of his stay on Death Row. Caro delivered his last meal – plates of photographed food torn from *Good Housekeeping*'s recipe pages – which she forced him to chew and swallow. Gordie recited the Lord's Prayer while leading Gerry across the hall to where I waited in my Lone Ranger mask. I informed him that we hadn't found a rope to hang him by the neck until he was dead, so Gordie and I would have to strangle him with our bare hands.

The room at the end of the hall was out of bounds. Toby and Glory's bedroom. Naturally we went in. The bed was always unmade. Caro would snatch up a lacy nightgown off the sheets and hold it in front of her, wriggling her hips. Gordie riffled through drawers, and slipped his arms into the straps of a brassière. Gerry danced with a pair of Toby's under-shorts on his head. A strange, tight feeling always moved in to sit in my chest whenever I stepped into that room. Why was this bedroom, like my parents', the only room in the house we'd been warned not to enter?

When we grew tired we sat on the steps with cookies and glasses of milk and listened to the adult voices below. Gerry fell asleep against the wall. Gordie reread his Green Lantern comic books. Sooner or later we would hear Kitty begin to cry. She wanted children, she couldn't stand it that she wasn't 'expecting' yet, even after years of trying. "Jesus," Aunt Edna said. "Enjoy it while it lasts. Afterwards you won't remember why you wanted them." They laughed good-naturedly over Glory's baking disasters. When a cake that was meant to be high and fluffy was more like a slab of rubber, my mother sug-gested that Glory dump a jar of raspberry preserves over it. "Then bury it in whipped cream and pretend that's what you wanted. That's how the rest of us started."

Eventually they pushed back the furniture, turned on the radio, and started to dance. We were sent up to lie on the naked beds, to huddle under coats and blankets in the opened-window scent off the ocean. We didn't sleep. While their music and laughter drifted up the stairs, we lay in the dark and talked about the people who'd slept here once – imagined who they were and where they'd come from, movie stars and royalty and criminals from the farthest corners of the world. We imagined they'd all come back to join the party below, dancing with the Macken brothers and their wives. "The Old Lamplighter." "String of Pearls." On summer evenings we picked armloads of roses from outside the windows, and tossed them down the staircase so they could be worn in people's hair.

But Glory was wrong when she said we didn't need to worry about Stokes until we were older. Sooner or later, just as we'd feared, our separate worlds would overlap. And everything would change.

We played the same sort of games in the pasture behind our barn as we played in the hotel. Ayrshires grazed on the tufts of grass or lay blinking at flies. Bluebottles hovered above the drainage ditches. As a band of noisy pirates we shouted from the upright roots of a great fallen log. As invaders from Japan we crept through blackberry vines to strangle innocent children in their sleep. Knights and crowned nobility plotted crusades inside the tall black castles of hollow stumps – more than twice our height and broad enough for any furniture we could drag through the tunnelled entrances. Inside, the air was seasoned with a sharp smoke odour from the wood-ash floor. Shining with black-diamond scales, the walls leaned up to the circle of sky.

To furnish the castles and pasture fortresses, we went on periodic excursions down towards the beach. Twisting through jackpine and second-growth fir, the dusty road was so narrow, its corners so sharp and the bordering brush so thick, that drivers honked their horns at every bend.

This was where people drove out in the dark of night to get rid of their junk: rusted cars, rolls of linoleum, mildew-smelling iceboxes, bottled tomatoes gone bad, chesterfields with stuffing torn out by pets and children. These prizes could be found all through the woods, in hollow logs and under huckleberry bushes. They lay in craters dug by people helping themselves to sand and gravel for cementing the floors of their barns. Washing machines and radios were inhabited by families of raccoons. Things that people couldn't stand to have around, my father said; remnants of a past that wouldn't go away on its own.

The rule was that we could salvage only what would fit

inside the stumps. It mustn't be seen. It especially must not be seen from the road. But one spring day we came upon a cook-stove behind a flowering red currant bush. White fawn lilies bloomed around its feet. It was old, with blistered enamel and scaly flakes of rust. But it still had all its accessories: firebox lids, oven racks, even a short elbow of stovepipe attached to the back. It stood on elaborate dainty legs. A little round piece of discoloured glass was set into the oven door, containing a red thermometer. It wasn't as big as the woodstove that out-lived the hotel but it was far too big for us. It broke the rule. But we knew we had to have it all the same.

With two-by-fours we levered the monumental piece of kitchen machinery up a ramp of splintered lumber and rested it across two of our wagons side by side. Sonny pulled one, I pulled the other; Gerry and Caro and Gordie leaned their weight against the stove.

The narrow wheels cut troughs in the sand. When the wagon tilted, the stove slid off on its side. We worked to get it upright again, then slowly moved on. Skunk cabbages, which bloomed like gaudy yellow lanterns in the swampy ditch, filled the air with their stink. Gordie went thudding ahead at every corner to see if cars were coming. We had no horn to honk.

"Where we gonna put 'er?" Sonny said.

"Inside the biggest stump," I said.

"Behind the barn," Gerry said, "so they can't see the smoke from the house."

"We're lighting a fire in it?" Sonny said.

"We can't," I said.

"We can if we want," Gerry said. He showed me his fist. He might be little but he could do a lot of damage before you got him down and sat on his head.

"They'll kill us," I said. Forest fires had twice gone through the district when our parents were young, wiping out half the settlement. It could easily happen again, though last night's rain had left everything wet.

Gordie whimpered. He turned down his face and walked almost horizontally behind the stove. "I hate it when you two fight."

"Shut up, you boob," Caro said.

"Okay, okay, we'll light it," I said.

"And cook on it," Gerry said, never satisfied to win just the once. "Who's got allowance?"

"We'll go down to the Store," I said. "A can of something we can heat up."

"My dad heats pork 'n' beans cans over the fire," Sonny said.

"How'll we get it inside a stump?" Caro said. "None of them's got doorways wide as this."

"Maybe we'll have to take it apart," I said. "And put it together inside."

Gordie threw up his hands. "I can't stand it." He appealed to the sky. "This is too much work!"

Hunters, gatherers, warriors, bringing home loot from ransacked villages. We pulled that cast-iron treasure for more than two hours along the sandy road of countless bends, potholes, and stones that had to be thrown out of the way. The sky grew dark; it was going to rain. Victorious warriors joined voices to celebrate this conquest with a song, composed in bits and pieces throughout the afternoon:

> "Yo ho ho and a bottle of rum,
> we've attacked the enemy and whipped their bum,
> we've taken their gold and home have come,
> draggin' the spoils behind us."

We'd got out to the highway and down the slope, and then had crossed the road and the culvert and passed in through the pasture gate before our load tilted sharply again, and again toppled off. This time the stove rolled over and lay with its dainty legs in the air. The accordion elbow of the stovepipe clattered free. Caro swore. Gordie threw himself beside it and pulled out handfuls of grass, yelling, "I can't stand it any more!"

We worked to get the stove upright. But we hadn't got it onto the wagons when Sonny grabbed my arm. At the top of the slope was the familiar Model T. Old Man Stokes stood by his open door, watching.

We were being looked at by eyes that had never looked at us before. A man who had killed his own son. Ice crystals started forming around my kidneys, spreading up through my chest.

Gordie whimpered. "I'm goin' home." But couldn't seem to move. Caro told him to shut his trap, big sissy.

We'd still not got that stove onto the wagons when the Model T started moving slowly down the slope.

"That's it," Gordie said. "I'm leaving."

"He'll catch you alone and eat you," Caro said. "Push."

Gordie pushed against the overturned stove, but he'd already started to cry.

The Model T moved slowly along the road outside the fence, and came to a halt by the gate. The door opened and again the giant got out. He crossed the road and stood looking our way, his murderer's hands in the pockets of his baggy black wool pants.

"Oh cripes," Sonny suddenly cried. "Run!"

We did. We abandoned the stove and raced for the nearest fortress, a high wide stump with a tunnel entrance under the farther side.

Inside, I scrambled up the wall to look over the top. Sonny came up behind me. Fifty feet of pasture and a barbed-wire fence lay between us and Old Man Stokes. A light rain had begun to fall.

He didn't move. For a moment we looked hard at one another, Old Man Stokes and I. What was there to say across that space?

"Get down, you stupe," said Caro below me. "He'll see he's got us trapped."

Sonny pushed his forehead against the inside wall of the stump. "He'll pick us off one at a time."

A sob escaped from behind Gordie's fist. Gerry offered to go out and poke his eyes.

"I don't think he cares about us," I said.

The man had removed the hat from his head and let it rest against his thigh while he walked through the opened gate towards the stove. Up at the house, my mother and Glory had come outside to see what was going on.

I shouted, "No!" and jumped down (Sonny yelling, "Don't! You idiot!") and crawled out through the tunnel and started to run for the stove. Did I think he intended to hoist it onto his shoulder and carry it off? I don't know what I thought I could do to stop him. Maybe climb on the stove and fight him off with stones. I ducked and scooped up a fist-sized rock from the dirt. I was every bit as afraid of Stokes as the others were, but there was something about that stove that drove me beyond myself, though my heart was pounding in my throat.

At any rate, he beat me to it. He stood over our great rusted treasure with one hand brushing the erupted surface as if it were something familiar. Those bushy eyebrows formed a terrific frown.

I climbed onto a pirate-ship log and pulled myself into the crow's nest of tangled roots. The dirt caked to the rock in my hand was turning to mud in the rain.

"It's ours," I said. "We found it." I shouted it loud enough for even Glory to hear.

He glanced my way, but did not raise his hand from the

stove. His head may have tilted slightly to one side, like someone listening with interest for what you might say. But I had nothing I would dare to say to him. Could I tell him I'd only now begun to understand why the fear rose up whenever I saw him drive by? I wouldn't have the words for years. He knew things you'd rather not learn, about having to be a grown-up in this world. Just by drawing himself across the edge of our vision he threatened the one fixed assumption of our lives – that growing up would mean achieving safety in an adult world. How could we stand to think anything else?

From the way he rested his hand on that stove, anyone could see why he'd stopped. In a sense, we'd forced him to. (The heads of Sonny and Caro and Gerry appeared above the stump, to watch his fingers touch the blistered enamel.) How could we have known the stove had been his? When he buried it deep in the woods, he must have believed that no one but squirrels would find it. No one had, for years.

All at once he returned the hat to his head and, looking straight at me, touched a finger to it in a quick salute. Then he returned through the rain to his Model T. He pulled his door closed, and with nose and pipe and bushy eyebrows straight ahead once more, drove off.

I got to the stove before the others but didn't touch it. Nor did the others touch it when they arrived. We stood at a safe distance and contemplated its rusted sides, its upturned dainty legs. We might have been waiting for the thing to breathe.

Gordie wiped the back of his hand across his wet red eyes. Gerry and Sonny and Caro held muddy rocks. If the stove had breathed we wouldn't have been surprised, but we'd have stoned it to death on the spot.

It didn't breathe. It didn't move. While Glory and my mother crossed the field towards us, we stood as motionless before this thing from the past as the tall hollow stumps behind us – all of which had stood black and disfigured in the pasture since the fires of our parents' youths had gone roaring through.

Once the stove had been installed inside a shiplap lean-to behind the largest stump, Glory would sometimes cook us recipes collected on her mother's singing tours. Gumbo, as it was made in New Orleans. Kentucky fried chicken. French Canadian pea soup. She baked bannock in the oven, cooked cabbage rolls on the top. She was not a very good cook, but we ate it anyway. And every time we sat to eat, she would think aloud about that poor sad Mrs. Stokes, the warbride, cooking on this stove for the husband and little boy who would be snatched from her in a flash. She would imagine what went through that poor man's head at night. "What must it be like, to kill your own child? I don't know how that gentleman can stand it. Can't you see what a wonderful movie you could make?"

Of course we didn't know that she had begun to visit Stokes. We didn't know for years. "Doesn't it break your heart," she would say, "to think how people's lives can be ruined in a single minute?"

9

CARO would not abandon her log to eat with the rest of us. She squeezed a worm of Nivea Cream into her hand, then rubbed it over her face and down her throat. "Let's get out of here," she said.

"I tried that once. You saw how far I got."

She smeared the lotion across the tops of her breasts, running fingers down inside her bathing suit. "If you don't have the guts just give me your keys, I'll go myself."

"Where to?"

James Dean's face fluttered in the breeze. "The creek," she said. She narrowed her eyes, waiting for me to understand.

For a moment I didn't know which creek she meant. Then I could not believe it. "You *want* to see it?"

"Don't tell me you don't."

I'd been trying not to think about that creek since we'd heard the news. Of course I wanted to see it. "Maybe after we eat."

"Puh!" She flipped a page of her magazine, to show she had serious doubts about me.

By late afternoon, the original circle of chairs had become a gathering of grey-haired women in cardigans: Aunt Nora, cousins of Nora's generation, older women of the community. The rule at Macken family picnics was "anyone who doesn't look after themselves can bloody-well go without," but these were the people who considered themselves exempt. They would sit there forever, if necessary, waiting for someone to serve them. "The royal invalids," my mother called them. Eventually, when she saw they would rather starve than lift a finger, she'd sometimes wait on them herself. She didn't want to give them a martyr's satisfaction.

Today she wouldn't even pour them coffee. "Do them good to find out they still got legs that work. I'm feeling old myself – that funeral did it." She let herself collapse against me, an ancient, trembling crone. "Put me in an old folks' home, I'm sinking fast!"

"Not fast enough for me," I said, twisting her arm behind her back. "I can't wait to get my hands on your fortune."

"Too late," she sang out. "I've used up several fortunes feeding you!" She ducked free. "Maybe it's about time you were across the water there, fighting for space amongst strangers."

My father stood behind a picnic table, carving slices off the barbecue beef. "Time to put the nosebags on!"

Beef, baked salmon, turkeys, chili con carne, salads of every colour, homemade bread – paper plates were heaped until they buckled, then carried to shade beneath the firs. Some people sat at picnic tables, some on chairs. A few opened out blankets on the ground. Most found a spot of grass and took root. The smallest children took their supper back to the beach. Men who'd spent the afternoon leaning into the sides of a pickup – passing judgement on bosses and exchanging opinions on the best locations for shooting deer – filled plates and returned to take up passing judgement and exchanging opinions where they'd left off. Women who'd gathered at Ethel Price's feet to learn their futures from the Tarot cards hurried back for more.

Players caught up in a horseshoe tournament balanced their plates on a log and kept on clanging horseshoes against the spikes while they ate. Mackens spread themselves across this whole expanse of property that my father had compared to famous battlefields but which was really only a kind of neglected playground going back to underbrush and weeds. Crows gathered in the boughs above us.

After changing back into my jeans and T-shirt, I loaded my plate and joined Colin and Theresa on a length of driftwood someone had dragged up from the beach. The tiny red and green leaves of wild strawberries shone here and there amongst the parched grass, each plant with its own roots but still joined to all the others by a network of dark red runners. Theresa held the baby beneath her shirt, slurping. "He'll holler the place down if he isn't fed," Colin explained. He seemed to think this was something to boast about.

"Eats like his old man," Theresa said. "A real pig – look at that belly." She pinched the roll of fat that hung over Colin's belt.

"So what?" he said, swatting her hand away. "I ain't no high jumper. Rusty's the one got to watch his weight."

"I probably won't even see a vaulting pole over there," I said. "I'll be buried under books."

"You won't be skinny for long, either," Theresa said, looking at my plate.

I had no more appetite for potato salad or chili con carne than I had for Kitty's mottled slabs of Prem decorated with pineapple slices – her usual. I'd loaded my plate with brownie squares, cinnamon cookies, and lemon tarts, making my selection before the others had even begun to think of dessert. The chocolate cake with layers divided by whipped cream and mousse and custard was Mrs. Korhonen's – Theresa's mother.

She'd watched me cut myself as large a piece as I dared, and smiled. "Track season's over," I said.

"I make-it one just for you when you gone," she said, her voice small and shy, "and sending it in the mail."

I saw myself eating Mrs. Korhonen's cake in Vancouver, but could not imagine my surroundings. Aloof scholars in a stone library? Drunken bums on a park bench? Shady men hissing at me from recessed doorways? ("Don't ever take a cigarette from a stranger over there," my father warned. "They fill them with dope, to get you addicted.")

Mr. Korhonen watched from where he leaned against the trunk of a nearby fir, then winked when he caught my eye. He preferred meat and potatoes to his wife's baking, but it gave him pleasure to witness my love affair with her food.

Colin spoke through a mouthful of turkey. "We tell you we're gonna build? Old Man gave us ten acres at the back of his place."

Mackens who married young were often given a piece of their parents' farm. Lynette's father, who'd noticed this, once asked me if my father intended to divide his property amongst his kids. Probably not, I told him, since my father's children all had plans that would eventually take them away. Gerry wanted to be a commercial pilot. Meg planned to dance for the Royal Winnipeg Ballet.

"A good thing that mother of Glory's isn't here," Kitty said, circling around while she decided where to settle. She ran a hand down the back of her leather-fringed skirt, then folded her tiny legs and sat on the grass. "Imagine what she'd say about eating like this on the ground. No tables. No linen serviettes. No silver flatware."

"Don't bring that old biddy into this!" Edna cried. She removed her gum from her mouth and stuck it to the underside of her plate. "Size of a Hereford bull." She held a forkful of lettuce up close to her eyes, then pulled a face and scraped it onto the edge of her plate.

"This turkey's drier than I like," said Reg.

"She thought we were all a bunch of hillbillies anyway," I said.

I'd meant it for Colin but indignation was shouted by several at once.

"Glory told me this," I said. "She took one look at that shack over there and called her Daisy Mae!"

Kitty's hand fluttered around her face, as though there were thoughts she wanted to keep from landing. "One single visit in all those years! Sailed in unexpected. Invited herself to Frieda's dinner party so she could meet all Glory's relatives – and never stopped talking about *herself*! This city, that city, one famous singer after another. Pee-ew! And guess what she said about the food!"

"I remember!" Edna cried, throwing up her hands. "Old battleaxe said she *loved* plain home-style cooking!" The last few words were sung out by Grace, Kitty, and Edna all together. Then Edna said, "Frieda's cooking plain!"

Everyone laughed except Edna herself, who frowned down into her salad, pushing green leaves this way and that with her fork.

"That woman didn't know turnips from toothpicks," Kitty said. "Who's a better cook than Frieda? I bet Frieda made these Parker House rolls." She held one up, to examine every side.

"Frieda didn't make this salad, I know that," Edna said. "I'm not the kind that likes to complain, but dammit, what I'm finding here is little white slugs."

Kitty lowered her voice. "Em's."

Edna widened her eyes at Kitty, then turned to Em Madill, who was about to join us. "For chrissake, Em, did you never hear about washing lettuce? Or did you think we needed the protein?" She laughed, to show she wasn't being cruel.

Em stopped in her tracks. "Good heavens, I'll wash it now!"

"Too late," Edna said. "I cleaned out the bloody bowl." She tugged at Em's arm until she sat beside her. "No point in telling the others, they might be jealous!"

Em used her serviette to wipe her front teeth. "My horoscope warned me to watch out for careless mistakes."

"Frieda's potato salad." Grace identified what she was tasting. "She cubes the spuds. Am I the only one who misses the kind that's mashed? Thick and creamy?"

"That was the only dish that Glory ever brought to things," my mother said, finding herself a spot beside Theresa.

"It was the only thing she could make," Edna said.

"That isn't true," Aunt Kitty said. "It was the only thing she would make for a crowd. She didn't have the confidence to try something new."

"That was her mother's fault," Grace said. "Never taught her nothing. Glory was not a cook!"

"She liked to read cookbooks though!" Em cried, though her mouth was full.

"Like Reg with his Zane Grey stories," Grace laughed. "Tore through them like she wanted to see what happens in the end, but she never tried none of the recipes."

Reg's chuckle rumbled deep in his throat. It was his way of getting you to ask what he thought was funny.

"What!" my mother said.

"When I heard that old hotel burned down I figured it musta been Glory did it – trying out some recipe from her books." He explained to Em Madill: "They were living with the old fellow then, same as Frieda and Eddie before."

Uncle Buddy said, "Glory wasn't even in it when it burned. Her and Toby drove down-Island for the weekend." *Flick, flick,* went his tongue across his upper lip. "Old Great-Uncle Jimmy Macken let it burn. Drunk as a skunk as usual."

"*If* it burned," Reg said. He glanced my way and winked.

"Hold it right there!" Em cried. "That hotel burned – a thousand people told me. Go look at those charred boards."

"Nobody seen it go," Reg said. He held up his fork and straightened a tine. "We got a big dump of snow that night, blocked roads – no traffic was passing by. They claim they never even seen the smoke from up the coastline there at Willow Point. Isn't that right, Tuomo?" Mr. Korhonen nodded to confirm it. "By the time Toby and her got back, the snow had melted and rain had washed 'er clean. Old Jimmy, he'd tidied everything up so neat you couldn't be sure there was anything there at all. It might have been taken by wind." Again he glanced my way and this time smiled. "Nothing left but foundations and that stove."

"And the *smell*," my mother insisted. "I know the stink of ashes when they're wet." She made a face to show she wished she didn't.

"You couldn't ask the old bugger what happened, neither," Buddy said. "He took right off. Year later he went and died in Halifax, willed the property to the eight of us to share."

"I can see the stove from here," Em said. "I seen charred rafters in that grass."

"Anyway, the time I was thinking of, Glory wasn't married yet a month," Reg said. "She knew she wasn't no cook, but this one day she decided to whip up a feast."

"She was trying to roast a couple pheasants, I remember that," my mother said. "Toby shot them, strutting across that grass over there."

"But she didn't know how to handle that stove." Reg tilted his head in the direction of the giant woodstove in the weeds.

Edna laughed. "Them birds were little charred bones! 'Jesus Murphy, girl,' I told her, 'can't you tell *cooked* from *cremated?*'"

166

Reg's laugh rumbled beneath his words. "Toby said he come home from work and smoke was pouring out every window. He figured the whole damn place was burning, he only hoped he wasn't too late to save Glory –"

"But found her bawling her eyes out over her ruined meal," my mother said. "She swore she'd never cook again."

"She had to," Grace said, stabbing her fork all over her plate, gathering peas. "But she hated cooking for company. How many invitations did *you* ever get for a meal?"

"Glory was a city girl," Em said. "She never got around to fitting in."

"City people think they're better'n us," Grace said. She looked as though it pained her to say it. "I'm not saying nothin' bad about Glory, that's just how she was raised."

"Anyone could tell she was from the city!" Helen said, laughing at some memory. "She couldn't get her mind around 'miles.' She'd ask you how many blocks was Nora's place from the Store – blocks!"

"She asked when Reg was going to paint his barn!" Kitty tossed in – more evidence.

"Now wouldn't that be something," Reg said. "Didn't she notice there's hardly a painted barn on this Island? It wouldn't *be* a barn if it was painted, it would be something else – a cow palace!"

"And," Grace said, about to deliver the clincher, "she went and started using her front door!"

Mackens did not use their front doors. Strangers who came to the front were asked to go round to the back. Otherwise they might be required to step over the vacuum cleaner and Sunday's chicken and a stack of extra chairs in the entrance hall. Mackens who built from commercial blueprints didn't even bother putting steps at the front, since they knew they'd never be used. Doors floated six feet above basement windows and grass.

"Anybody too good to come through the kitchen's not someone I want in my house," was Kitty's way of explaining this.

"Frieda was a bad example for Glory," said Grace.

My mother bristled; that is, she acted the role of someone bristling with indignation. "What do you mean by that?"

"She wanted a marriage like yours. She didn't know that Toby wasn't Eddie."

"She wasn't Frieda herself!" Grace said. "Frieda never kept herself apart!"

"Well, Glory *tried* not to keep herself apart," Kitty said.

"She didn't try as hard as you seem to think," said Em Madill, glad to be into the fray.

"Oh Em!" my mother said, sad and disappointed.

"I'm sorry to say this but it's the truth. She never learned how to be family." Em looked off towards the highway and added, "Mind you, I'm only a distant relation so she didn't need to try at all with me."

"Stop it, you!" my mother shouted, slapping one hand on the grass. She looked as shocked as anyone once the words had escaped her mouth. She said it a little softer a second time. "Just stop it. We can't start doing this."

The baby snuffled and squeaked inside Theresa's shirt.

"If Glory wanted to be like Frieda she shoulda looked harder." Kitty lowered her voice for this. "You don't see Frieda rushing off to visit men up gravel roads. What did she think she was *doing?*"

"We aren't listening to this!" my mother said.

"She put herself outside the world she lived in," said Uncle Reg. "She made her friends outside the family. Outside the community too. When she saw what she done, she couldn't face it. That's my theory and I'm stickin' to it." He dropped his bottom jaw and read messages in the clear blue afternoon sky. "That's what she added to the Macken history. One pretty girl glanced off the edge and went spinning out to nowhere. Who let her go?"

"She loved that shack when it was new," Grace said. "Being from the city, she'd been raised with all the conveniences, but you'd think she was the first one ever had a house built just for her."

For a moment everyone looked at the shack she'd had to live in. A drab desolate thing. Moss grew on the cedar shake roof. The tarpaper had been torn away in patches, exposing the boards and the rusted stains of the nails. Across the front, the eavestrough had come away from the house and slanted down on its own. Toby's climbing pole looked more deserted than ever, off to the side, rising up amidst the people who sat at the picnic tables.

"Her little doll's house," Kitty said. "That's what she called it."

"Seems to me she started finding fault with it right away," Aunt Helen said. She held her twin grandchildren on her lap while she ate, and kissed the top of one twin's head, and then the other.

"Not until it started falling apart," I said.

A moment of silence followed this. Sometimes when I spoke up it seemed that everyone had to make an effort to remember that I wasn't still in diapers. Especially if they didn't like what I'd said.

Em Madill did not like what I'd said. "She'd be thinking of her city friends. It wouldn't be good enough for them." To her I was the one who'd hung around her store every Saturday trying to read the *Star Weekly* coloured comics without paying. "Pretty soon it wasn't good enough for her."

"He told her she wouldn't have to live in it for long," I said. "Ten years seems long to me."

"He had a living to make," Grace said.

"He just, he just never *thought*," said Uncle Buddy, in the voice of someone who regrets saying what has to be said. His long skinny legs were pulled in so close that his knees were up by his ears.

"Glory picked 'im!" Grace reminded us, gathering scraps of food with the side of her fork. "She ought to have known what she was getting."

Theresa drew the baby out from inside her shirt and placed it, wrapped in the blanket, on the grass. "I wouldn't ask a hog to live in a dump like that," she said.

Uncle Martin drove in off the driveway then, and parked and got out of his truck. He paused here and there to exchange words with groups of people eating. "Gone!" he announced when he got to us, and showed his large pink callused palms. "So help me."

"Toby?" My mother's surprise drove her to her feet.

"Broke out, I bet," said Nora, who'd come over to see what Martin had to report.

"Didn't have to," Martin said. "He talked himself out – you know him. They couldn't tell me where he was going."

"Somebody should've been with him," Nora said.

"He's a hazard on those roads," said Uncle Reg.

"He, he won't go back to the bridge," said Uncle Buddy. "That wasn't *planned*. Maybe he went somewhere to sulk."

"Where he ought to be is here!" Nora cried. "We're family. We ought to spread out and look."

"Look where?" Martin said. "If Toby don't want to be found we aren't gonna find him. He'll come back in his own good time."

"He's probably ashamed to come back here," I said. "He'd have to look at what he made her live in."

"Well, well," said Uncle Martin. "Is Toby's shadow turning against him here?" To show that he wasn't being unfriendly he

170

gripped my upper arm and squeezed as hard as it was possible to squeeze without breaking bones. Then he gripped Colin's shoulder and gave him a few good shakes. "I hope you gluttons left some food."

"I wouldn't turn against him," I said to Uncle Martin's back. He was heading towards the tables. "But I think Toby would agree."

"That he let Glory down?" Em cried. "You better think again."

Em Madill was the one who knew I'd sent a letter to Howard Hawks but got no answer. She knew I'd received a parcel in a plain brown wrapper once, precisely the size and weight of *Sex, Marriage, and Birth Control*. She knew that Johnnie Strauss used our family's mail slot without postage to pass along his copy of *Peyton Place*.

"That's why he's out there somewhere taking it hard," I said. "We sit here making excuses but he doesn't have any excuse he believes himself. He knows what he should've done better than we do."

We sat in silence for a few minutes after that. A disgusted Nora returned to her circle of cardigans. When I looked at my mother she raised her eyebrows and made the sort of face that said: Close call, but the universe didn't collapse!

Now Reg was rumbling again.

"What now?" my mother said, with her waiting-for-the-surprise smile on her face. She was always Reg's best audience.

"You were saying she never learned to cook but she sure learned how to cut up a beef in a hurry! Remember that? Musta broke a record, them two between them!"

Everyone laughed at this. Everyone knew this story, but that wouldn't stop Reg and Buddy from telling it. "Here's one for your cameras, Rusty," Buddy said. "I'd pay money to see what you'd do with this!"

"Make sure you sign up Audie Murphy for the part," said Em Madill.

"Audie Murphy don't look like Toby," said Grace.

"This must've been – when was it?" Buddy said. "They hadn't been in that shack for long. Ol' Sam Williamson was running some of his white-faces on the golf course here for a while, paying Toby for it. Half a dozen heifers nearly ready for the bull."

Reg listened with the distracted smile of someone monitoring what he heard to make sure it was right. "Them little heifers were crazy about Toby," he said. "Followed him everywhere with stars in their eyes. Used to come right up to the house and look in the windows, mooning. He couldn't walk out to his truck without them drooling and shoving their noses into his shirt. He'd curse and swat but they'd just come back for more. He would've sent them home except he liked that little bit of money he was getting."

"Toby never had cattle of his own," Buddy said. "Him and his pal Ray George, they used to go out hunting once a year and get themselves a deer. The year we're talking about, Toby shot a three-spike up behind Gosling Lake. Brought it down to Ray's place and put it in his deep-freeze."

"Ray needed the space himself," Reg said, "but Toby kept forgetting to do anything about it. They started to get a little testy with one another after a while."

Buddy said, "Toby rented a cold-storage locker in town, to stop Ray's nagging, but he still forgot to pick up that venison. Whenever Ray reminded him, Toby got so mad he put off doing it on purpose. Then one day Ray phoned up and told Glory, If he don't come get it today I'm dumping it in the swamp."

"Toby was under the lumber truck when Glory come out and told him about this call," Reg said. "He had the driveshaft out and everything all apart. He wasn't going anywhere. 'That sonofabitch is trying to drive me crazy. Tell him I'll pick it up when I get this truck on the road.' But Glory started to worry. Later she comes out again and says, 'He sounded like he meant it, I think you better go.'"

"He only had to call one of yous to get it for him," Grace said. She hunted through the needles on the front of her smock, then removed one that trailed green thread.

"Ray could've delivered it himself," my mother said, "but one of them's as stubborn as the other."

"Anyway, Toby drives over in Glory's pickup," Reg went on. "When he comes into the yard, Ray is putting the tractor away. 'Too late,' he says. 'I just hauled 'er down and dumped her in the mud, that meat is deep in frogs' eggs by now. If you want 'er you'll need a deep-sea diver's suit.' Toby hauled him off that tractor by the shirt front and they fought it out right there in the yard. Both had bloody noses and a few loose teeth by the time they were tired enough to quit."

Reg's grin was wide enough to show every one of his own sturdy teeth. "So when he got back, Toby didn't have much patience with them heifers when they come trotting over to the truck. He yelled and swatted at them and come growling up to the door there, still wiping the blood off his face and cursing. When he got into the shack, Glory is at the sink with her back to him. 'You got it?' she says. He was ready to tell her he wasn't in any mood to talk about it but then he sees these white-faces looking in through every window, their big cow eyes full of love. One's in the open doorway, drooling onto Glory's lino. He said he never even thought – when Glory turned and said, 'Where's that meat you went for?' he answered quick, 'Just give me a minute, willya' and took his 30:30 down off the wall."

"He didn't!" Several people said this at once, though of course they already knew that Reg was telling the truth.

"She didn't know what hit 'er. Toby said he felt terrible as soon as he done it. Glory was horrified."

"I woulda turned the gun on *him*," said Em Madill.

"But she didn't," Buddy said. "She was making an effort to adjust to country life. 'We can't just stand here,' she said. 'We've got to get rid of her quick!'"

"Toby agreed. They had to get rid of the evidence," Reg said. "So Glory got her first lesson in butchering. He said she handled that knife like an army surgeon. Stood and cut for the rest of that afternoon and never said a word until that beef was wrapped in butcher paper and driven to the locker in town."

Edna prompted. "What did she say when she finally spoke?" She waited with mouth wide open for what came next.

Grinning and chuckling and hardly able to speak, Reg shook his head. "She said, she's wiping off the table, right? and first she says, I hope this don't happen often, the blood can't be too good for my hands!"

Reg waited. "Then she said to Toby, she says, A good thing it wasn't another woman followed you home, I wouldn't be too happy about her taking up space in my locker!"

Reg's whole body was shaking now. "Then she wipes the table off a little bit more and says, But if it *was* another woman you might've had a fight on your hands, to get that gun off the wall before me."

Grace said, "Don't fall in love with Toby, it could be fatal. Too bad that little heifer didn't know." She sorted through a tangle of embroidery thread for more.

"He cut wires in his fence so the rest of them heifers could escape," Buddy said. "Ol' Williamson was mad as hell when he rounded them up and one was missing, but he never knew who it was that got 'er."

If Mr. Collins were here to see this he'd be sure to bring up

Chaucer's pilgrims. And the people of Florence, telling tales while they waited for the plague to end. That was the sort of thing he did. In English classes he insisted the people we talked about from books were much like us. No one believed him. No one believed the world out there had much in common with us.

Of course we weren't medieval pilgrims or wealthy Italian nobles, we were only Mackens from the Vancouver Island bush, doing what came naturally. Could I imagine Uncle Reg with the Oxford clerk, or Edna amongst the Florentines? This place was hardly the civilized garden terrace of the Palmieri villa, with its statues and fountains and fancy hedges that I'd seen in the *Book of Knowledge* photograph. Those people from Florence would have sneered at this expanse of dry, thin, grassy stubble, untidy with giant cones, populated by monstrous trees and haunted by dozens of crows whose squawking was sometimes louder than the human gossip below.

Mr. Collins would make something of it, he saw symbols everywhere. Crows, trees, water, food. He would keep us listening for half an hour while he explored this colony of wild strawberries for its meaning. I imagined him telling me about it from the front of the classroom, English 91. "There's your title image, if you ever make a movie about your family."

Of course he would never say such a thing. Though he often made references to movies when he was trying to point out something in the stories we read, he never let on that he knew my elaborate hopes.

"For a while Glory talked about taking a hairdressing course," my mother said. "She thought she might be good at that."

"I doubt it," Kitty said. "I wouldn't let her touch me with a pair of scissors but I let her dye my hair. God knows why. The first time she turned it pink by mistake. She didn't bat an eye. She tried to tell me everybody in Vancouver was going pink.

I didn't believe her so she did it again. We had a good laugh anyway. She said I may have buggered up my chance at a singing career, I coulda been the Pink-Haired Sparrow of Nashville."

"Well, I let her have a go at this bush once in a while," said Grace, driving fingers into her Orphan Annie mop. "How much damage could she do? Wait a minute – I forgot! The first time I didn't think to tell her what happens to curly hair when it dries. She nearly scalped me! We laughed until there were tears. I said, 'I can't go nowhere lookin' like this,' so she says, 'Oh hell, there's nothin to fixing that.' And she whips me up a turban hat out of an old piece of skirt. Then she makes herself another one just like it. 'Tell 'em we're Hindu spies,' she says. We wore them the rest of that day, laughing like fools, even wore them to town – but I never wore the damn thing after that. A person forgets."

"Well, there you are – she tried," Edna said. "Maybe she shoulda taken up sewing. Too bad she didn't get to stay longer in that hotel. I bet she'd be happy there."

"She loved that hotel," my mother said. "So did I. A wonderful place for a honeymoon."

"Honeymoon!" Kitty said. "You were in it a year!"

"No wonder it lasted a year!" Edna cried. "Thirteen empty bedrooms!"

"You can only sleep in one at a time," my mother sang out, pretending she didn't know what was meant.

"Yes, but you can *visit* more than one if you're strong enough!" Reg grinned at his audience.

"Look who's talking," Kitty said, tossing her soot-black curls. "You'd be snoring after one."

Reg sat back on his heels.

"Oh, I'm sorry," Kitty said. "I'm only teasing. Thirteen bedrooms wears me out just thinking."

"Where's Eddie? What's Eddie got to say about this?" Buddy stretched his neck to peer through the crowds.

"Over by those trucks — where else?" my mother said. "Logging with Shorty Madill."

"Slack the haul-back!" Grace called out.

Everyone laughed. My father and Shorty Madill looked over but went on talking. Their plates sat on the roof of someone's car.

"Who's a whistle-punk here?" Kitty said. "How many peeps to say 'quittin' time'?"

"There's no quittin' time for loggers, you know that," my mother said. "Put two of them together and it's 'spar tree' this and 'rigging slinger' that until they drop."

Grace put down her sewing long enough to light a cigarette. Then she went immediately into a coughing fit, *horrack, horrack,* and waved her hands about until it stopped. "Buddy, get me a coffee while you're up."

Uncle Buddy wasn't up, but he jumped to his feet and set off with his long-legged strides towards the stove. Grace raised her embroidery again and stabbed the needle down through the cloth, squinting through her smoke.

Helen said, "I remember the time I dropped in and found Glory all red-eyed from sobbing."

"We don't want to hear about that!" my mother said, holding up a hand to ward off something bad. "Let's get dessert. There's sixteen pies over there."

Nobody moved. "You telling me to be quiet?" Helen said, her shoulders high and stiff.

"Anyway, Helen's not the only one that knows why Glory was crying that day," said Kitty. "This was when she'd just come?"

"'There's a story comes with me,' Glory told me once," Grace said. "Frieda remembers that."

"Part of the story is this!" said Kitty. "She thought she was having a baby when she come here. We're talkin' about the day she found out she wasn't, aren't we Helen? She was broken-hearted."

"Whose baby?" Edna cried. Then, to the silence, she said, "Oh, hell. I'm sorry. Damn."

"It was Toby's," said Kitty. "At least she didn't say it wasn't."

"Don't tell me any more," Edna said. "You know I'm the kind that can't stop bawling once I start." Most of the time she was one tough cookie but, as she liked to put it herself, even ginger-snaps would turn to mush if you dunked them.

"Don't make too much of this," my mother warned. "She didn't pine for babies." She looked at Colin and Theresa's nameless child. "There was more to the story than that."

"Where's Marty?" Edna said. "I need the truck keys for some Kleenex."

"Martin locks his truck at a family reunion?" Colin bel-lowed.

"Nobody here would steal a GMC," Reg said. "Not even if he left the doors wide open and the motor running, with a Help Yourself sign on the windshield."

"Oh hell, it don't matter," Edna said. "Forget it."

Crows sat in every tree now, hollering. No one seemed to mind – they just raised their voices to compete.

"She was just a little girl herself," my mother said, "but I'd like to think she'd've made a good mother if she had the chance. Who remembers the time she piled everybody's kids into her pickup and drove them up to Campbell River for ice cream? She came home with two more kids than she left with, couldn't figure out why. Not one of them would admit they didn't belong – others wouldn't squeal. Finally she brought them all to our place so I could point out strangers. Then she drove the whole way back and delivered them to their doors."

"Kids loved her," Kitty said.

"She was wonderful with children," my mother said. "There was one little guy, she said she would've kept him in a minute if she thought she'd get away with it. I remember the one she meant – cute as a button – you could've believed he was hers."

"Too bad he wasn't," said Kitty. "If she'd had kids like the rest of us she might have saved herself some grief, she'd have been far too busy to stray!"

10

THAT Glory had got into the habit of visiting Stokes was only muttered at first between adults, or referred to in such an indirect way that you had to guess what was meant. Maybe no one wanted to say it out loud, in case that made something real. You overheard. "He" lived like a pig in a sty. Did "she" go up to help him clean? He ate poorly – porridge and boiled potatoes. Did she drive up to cook him a decent meal? "A terrible cook like her?"

Of course it wasn't difficult to figure out who they meant. Stokes wasn't the only old man in the picture either, it was eventually learned. Sandy Roberts. Howie Twist. The ancient Spivac twins. All old, all runny-eyed, all shaky. What sort of woman hung around with lonely old men? She was forever driving off to visit one of them – a bakery pie or loaf of bread beside her on the seat of her half-ton – filling the world with dust. "Food some relative could have done with," Nora used to say. "But she'd rather waste it on *them!*"

They drank. That was the general assumption in the beginning – perhaps still was. A lonely old man was so grateful for female company that he was happy to share his booze. Nora suspected that Glory was a secret drunk. "Not enough excitement here for her. Not enough boozing, not enough hanky-panky. Toby ought to take the boots to her, or send her back to the city. Either that, or give her a dozen babies to keep her busy."

Others were not so hard on Glory as Nora was, but most felt much the same. My mother didn't like what she heard either, but refused to join the critics. "Anyone marries into this family has some shocks ahead," my father said. "Sooner or later that girl'll grow up. Meanwhile she does what she can."

Of course when Glory saw how she was upsetting the others she tried to explain the attraction. Stokes owned a piano. He'd been a lover of classical music and opera before the First War, in Nova Scotia. He sometimes played for Glory. She sometimes played for him. Around here, cowboy music was what you heard on the radio most, or Red Robinson's rock and roll. Glory had been trained to accompany her mother in rehearsal – *La Boheme*, *The Marriage of Figaro*. When she visited Stokes – or those outcasts from Europe – it was a chance to practise her skills at the keyboard while bringing pleasure to someone else as well.

Whatever the reason, there was still how it looked. Nora had never heard anything like it. "What kind of woman would risk her reputation to play music? She's more peculiar than we thought if she thinks tickling the ivories is a good enough reason for embarrassing an entire family."

For a while the mystery was why Toby didn't stop her. Davy Morgan spent a month in hospital for something he'd said about Glory that Toby overheard. Uncle Buddy had had to duck a flying hammer after some joke he'd made without thinking. Toby chased Charlie Calhoun right off the Island for touching Glory where he shouldn't, and Charlie never found the nerve to come back. Why didn't he do the same to Stokes? Toby never laid a hand on Glory either, never raised his voice. He could have insisted she stay home.

"City people do that sort of thing," he told me. He was proud of her. City people who didn't have to go to work every day did favours for the poor. Rich people did that, and people with education – helped others, visited the needy, shared what they had with those who had less. This was what you called civilized behaviour.

And he knew how Glory loved music. One day he would buy her a piano of her own, he said. He would buy her a big shiny concert grand in Vancouver, and have it shipped over. She could stay home and play, she could take students and charge them for lessons. He would build her a lean-to with an outside entrance, with a welcome mat for students to wipe their feet on. He would make her a little sign to hang by the gate, he said. But of course he never did.

What would Gordie say about the way Old Stokes kept showing up in our lives? I still missed Gordie – enough to imagine seeing him now and then, even to having conversations with him when no one else was around. He was never mentioned between Caro and myself. So far as I could tell, he was never mentioned at all.

It may have been because of Gordie that Uncle Martin moved his family away. Gordie embarrassed him. He cried too much. He daydreamed when he was supposed to be carrying firewood. When Uncle Martin discovered that Gordie wore an apron to serve the warmed-up pork 'n' beans in our stump, he whipped off his belt and thrashed him. Gordie was five years old. Uncle Martin referred to Gordie as "Missy" for a week. He told Caro to think of Gordie as a sister. "That ought to cure him fast!"

Gordie didn't know what he was supposed to be cured of. He didn't want to be a girl, he hoped to be a fighter pilot one day. Uncle Martin may not have meant to be cruel, he never called him "Missy" again. But when we started school, word of the incident had preceded him. Gordie was addressed as "Gordella." Instead of laughing, Gordie blushed. His eyes filled up with tears. Although he wasn't bad at softball, he was jeered at when he tried to join in, and told to skip rope on the other side of the school. Any attempt I made to defend him only made things worse; Gordie told me not to do him any favours. On the schoolbus older boys stretched his neck in a hammer-lock and pinched his bum. I pretended not to see.

On weekends we played as we'd always done. The world of school was forgotten when you swarmed out to attack stumps inhabited by cousins who would try to repel you with clubs. Schoolyard bullies meant nothing when you were rebels armed with wooden rifles, creeping up the roof of the barn to leap upon soldiers hiding below in the loft.

But weekends were short. When I asked Toby how I could help Gordie at school, Toby said he'd be glad to pay a visit himself to the school that had booted him out for breaking a teacher's arm. He'd show the bullies what measures might be taken against them. He'd read soldier magazines and knew a variety of tortures. But getting wind of the plan only made Gordie feel worse, to think this sort of help was needed. He threatened to run away from home if Toby came near the school. Grade three boys forced Gordie to wear his pants back-wards, so that he'd have no fly in the front.

Maybe Uncle Martin thought Gordie would get a new start if they moved. I don't know if moving made any difference, I didn't see much of Gordie after that. He didn't write. I didn't hear much about him either, until we got word that Gordie had disappeared. One day he didn't come home from school. This was a few days after my thirteenth birthday – I'd wondered why he hadn't sent a card, or phoned. He never contacted his family, he was never found. For years I half expected him to show up at our place and ask to stay. But I suppose that wouldn't have been allowed. Someone in the family would have taken him back, to keep him where he belonged.

We learned of Gordie's disappearance the week before Uncle Buddy was finally to marry his housekeeper. I decided not to go to the wedding, in case Gordie chose that day to show up. He could live secretly in the barn or in one of the stumps. I would smuggle food out every night and do my homework with him so he would get some education.

I imagined he would have taken a new name. If Gordie had changed his name I didn't want to be Rusty any more. From now on I would be known as Joe. I told my family this. Joe Macken. "Don't be stupid," my father said. "Your name is Russell – Rusty – we've already sort of changed your name once." My mother said if I insisted on a different name she would call me Winston Roosevelt Stalin. Gerry suggested Mortimer Snerd. Nobody took me seriously. When I begged to be called RJ on a trial basis, they laughed. Gordie wouldn't have laughed. When he arrived we would make a pact not to say "Rusty" or "Gordie" again, though I'd have to leave home before I could make it official.

Before most family weddings, the bridal party and closest relatives gathered at our place for a long and leisurely steam bath. First the women, then the men, went out to the un-painted hut my father had built at the back of the stumpy pasture, an imitation of the saunas built by the neighbouring Finns. Inside, they sat for as long as they could bear the steam. Talking. Drinking beer. Telling jokes. Planning. Remembering. Scrubbing one another's back with the scratchy loofahs.

The day of Uncle Buddy's wedding I'd gone to the largest stump to do my homework in the one part of the world untouched by adult lives. I was wondering how long I would have to wait for Gordie when the women went past on the trail, carrying towels and folded clothing. Grace, Kitty, Frieda, Glory. I knew their voices. My sister, Meg. Sonny and Gordie and I had long ago joked about sneaking up to listen when there were women inside – what did naked ladies talk about? We'd even loosened a knothole that we imagined having the courage to peek through one day. But it had never occurred to me that I might do such a thing myself. Watching the women go in through the door, I considered it. Would Gordie have gone along?

Gordie might, but Toby would not have approved. Anyway, it was enough, for now, to imagine: the women were something of a blur, stepping out of their clothes in the dressing room and rushing in to sit on the benches around the oil-drum stove. White thighs. Heavy breasts – Grace's heaviest of all. Kitty's "two fried eggs," as she liked to call them herself. They poured a dipper of water over the stones on the oil-drum stove, and hummed with pleasure at the steam. (Smoke rose from the chimney to shred out through the upper boughs of the willows.)

Glory would not be rushed. She removed her clothing slowly, draping it carefully over a chair. Her dress, her slip, her brassière. Finally her white silk panties, trimmed, I imagined, with lace. Naked, she arched her back and reached behind to push up her hair, and to pin it all up on top. Her long, long slender throat. Then, finally, she walked in her exquisite naked beauty through the connecting door to where the others sat around the horseshoe tiers of benches.

I imagined her settling in a top corner. Inside the stump, I ran one hand over the nearest leg of the stove and up the enamel surface of the oven door. Glory leaned back against the wall and lifted a knee, pulling one foot in close, and ran a hand from her ankle right up her leg. She laughed at something Grace had said, and let the hand run up to hold one of her breasts for a moment. Something convulsed inside me. I raised a hand and ran the palm down the inside wall of the stump. The charred surface was silky, cool. Female flesh, lightly powdered. And curved in places, cleft in places, creased where hard wood grain had resisted fire.

I did not look out when they passed the stump again. To seek a glimpse of Glory would be to risk being found with a flaming face, my guilt advertised to everyone. Charcoal smudges on my arms and chest, on my pants. I waited until their voices had faded, then ran for the steam-bath house. Before the men arrived, I wanted the place to myself.

Stripped, I went into the little room and ran a hand along the benches. Where had she sat? I decided on a corner, the upper level. She would set herself apart. Sitting where she may have sat, I felt the hot smooth texture of the wood, velvet from years of moisture. I lay out on my belly and pressed my face to the hot damp spongy wood. This was something I couldn't tell Sonny, or anyone. Not even Gordie, if that were possible. I inhaled the steam and imagined Glory's secret flesh. Against the bench, my own flesh felt that this was close enough to real.

I should not have thought of Gordie. Now it seemed he might be across the room from me. Sitting on the highest bench. "I'm trying to remember if they told us growing up would be like this. It looks ridiculous. What if the others come in and catch you at it?"

At the sound of someone entering the change room, I sat up fast. Crossed my legs. Bent forward. If the men came in and found me like this, I'd be hearing about it for the rest of my life. One of the family tales.

But it was worse. Glory. She pushed the door open, calling,

"Someone in there?" God knows what I looked like when she saw me – trying to shrink into the corner. "Oh – I! Sorry. I came back for my sweater."

She turned away, but then turned back. "You look so embarrassed!" A laugh – she seemed surprised by this.

Couldn't she see that I was in agony! I tried to laugh too, to suggest that I knew how ridiculous I looked. But it didn't come off.

"You look like a whipped dog, trying to make himself invisible in a corner."

"I'm not used to women bursting in when I'm out of my clothes."

"You mean it isn't something you *hoped* might happen?"

"Right now I feel silly." Skinny and white.

"And running out of steam as well. How can you have a steam bath without any steam? You going to pour more water on, or do you think I'll do it for you?"

I could see in her wicked smile that she wouldn't. I could see that she didn't intend to leave, either. I stayed where I was.

She lowered her voice to one of her movie-star growls. "You're scared to stand up and show me you aren't ashamed?"

She laughed, to suggest she was putting on an act, but I knew she was serious. I couldn't believe she would say this. I couldn't believe I was capable of doing what she said. And yet I stood up, in my corner, and stepped down onto the floor. I walked to the cold-water tap, lifted the dipper from the bucket, and walked to the oil-drum stove. Aware of air on my skin. Aware of my hands, of my feet, of my awkward legs. Aware of my long, narrow, naked, and vulnerable front. I tossed the water onto the rocks and replaced the dipper. Then I stepped back onto the bench. Nothing had prepared me for this. I was amazed I hadn't forgotten how to make my legs go through the motion of walking.

"Oh, you're beautiful, of course! What did you think?" She seemed delighted with herself. "You'll be Toby's twin one day, but taller." She stepped inside the connecting doorway, but quickly moved back. "My gosh, you're growing *up*! Be glad."

Was she being an aunt, now, or just Glory, who could make you feel grown up just by lowering her voice and smiling like Rita Hayworth? Perhaps she was only playing it safe. At any rate, I was weak with gratitude.

"Any whipped-looking man will break my heart," she said. "I can't help it. I ought to run an orphanage for males. I can't stand to see a man or boy that doesn't know what he's worth. You'd be surprised to learn how many there are in this world."

Once she'd gone, I dressed quickly and returned to the stump. Yet I continued to feel the film of steam on my skin, the warm and clammy slick of shame. When Gerry came looking for me I told him I didn't feel very well. I told my father the same when he appeared. "Suit yourself, if you want to be a grouch." He seemed to find this amusing. "I don't suppose they'll stop the wedding just for you."

Excited and ashamed. The steamy slick would never leave my skin. It wasn't just the wedding I would avoid. I'd never go anywhere! I couldn't, until I'd sorted things out. I hadn't asked for this, I had no business feeling this shameful interest in Toby's wife. When I looked around the inside of that charred dead stump, at the streaks from my hands down the wall, at Stokes's old curved-leg cookstove, I knew that all of this would soon be left behind. Was left behind already. Where was Gordie? I suspected this world of pasture stumps was already a thing of the past.

II

THE creek was beyond Kruegers' last field and a mile or so into woods, past mottled alder thickets and a cedar swamp. A few small firs grew up from decaying stumps. The bridge was old. One of the dusty wooden planks was loose, another was thicker than the others, a replacement.

"This can't be it," Caro said. "There's no water."

We got out and looked down from the railing. Gravel. Swamp grass. Dusty willows. Patches of unhealthy-looking bull-rushes. Someone had pulled a small blue wooden punt into the midst of the salmonberries and bracken ferns.

The creek was a dry narrow cleft in the world, a crooked slice like the sort of unnerving fissure an earthquake might leave. It was only one of the many nameless streams that wandered through the district, hardly more than drainage ditches, to empty eventually into Portuguese Creek. It was impossible to know which one it was, which farms it crossed, without following it for miles.

A dragonfly hovered above its own reflection in a stagnant puddle. "There's water," I said. "Look."

There was a series of small, dead puddles along one side. Weeds and slime. Cattle had crossed here, leaving a strange confusion of punctures where their hoofs had sunk into what had been mud – dry as baked clay now.

The only sound was the far-off hum of a vehicle, on this road or another. Things were so quiet that a young deer had come down to sniff at the shallow water. She looked up, ears alert, to consider us. Then lowered her nose to the puddle, as though she recognized my car and knew she wasn't in danger. But Caro leaned an imaginary rifle across the Meteor's hood. "*Blam!*"

The startled doe leapt back, and went crashing through the woods.

"There's nothing here," I said. "Let's go." I wished I had never come.

"We haven't *seen* it yet," she said, starting down the bank. "Aren't you curious?"

It wasn't a matter of being curious. I was worse than curious. Death scenes had their pull – this one more than others. I'd never seen a dead person. Didn't really want to, but knew I wouldn't be able to resist an opportunity. Grandparents had been whisked away before you were even told what had happened. I sometimes stopped my car by Cooper's Corner, where a friend from school was killed when a bus ran into his bike. To imagine where he had fallen, to think what it must have been like for him to know he was dying, to imagine what sort of thoughts went through his head. I hated this, but felt that if I could stare hard enough at one dead body, or imagine the thoughts of a dying person, I would understand something important about the world.

But not this time. This time there was something else. This time there was something I couldn't explain, even to myself. I didn't want to know what Glory had been thinking, I didn't want to imagine where she had been. I wished I had never agreed to drive Caro here, never got out of the car.

190

There was little water upstream of the bridge – mostly gravel, and more baked mud with skin as smooth and shiny as the surface of chocolate pudding. Caro pushed through flowering spikes of hardhack. "Not a drop this way." Flies buzzed above the cow-pies on a pebbled slope.

I went to the downstream side of the bridge to see what had happened to the creek. There was only more willows, more gravel, with irregular connected puddles that looked no deeper than a finger's length. How could anyone drown in that?

I climbed down the bank for a closer look. Green slime lay clotted around the edges of the puddles. Leaves and twigs floated. Something small as a needle darted across. One pool may have been eight, ten inches deep. What were we looking for – handprints? The impression of Glory's profile on the muddy bottom?

"Godalmighty," Caro said. "Just think how hard it must've been."

You couldn't avoid imagining: Glory walking up that road, stopping to look from the bridge (was she crying?), Glory climbing down that bank, staring at her own reflection in the shallow water and seeing how hard this was going to be. Then Glory's skirt across this patch of starved clover, one hand on the dirty bottom of the pool. I didn't know what she was thinking, I'd never know what she was thinking now.

"It would've been easier in the bathtub," Caro said. "Why didn't she slit her wrists?"

"Don't be stupid," I said.

"She knew we'd talk about it afterwards."

"She might not've meant to do it."

Caro's laugh was a sort of choked cough. "One thing we know for sure is she meant to do it. Look at this – you'd have to be pretty damned determined to drown yourself in here!"

Did she think she might not be found, and that heavy rains would some day carry her like Ophelia or the Lady of Shalott through the family farms until she floated past Toby's mill?

"I mean, when she set out for a walk. She might've just got feeling worse the farther she got from home."

"Bullshit. She wanted to make sure it was something the others couldn't get out of their heads."

"You're wrong," I said. "Let's go."

But Caro sat on her heels to stare into the hardened mud. "Doesn't Old Man Stokes live up this road? I bet she was walking up to see him –"

"She'd take her truck."

"– and all of a sudden just couldn't help herself."

I glanced up at the underside of the bridge. How often had her pickup rumbled across those planks?

"Don't forget she was a little bit crazy," Caro said. "It wouldn't take much to push her over the edge."

"She wasn't crazy, she was different – a little different from the rest is all."

Caro looked at me as though I'd proved her point. "How long you think she stood on that bridge, before she made up her mind to come down and do it?" When I ignored her and climbed up the bank, she called after me, "Scares the hell out of you, don't it?"

By the time she'd come up to the road, the sound of an approaching car had grown louder. It was Sonny Aalto in his old man's yellow Jeep. He pulled up, but didn't get out. "They told me you took off but didn't know where. I guessed."

His fishing pole lay in sections behind the seat. "I thought you'd've gone long ago," I said.

"Old man needed the Jeep."

"You remember Caro."

"Sure," he said. He didn't quite look at her. His throat went red. He tucked his chin down and lit a cigarette. "Come for the funeral, eh?"

"I sure as hell didn't come for the fishing," Caro said. "A good way to bore yourself to death." She picked a handful of salmonberries off a roadside bush, blew off the dust, and tipped them into her mouth.

"It hasn't killed me yet," Sonny said, looking as though there was something up the road he was interested in.

"I wouldn't know," Caro said. "All I seen of you so far is the boils on the back of your neck."

Sonny's hand slapped at his neck. "Git out! I never had boils in my life!"

Caro laughed. "Maybe not, but you got a bad case of *something* red that's spreading round your collar. You got a funny way of showing how pleased you are to see me."

"You any idea where Toby might be?" I said.

Sonny made a face and shook his head. "Leave him alone. Go back to your party." He got out of the Jeep and leaned against the closed door.

"You still driving up to the lake?"

He tilted back to suck at his cigarette, looking down his nose at the distance. "Beth don't want to go because Lynette's not going. What's the matter with you two? Beth thinks you want to see how long it'll take her to apologize. She won't."

"She already has," I said. "She showed up at the funeral home."

"So we'll pick her up," Sonny said, ready to go.

"Forget that," Caro said. "Come back to the beach, have a beer and we'll go for a swim."

Sonny ran his gaze down Caro's legs.

"Me, I'm goin' skinny dipping," Caro said. "You can come if you got the nerve, you lucky dog. Ol' Rusty here, he won't. He's afraid his balls'll freeze off."

193

"And mine won't?" Sonny said, stretching his neck to look off into the woods. No girl we knew had ever talked like Caro.

"Not if they're as hot as I think they are. I expect to see *steam.*"

Sonny laughed, but wouldn't let his gaze near Caro.

"Jesus," Caro said. "When're you morons gonna grow up? Come on, let's get outa this hole!"

They would still be talking back at Toby's, spread out across the neglected playground and trying to hold off time while they fitted Glory into history. Even as the sun began to drop towards the Island mountains, they would be still trying to cast the charm that kept Mackens together inside their idea of what Mackens should be. A few would have started a baseball game. Others would have erected a volleyball net. Kitty and Reg would be setting up for a concert, where they – The Singing Lariats – would again be the stars of the show. I wasn't in any hurry to return.

"You can go back if you want," I said. "First I think I'll take a gander up at Stokes's place."

They insisted on going too. They wanted to see where the man had come from who'd once had the power to scare us half to death. It had never before occurred to us to do this. Sonny left the Jeep where it was and climbed in with us. Caro slid over to the middle and put a hand on his knee.

"We going to accuse him of something?" she said.

"He won't tell you nothing," Sonny said. "He don't talk to people."

"Tie him up and stick a pitchfork into his throat," Caro said. "Don't let him go till he sings." She turned the radio on. Gogi Grant was into "The Wayward Wind" again – she'd been singing it all day long every day this month. I turned it off.

I hadn't anticipated the queasy feeling that settled in my stomach as I drove up that road. As though I were going where I had no business going. The trees were familiar, the washboard gravel was familiar, this was a public road. And yet I could not shake the sense that I had come over to the wrong side of that bridge. The Shippits lived up this road, and the Hawkins brothers – beyond Stokes, in makeshift shacks on the site of the old original logging camp. People sometimes spoke of the place as Dogpatch, sometimes as Maniacs Row. Wives were swapped up there, they said. Home brew was consumed, and illegally sold. You heard rumours of wives who were beaten nearly to death, of children sold to strangers, of men removing the ears of other men in acts of revenge. Once a Hawkins had killed his wife with an axe before using his gun on himself. His son walked down to the bus stop every morning but ran to hide in the bush when the bus appeared. Those children who did come to school rarely spoke but they would beat you bloody if they didn't like the way you looked at them.

Heading up this road didn't seem to bother Caro, who was more interested in playing with the buttons on Sonny's shirt. Sonny appeared a little nervous, but that was probably because of Caro. This was stupid – I told myself this – it was stupid to feel anything different at all. We might have come up here to pick early Himalaya blackberries along the ditch.

A woman with long grey hair watched us from the entrance-way to a grass-roofed hut. She waved, though she wouldn't know my car. "Rabbit Fitzgerald, looking for business," Sonny said. "World's first underground hoor." We slowed when we came to the Freemans' circle of converted bread vans and buses – each a separate room around a central canvas roof, as messy as we'd been told. No one seemed to be home.

We knew we were alongside Stokes's land when the barbed-wire fences began to sag. Rotted fence posts leaned against huckleberry bushes, all that kept them from lying flat to the ground. Uncleared bush gave way to fields grown up with Scotch broom and second-growth fir amongst the stumps that had never been blasted out nor burned. Dead and dying orchard trees were choked with morning glory.

The house was built at the same time as our own but in the style of most of the originals – a long narrow one-storey box with verandah across the gable end. It sat fifty feet back from the road, with the woods at its back. It seemed naked, the house, like an old man's face without eyelashes. There were no curtains in the windows, no paint on the walls, no proper steps at the door – just blocks of wood. Little grass grew in the yard. Chickens scratched at dirt where a black Hillman was parked. The Model T sat beneath the roof of a sagging garage.

"We'll stay in the car," Caro said, when I'd stopped near the gate. "Me 'n' Sonny have some catching up to do." She slid her hand so quickly up his thigh that Sonny slapped his own hand down to stop it. "You go give 'im hell."

"We should all go in," Sonny said. "But I don't know why we're here."

He was looking at Stokes's house across the pasture. Stokes had come out his front door to stand on the porch, looking at us. Blood, gone cold, seemed to have escaped from my veins to go sloshing up and down inside my chest.

Nosy Caro opened the glove compartment and poked her fingers into the mess – flashlight and air gauge and papers.

"I don't know why we're here either," I said. "But I need to take a good look at him. Maybe he'll have something to say, after all this time."

Caro slipped my Bell & Howell out from the glove compartment and held it to her eye, aiming it at the figure on the porch. "We'll make a movie of it. Exhibit B at his murder trial – your body will be Exhibit A."

"Put that back," I said. I grabbed for the camera but she held it out of my reach — across Sonny and through the open window.

"You'll make me drop it," she said.

"It's already broken," Sonny said. "It's always been broken."

"What good is it then?"

"He's kept it in there since he bought the car," Sonny said. "Waiting for a miracle."

Caro laughed. "Y'oughta toss it down the beach road with the iceboxes and goddam canned tomatoes."

When Caro brought the camera back inside I snatched it from her and swung it over the back of the seat. Then I grabbed up my cotton jacket and slipped the camera into the one pocket that wasn't already bulging with cigarettes and lighter and change. "Leave it." I removed the key from the ignition and got out.

Sonny stepped out and stood inside the opened door. Caro got out beside him. "We'll come if you scream for help," she said. The space between the road and the fence was a dense snarl of young alder, blackberry, orange rose-hips, and Scotch broom whose black pods were almost dry enough for their yearly explosion of seeds.

Walking towards Stokes's gate, I felt a little light-headed. The old man had come to the edge of the porch to scatter feed for the hens. He was still unusually tall, but badly stooped. A dark cardigan was caught up on one side against the gaping waist of his tweed pants, which were held up by wide suspenders.

To one side of the gate, a few cartons of eggs and several baskets of blueberries sat on the lopsided milk-can stand. A tobacco tin with a slit in the lid was where you were meant to put your money — "40 cents per doz/pint."

At the head of the driveway, Stokes looked up and halted the sowing movement. We looked at one another as we had looked across that stumpy pasture a decade before. Long grass grew between the tire tracks. A garter snake lay squished not far from my right foot, its jelly entrails coated with dust. I started down the driveway towards him. I would think of something to say before I got there.

The house looked even more squalid and filthy at close range than it had from the road. Chicken droppings decorated the step – some dried and smeared, some freshly gleaming. On the porch an axe was imbedded in a blood-stained block of wood, amidst a mess of feathers and boards and cans.

The old man watched me with suspicion from under a heavy fringe of eyebrow.

"Rusty Macken," was the best I could do.

His eyes had a blurred look to them, as though they'd been smeared with Vaseline. His flesh was coarse and loose, with large pores. In a furrow that ran down from his nose, a tuft of whiskers had been missed by his razor. Eventually, as though it had taken a while for my name to register, he nodded. "Saw you in the paper once."

"For the forestry scholarship," he must have meant, though you wouldn't have known from the tone of his voice that he hadn't meant "drunken driver."

A shriek from Caro caused me to jump. She went running off down the road with Sonny after her. When he caught her, they struggled until she broke free and ran off again, squealing. Again he followed. Dust rose up behind them.

Stokes's gaze followed them for a moment. "What kind of people you hanging out with now?" He turned his blurry eyes on me again, as though there was something unpleasant about me he wanted to study.

"Same as always – friend, a cousin. She's been after him for years."

His face did not betray much interest. "Sounds like she got

him." He spoke to the chickens. "Now, you selling something, or only come to gawk?"

I took a fast deep breath. "You were at the cemetery."

He continued to look at me from under those brows, waiting for more. "You come to arrest me for that?"

"Nobody understands why she did it," I said.

He cleared his throat of phlegm and spat onto the floorboards of the porch. "They think lives should be tidy, your lot. Fit into narrow slots. They're much like children that way. You coming in?"

I would rather not go in, but he turned and disappeared through the door. I crossed the porch and followed him inside to a world of disorder and shadow. Patches of linoleum had been torn up, exposing raw boards. Wallpaper curled away from the walls, drooping floorward in faded strips. The air smelled of fried grease. I pressed one hand to my stomach – cramps.

But he didn't stop in that first room, he walked right through it and seemed to assume I was following. Boots and rubbers and bedroom slippers had to be kicked out of the way as we passed down a hall. I wondered if I'd be murdered while Caro and Sonny were fooling around in the bush. How did I know that Glory's death hadn't deranged him? That he wasn't heading now for his shotgun to blow off my head? He could bury me back in the woods. In a movie an old man in this house would torment a trapped outsider for a while before committing the deed.

The room he led me to may have been the only room in the house he'd kept clean and tidy – an old-fashioned parlour, with stuffed red chairs, fancy-legged tables, and tall vases. Glasses of different shapes sat behind the doors of a tall cabinet. Portraits hung on the walls, and prints of pale watery pastures. Sunlight flooded in through windows that looked out the back of the house in the direction of the woods, across a garden of

blooming roses and daisies and tall bright flowers I didn't recognize. An upright piano sat at the very centre of this light,
on a circular Persian carpet.

"She brought it with her," he said, standing beside the piano
in a manner that made it clear I was to admire it.

"This came from England?"

He nodded, but frowned, as though he had reservations
about this confidence.

"Your wife's?"

He nodded again, his frown grown even fiercer.

"And Glory played it too?"

He smiled, or almost smiled, and nodded. But then pulled
all of his mouth in, as though he would swallow his lips.

Amongst the wall portraits there was one scene that might
have been religious, in a fancy gold-leaf frame. A robed figure
on the shoreline looked out towards a little sailboat danger-
ously tilted to one side.

"Sit down," he said. "Play."

"I don't play."

He raised his furry eyebrows. "She didn't teach you?"

"We don't have a piano," I said.

He nodded again, and sat on the piano bench himself. His
hairless spotted hands curled above the keyboard. Books of
music sat on the ledge – *Great Arias*, a thick hymnal open to
"Nearer My God to Thee." He smelled of pipe tobacco – a
leather pouch bulged in the pocket of his checkered shirt.

"But you jump," he said. "The high jump?"

"Pole vault."

"Yes. I've seen you. She told me about it. I stopped to watch
from the sidelines at a school track meet in town. It must be
more than having those long legs."

"There's some skill," I said. "And practice."

"That moment, when you let go of the pole and are about to sail safely over the what-is-it – "

"Crossbar."

He shook his head. "A remarkable feeling, I think, even as you're starting to fall." A finger of his left hand struck a single note, which rang in the room like a bell. Then a second note, and a third. Notes began to fall tumbling after one another, until his right hand joined in with something else and a melody of some sort began to distinguish itself from the rest. He leaned into the piano, then shifted to one side and came back. Everything above his hips moved with the music.

"What is that?" I said.

"Donizetti," he said, without stopping. "Lucia is singing of her wedding. To the man she loves. Though of course the wedding has never happened, and will not."

I had never seen an opera but I had no trouble imagining that this music came from a woman who believed she had married someone she had not. On stage, she might be old and fat – Glory's mother, stuffed into a young woman's dress – but the music itself suggested a young and graceful woman, whose heart must surely know that she only imagines the joy she sings of. I had read Sir Walter Scott. The woman would soon be dead.

The silence that followed his final note was almost a hollow ringing, a loud absence. The house itself might have gone rigid and cold. Chickens had stopped clucking, even the ants that were surely eating the walls must have stopped their chewing. All at once you knew how alone this man was, here in this house.

No family lived here. He *had* no family. Stokes had killed his family with a single stone. There were no Stokeses, there was only Stokes. Perhaps that was the point, for Glory. When Glory played the piano there was only Stokes to play for. No other audience to pass judgement. No army of Stokeses to tell her that being a refined city girl, useless for anything else, it was a good thing she had at least learned to play the piano. No sisters-in-law to suggest that she play at dances, play for singalongs at family reunions, learn to play something you could strum along with on a guitar, or yodel.

The colours of the religious painting were faded. It may have been torn from a magazine and slipped behind glass over some ancestor's face. The little sailboat which interested the robed figure was tilted so sharply because its net was swollen with too many fish. The water on that side was dark with thousands of other fish as well, all trying to leap into the net. On the other side of the boat the water was as transparently vacant as sunlit ice.

"You go to church?" I said.

"Used to." He turned down the corners of his mouth. "Too much blood, too much anguish. That picture reminds me how the story goes right on past it."

"How?"

The silence lasted so long that it seemed he wouldn't answer. I'd begun to hope he wouldn't. The squeamish beginnings of a Macken-style embarrassment had begun to creep under my skin.

Finally he said, "I keep it there to remind myself there's choices – which side you fishing on today, Howard Stokes?" He smiled, suddenly. "You think those fellows in the boat got the point? We can read that they didn't drown."

I had no trouble imagining Glory in this old-fashioned room, kept perfect at the centre of a decaying farmhouse. Had he kept that garden flowering outside for her, or for the memory of his son, his departed wife?

He began to play again – something different. "You taking care of my stove?"

"We're too old to play with it now," I said. "Visitors sometimes do, but nobody lights it."

"Go to the window," he said.

I crossed to the window that looked out on the garden. "He's waiting for me to go out," Stokes said. "He's been up there for a good hour now. He doesn't know I've seen him, he thinks I'll go out in the yard where he can shoot me."

On the peak of the barn roof, Toby sat with knees apart and his rifle across his thighs. Trees must have shielded him from the road – I hadn't seen him, or noticed even the barn. He took a cigarette from his mouth and released a long blue ribbon of smoke, and looked off, for the moment, into the woods.

I went out the back door shouting. "Are you crazy?"

Toby tossed down the cigarette butt to the yard. "Go away, kid. What are you doing here?" He didn't seem surprised; he may have watched me come in.

I laughed, or tried to laugh. My father's approach to things: act as though you can't believe he's serious. "You think you'll like jail better when it's permanent? Maybe you think hanging will make you feel better."

"I wasn't going to kill him," Toby said.

"Then why are you up there, why've you got a gun?"

"I'm gonna shoot the bastard's kneecaps off is all."

He could do that too, he was a good enough shot.

"You think the judge will give you a medal for that?" I hated this sarcastic tone that came from my mouth, but seemed unable to speak in any other way.

Stokes's barn was a small one. Like many old barns, it had a sort of ladder nailed up one wall, leading to the gaping doorway of the hay loft. From there I could reach out and throw my leg up onto the slope of the roof.

"Where you going?"

"Coming up."

"Don't waste your time. You know you're not strong enough to get this out of my hand."

"I know that," I said, climbing up the ancient cedar shakes. "I just want to watch." I sat on the peak beside him – a couple of yards away. "I've never seen anyone shoot an old man's kneecaps before. You want to give me a cigarette while I wait?"

"Bugger off." He was not just annoyed, he was mad. "Go back to the others."

"I will," I said. "But first I want to see what an old man looks like when his knee is shot out from under him. Then I want to see how you can hit the second kneecap when he's already writhing on the ground. How long you think you'll have to sit here before he comes out? Maybe you'll have to go right up and shoot through the window."

"You can be an asshole, you know that? Who gave you the right to talk to me like that?"

"You did," I said, "when you started acting like you sold your brains at an auction."

"I'd never do it," Toby said. "Whaddaya think, for chrissake! I just wanted to sit here a while and hear the bastard play."

"Anyway, you'd be shooting the wrong person." I looked off across the yard and the overgrown orchard in the direction Caro and Sonny had gone. "The last couple of years she didn't spend much time with Stokes, she spent most of that time with me."

"Get outa here!" He shifted his shoulders as though trying to shake off an irritation. "Son of a *gun*, Rusty, just go!"

"It's true. She still played Stokes's piano, but she didn't stay. She drove up to meet me at Wolf Lake, by that old explosives shack."

He made a show of sniffing the air. "You been into the hootch?" He could tell I hadn't. "Dreaming your picture shows again."

"She read my notes, we talked about ideas for a screenplay. Sometimes we'd have a picnic, or go in for a swim, but mostly we talked."

He kept his face turned away from me, as though he were studying Stokes's flower garden. "Well, bully for you!"

Now that I'd started this, it seemed I couldn't stop. "She knew you weren't interested in this kind of stuff, Toby. She tried to tell me what to expect in the city. She tried to think of how I could do the things I wanted to do, she tried to think of ways to get our hands on the money. She wanted to be my assistant, she said, so she could give me advice. She imagined that once I got off this island I wouldn't stop, I'd see New York and Montreal, and Los Angeles."

"You went swimming together?" He looked at me now as though he believed what I was saying but could not imagine how such a thing could come about. As though I'd been wearing some sort of disguise all my life.

"She wouldn't even let me hold her hand. At first I hoped to. Maybe I'd seen too many movies. But she didn't. I was glad, I guess, but I would have done it if she'd let me. I guess I loved her too, Toby. You must've known that. What do you think that was like?"

What a fool I would look now if I burst into tears. Yet I'd half-sobbed out the last few words, choking on my own racing heart.

I couldn't seem to bring this to an end. His silence kept me talking. I hardly knew what would come out of my mouth next. "I tried to talk to my dad about this, I needed to talk to someone – I couldn't talk to you. But when it came right down to it I couldn't tell him either, I didn't want to see him disappointed."

Toby looked down at Stokes's house and rubbed his free hand over his face, exploring his bones with his fingers, testing the bruise on his cheek. "Jesus," was all he said.

"My folks thought I was trying to improve my jump, or getting extra help for exams. Everyone thought she was at Stokes's place. We needed to talk. What other choices did we have? I used to stop by your place after school, but then she suggested we meet at the lake, after she'd been out on the road anyway. I couldn't stay away, though it made me feel like shit I'll tell you, because I couldn't stand the thought of doing something that looked . . . something behind your back."

This time when he looked at me he raised one corner of his lip in a sneer. It was a look I'd seen on his face before but never turned against me. "You better get," he said. "You better just bloody-well get away from me, okay?"

Then he raised the rifle, holding the barrel in one hand, and swung the butt at my head. He missed when I ducked, but in ducking I lost my balance. By the time he could swing a second time, if that was what he'd intended, I'd already started to topple down the roof.

12

Toby must have parked his truck beyond a bend in the road. By the time I'd got to my feet he had already gone. Stokes came out to check: a bruised arm, a scrape down the front of one leg – broken skin but little blood. I tried not to limp as I walked down the lane to my car. Every muscle ached, every cell in my body was tense with dissatisfaction. Was there anything I might have said to make a difference? How much should I have told?

Caro and Sonny were not on the road. Nor was Sonny's Jeep by the narrow bridge when I got there, above the creek that divided Glory's world. I drove alone to the highway and back to the picnic site, where the baseball game was coming to a noisy end and the concert had already started.

Normally the flatdeck of Toby's MACKEN LUMBER truck was the concert stage but today's performance took place on the back of Glory's battered half-ton. Kitty and Reg were running things as usual. Most Mackens believed that if only Nashville weren't so far away, Reg and Kitty would be singing on the radio every week. "You don't hear nothing better on the Grand Ole Opry," people said. Reg may have lost his nerve in the Nanaimo hotel, but he hadn't let go of his dream. I was never sure what I should think of this.

Kitty was hardly Kitty Wells but for "The Blue Canadian Rockies" she flung her voice off her highest sinus cavity – straight off the inside-top of her skull – as clear and sad as any country singer you could name. While he strummed on his ivory-inlaid guitar, Reg's face was the battlefield for a mighty struggle against tears. For all Wilf Carter songs they'd trained their boys to imitate the Rhythm Pals – the original Mike, Mark, and Jack – oooohing and ahhhhhing behind them in their satin shirts. Mackens, relatives of Mackens, neighbours, and friends, put fingers in their mouths and whistled.

"You missed Reg's song for Glory," Colin said, patting his baby's back and swinging his shoulders in time to the song.

"How bad was it?"

"Bad enough. Both got choked up, couldn't hardly finish. They switched to 'Live Fast, Love Hard, Die Young.'"

I laughed. "Too bad Toby wasn't here," I said. Faron Young was one of his favourites. At least he used to be.

Tap-dancing would come next. Girl cousins all took lessons from the same teacher, a distant relative up the Powerhouse Road. *Clickety clickety clack.* Curls would bounce, baby-fat jiggle, sailor skirts swish, the springs of the pickup creak. *Clickety clickety clickety clack.*

There was a chill in the breeze, now that the sun was down amongst the tops of the tallest firs, gathering streaks of narrow clouds the colour of apricots. I returned to my car and put on my jacket. Then I left the concert altogether and walked to the beach.

The tide had come in across the shallow bay, would come in higher yet. Some of the youngest cousins were playing in the shallow pools along the exposed flats of corrugated sand. I followed the curve of the bay and sat on a log, not far from the tilted hull, and removed the Bell & Howell from my pocket. The faint smell of oil and the feel of its shape in my hand could make my heart race, as the chilled metal warmed to my body heat. Guilt, excitement, frustration.

I held the viewfinder to my eye and watched Mike, Mark, and Jack come down to play where Meg was already playing at the water's edge. Maybe she wasn't dancing tonight, though I doubted it. She'd probably done a ballet solo already. Immediately, the boys had her screaming – pouring buckets of water on her castle. I stood up to go to her rescue. But she didn't need me – she laid into them with her fists.

I'd need a zoom lens for this, to do it right. And a crane, so that I could look down from somewhere in the trees, like the crows – children torturing one another on a narrowing world of ridged grey sand. The boys were in red, Meg in white. Was there anything here that I'd missed? There usually was – at least there usually was the feeling I could not see it all. Or couldn't see it clearly enough. What was here that I couldn't see? The family was in plain enough view, most of them, over at their concert. Uncle Martin with his button accordion started "Alice Blue Gown." I swung the camera to the left, across the sand and waves to the rotting planks of the hull.

People had been watching me for years, to see how serious I was. "You'll have to quit school and run away from home," a Seattle cousin of my mother's had told me once. Glory had said, "Why aren't you hitchhiking down to California? Make a nuisance of yourself until somebody gives you a break." Only mainland people could say things like that. Didn't they realize there were 300,000 people already down there working in the industry? I'd read this somewhere. Three hundred thousand people handling two billion dollars in investments. They paid some actors more money than the President of the United States. Was I supposed to thumb down the coast and say, "Here I am, hop to it – give me a movie to direct"? I'd end up under a bridge, murdered by someone for the look on my face.

"The man who started those Mr. Magoo cartoons was from somewhere on this island," Glory told me. "I think he drew *Bambi* too."

This was on Tuesday afternoon. I'd driven to town to see how Toby's defence was holding up against Macleod's stolen-steer charges, but didn't get as far as the courtroom. Glory was outside amongst the roses, wanting a ride home. "I don't even know why I came." A few hours later she would walk up the gravel road to that creek, though of course I didn't know that yet.

"A cartoonist?" I said. "No directors, though." We were back at the shack before she brought this up. She was pouring lemonade from a jug.

"An art director – won an Oscar for *On the Waterfront*. I've forgotten his name."

"I saw it twice! Marlon Brando and Eva Marie Saint are on my bedroom wall." Toby had stolen the picture from the glass case outside the theatre. Marlon Brando looking into that trusting face. "Anyone else?"

She seemed to change her mind about something and poured the lemonade back into the jug. Then she reached two more glasses down from the cupboard. "Yes! A famous director. Your old friend – Nell Shipman." This time she half-filled each glass from a bottle of Scotch.

For a moment, the name meant nothing.

"*Under the Crescent?*" she prompted. "You showed me the book, remember? You told me about your disastrous rehearsal. She's from Victoria."

"Nell Shipman?" The beautiful woman with pearls in her hair.

"She even made her own movies," Glory said, adding water from the tap. "Worked all over the world. *Back to God's Country* was shot in Calgary."

That lovely woman with pearls in her hair. Pyramids,

murders, an actress imprisoned in a harem. I could recall every grain of sand in those photos, and every ragged palm. She would be old by now, if she were still alive.

"That was before I was born." In my entire lifetime, so far as I could find out, only one English-language feature film had been made in this country by Canadians. Hollywood would not allow any more. This was a foreign business I was dreaming of. "So – how'd those people get there? How'd *she* get off the Island?"

Glory's expression changed. Sad. "The art director had a rich grandfather paid his way."

"Ha!"

"I knew you'd say that. The Shipman woman married a producer."

"Dammit, Glory, do you think Natalie Wood's going to come knocking on my door and ask me to marry her?"

She swatted at an open cupboard door, slamming it shut, and turned to hand me one of the glasses of Scotch. "You'll never get anywhere if you think someone ought to come and beg you to be a success." She put her free hand against my ear, then ran it down my neck and along my shoulder. She shook her head, smiling at me – exasperated. Then she laid her forehead against my chest.

She'd wondered – while I was driving her home from town she wondered if they would put Toby in jail. "It wouldn't be the first time." She'd rested her head against the window glass and watched the telephone wires. The Island Highway ran between rows of narrow hayfields, long driveways, houses set back near the trees. Axel Herman's family was picking raspberries.

"He told you about the high-school riot he started? He was behind bars less than an hour that time, Nora got him out."

211

"I mean on one of his visits to Vancouver. Before we were married. He never mentions it, it makes him so mad." She opened her purse and took out a package of Matinée Filters. Once she'd lit a cigarette, she pulled out my ashtray and dropped in the paper match. "He couldn't stand it that nobody in the city paid attention to him, however much he acted up." She tapped the cigarette over the ashtray – Glory did this after every draw, one quick tap with her long painted nail. "They considered him a jerk – this was what he thought. I suppose he was right. He got drunk one night and decided to climb the Marine Building again. He would dance on the top of the highest building in town."

"He didn't make it?"

"Instead of moonlight and ocean liners there were police. He spent the night in jail. You want one of these?"

I shook my head. I hated filters. "And that's why he never goes back?"

In front of the General Store, Em Madill stood talking to Ernie Coleman while he filled the gas tank of his station wagon. George Price was reading his mail as he walked to his car.

"He couldn't be Toby Macken over there, he was just another jerk that nobody noticed. At least that's what he felt. I suppose I should care what happens inside that courtroom today," she said. "Is there something wrong with me, do you think?"

"It doesn't matter what happens in the courtroom," I said, as we pulled up before the tarpaper shack. "It's only a chance for people to yell at one another."

I had never seen her so agitated. She laughed when the doorknob came off in her hand. "This house will collapse on our heads and kill us both." She pushed the handle back onto its axle and turned. Then she walked through the front room, tossing her purse on a chair. "Sit down."

I followed her to the kitchen doorway and watched while she

reached into the little icebox for the lemonade jug. She knew she was beautiful, she couldn't help it, but when she was pre-occupied she seemed to forget herself – more beautiful than ever.

Then she brought me the glass of Scotch and leaned her head against my chest. "What's wrong?"

"Well, I guess I'm frightened."

I put my glass on the kitchen table and pressed my face to her hair. To tell the truth, I was frightened myself – of this unruly hope that had risen within me again. With my lips to the side of her throat, I could feel her pulse beneath the skin. Amazed at myself even as I was doing it, I pressed a kiss into her neck and another along her shoulder, the scent of her freckled skin enough to justify anything.

"What are you doing?" she said. She leaned back and laughed a chirrupy sort of laugh, as though there were some sort of happy game going on that she didn't yet understand.

I kissed her shoulder again. She made a sound like someone intending to eat me. "Mmh! Mmh!" Then she put one hand on either side of my face and looked hard into my eyes. Longer than she may have meant to. She groaned, a long internal lamentation that sent electric charges out through every nerve in my body. Pressed this close, it was impossible for her not to know what she was doing. She kissed me quickly on the lips and backed away.

This had happened before. Something like this had hap-pened before. I had started it then, and she had stopped it. I was to remember the borders, if we were to be friends. So it wasn't possible to pretend this hope was new. In its various dis-guises I had been able to push it off.

Honour. Loyalty. Decency.

In my imagination it was possible to come up with circum-stances to sidestep inconvenient facts. Perhaps I would be for-given by Toby once I'd rescued him from a whirring saw blade.

Confined for life to a hospital bed, Toby would think it only natural – in fact he would insist that the nephew who had saved his life should take his place with his wife.

Such dreams meant nothing now. This seemed as natural and right as anything else.

"I must be out of my mind."

"I hoped for this," I said, pressing her hand to the racing pulse in my neck.

"You wouldn't have stopped?"

"I'd have done anything you'd let me, what do you think? If you wanted it too."

"Oh, Rusty. What I want – I have never known what I wanted. I'm a fool. A decent boy like you."

Decent! As though a "decent" person couldn't want. All at once my body felt more foolishly awkward than it had since that summer of my sudden growth – since that day in the steam-bath shack. I didn't know where to put my hands. Or how to stand. "Decent" might as well have been "young" or even "little."

"It wouldn't be like you to hurt anyone. Not when you know better."

"Who says?" I laughed, though it wasn't a joyful laugh at all. "Do you think this was decided before I was born? Maybe Nora stamped it on my forehead in the maternity ward. 'Macken, Russell Joseph – useless and incurably decent.' What if I was really meant to be more like Toby? What if I was meant to be a rip-snorting terror?"

She tried not to laugh. "You weren't." She turned up the palm of my hand and kissed it. "You've got more common sense. You've got more common sense than I have."

She left me then, and went back to the kitchen. This was not to be *Tea and Sympathy*.

Was I discovering that life would exclude a person with

common sense? A person with common sense knew better than to get mixed up in the messy aspects of life. You could not imagine a decent person of common sense experiencing the sort of abandon needed for a passionate devotion to love.

Except maybe on your final day on earth, when there was no having to face tomorrow. I knew what it would have to be as clearly as though I'd been planning it for years. Perhaps I had. The two of us were lying on the sagging bed, her head against my shoulder, her rich wild hair across my chest. In the midst of a night of love we laughed softly, knowing there would be no need to face ourselves or anyone else in the morning, since the tarpaper shack all around us was in flames.

"I've made a decision I want to tell you about," she said, returning from the kitchen with the second glass. She indicated that I was to sit on the chesterfield, while she herself sat on the unsteady chair in the corner, in the light from the narrow window. At once I realized how dark this room was, most of it in shadow. She had put herself in the only light. "I'm going too."

"To Vancouver?"

She nodded, biting her bottom lip.

"But you just got back."

"To stay this time. I'll go when you go – when your school starts." She jumped up, and started walking about the room touching things. In and out of light and shadow, sipping at the glass. She picked up a flower vase and put it down, then straightened a crocheted antimacassar on the back of the chesterfield. "We'll find apartments close together. Kitsilano maybe, not far from the beach." She brushed dust from the window curtains. Ran her fingers over a china panther on the sill. "I'll get a job."

"You mean you're leaving Toby?"

"I can't stay here." She lifted a photograph from an end

table, and studied it. Colin's baby. "I almost didn't come back this time, I came back to see."

"But I don't understand – why now? Has it got something to do with me?"

She put the photograph down and turned, her eyes wide. "Oh no, no!" She returned to her spotlighted chair, but immediately stood up again and went to the window that faced the beach. "Well, yes, I suppose. You'll have one friend over there, to start with. We'll go to the shows together, and sit in Scott's Café to talk about them afterwards. You'll make director's notes in your little book. We'll save money so that you can fly . . . maybe we could fly to Hollywood and knock on doors."

"You mean we'd be pals?" My voice cracked, saying it.

"I know what you think you feel for me." She didn't look at me, she wouldn't look. She'd found a broken china blackbird on the windowsill and concentrated on fitting its pieces together. "I've been a fool. I didn't think about you, what you were feeling. But you don't love me the way you'll love someone else some day."

"I'm sorry," I said. "I don't want you to go." I stood up, filled with an astonished awareness of my own dramatic position. There might have been cameras whirring somewhere behind me, zooming in on the alarm in Glory's eyes as she turned to face me.

"But Rusty!"

"Toby needs you."

She narrowed her eyes fiercely. "That's between Toby and me. He doesn't need me as much as he thinks."

"Anyway, I'm supposed to be going over there for an education. Not to keep my head filled with silly dreams."

She grabbed up her Matinées, shook out a cigarette. "You blame me? – when that's all you've ever talked about!" Her trembling hands struck three different matches before one

216

stayed lit long enough to use. "Am I supposed to believe you'll take that scholarship and go off to study for a *job?*"

"Maybe I will." I don't know why I said this. "Maybe movies were just a kid's fantasy I didn't grow out of. Held onto it too long." These were someone else's words – Aunt Nora's, though she'd never said them aloud. Uncle Reg's. I didn't want to say this; what I wanted to say was, "How could you do this to me – how could you be the woman I've been drawn to all my life, the woman I've grown up wanting, when you've known all along that it was impossible?"

"But you *should* have held on this long!" she said. "You shouldn't let go of it now!"

This was said to something outside the window.

She waited, but I didn't respond. I could have said, "You should have been more like the other aunts."

"So you'll play it safe," she said, "because you're scared to take a risk – you might fail." I'd never heard such bitterness in her voice.

"Anyway, I don't want you over there being my *pal!*" I said. "I don't want you to show me around the city! I couldn't stand it. Toby couldn't stand it. You wouldn't be able to stand it yourself for very long, I'd drive you crazy trying to have a life of my own. Let me go and start my life, you've already got yours here."

I went down onto the sand and stopped to roll up my pantlegs before wading into the sea. Salt bit at the scrape on my shin. By the time I ducked in through a familiar gap in the tilted hull, the water had risen above my knees and halfway up my thighs.

Inside, the rotting planks were hosts to a spatter of barnacles and clusters of large blue mussels that hung like luxuriant fruit. Where boards had fallen away, bolts that had held them together were rusted and bent. Dark water sloshed and sucked through the chinks, and splashed against one fallen plank that leaned, at a low angle, against the starboard side.

Toby had been the one to start us playing here, soon after the boat had been brought up from San Francisco for the breakwater. They'd blasted a hole in the bottom so that sand would move in and anchor it. It had been a gambling ship in its previous life, Toby said, and led us up a rope ladder to the deck. Tables. Chairs. Silverware! Abandoned remnants of the mysterious lives of strangers. We dropped cutlery and trays overboard, and buried them. Later, when we tried to dig them up we couldn't find them.

Toby brushed magic onto that hull with his stories and then moved on. We continued to give it life without him – set sail on waters infested with sharks, fought pirates, made newcomers walk the plank, abandoned the sinking ship. Sometimes Toby joined us, but not for long. He'd discovered women by then, he drove a car.

Of course much of the ship had been torn away by tides. What was left could be the ribcage of some forgotten sea monster. I sat on the slanted creosote-smelling plank, and dragged a hand through the cold water, caught a tiny green ribbon of seaweed between my fingers. Then I stretched out along its slope, lay on my back. No one could see this. Dampness seeped through my jeans. I stayed where I was while the frothy splash of the tide crept higher. My jacket, my shirt. Small strips of floating seaweed wrapped themselves around my wrist. I might have been feeling the little needle teeth of sculpins nibbling. Mudsharks waited their turn. (Suppose I'd been chained here, and left.) At the bottom of that great skeleton I imagined the water rising farther to fill my ears and lap at my temples, to leak in at the edges of my mouth and creep up my nostrils, seeking out my lungs.

I imagined what it would be like to will myself not to float, to hold myself to the bottom and refuse to rise above the intruding ocean's exploration of my throat and lungs and stomach, its insistent occupation of the body I had hardly got used to occupying myself. I imagined the struggle set up within myself, if I remained where I was, by those forces that wanted no part in this annihilation while I looked up at the slanted mast and the faded sky from beneath the murky layer of sea that moved in to extinguish me.

I became aware that again the hull was singing. A soft, low tremulous sound, a higher, thinner strain – several notes at once composed a kind of harmony. A breeze hummed through the spaces between the ribs, whistled in the darkened corners, whispered secret shreds of broken melody across the creeping surface of the incoming tide. Perhaps it had always sung like this. Maybe the hull had made itself a kind of instrument that my own confused and turbulent grief could play upon. I could believe it then. I could believe as well that this was Glory singing in the ribs of that old ship, preparing to leave or pleading to return or taking up a new vocation as spirit of the Strait. This was the sort of musical lamentation that seemed to promise an eventual break to more joyful noise, but never completed the change.

13

YEARS later, people would remember best the part of Glory's funeral that left the landscape altered. It was something to laugh about, a visible boast. "Typical Mackens – never know when to quit."

"I don't know what they must have been thinking," my mother would say. "They didn't *think*!" Eyes wide with innocence. "I was never as bad as the rest."

Some said she was worse. "Just got into a fight with Nora is all. And went for a walk on the roof!" But no one suggested that she had started it. I was there for much of it myself but couldn't say which moment marked the shift in the direction of things.

When I'd returned from the beach I changed into my dress pants and shirt again, leaving my damp clothes in the trunk of my car. Crows now sat in every bough of every fir, hundreds of them, black splashes amongst the green. Boughs sagged beneath their weight. They might have been some gleaming ebony fruit the trees had produced during the day. Some flew up and moved to another tree, causing others to fly up as well to another. Thousands of crows. Their racket was too dense for any individual cawing, more of a raucous one-note choir, countless blaring horns amidst the noise of a colossal highway wreck. The noise of a volleyball game was buried within it; horseshoes could be seen but not heard.

Outside Toby's shack I met with Caro and Sonny, back from their swim. From the step we could see through the open door that the front room was crowded. Shoes were off. Feet were up. Aunt Nora tipped back a bottle of beer. My mother and Grace sipped tea from Glory's cups. Buddy and Uncle Martin leaned against a wall. Uncle Curtis, a late arriver, sat in a corner chair with his hands between his knees. A tree-pruner down in Washington State, he was known as "the quiet Macken." He seldom had much to say. It seemed that no one else had much to say at the moment either.

"It's too quiet in here," I said to Caro. "They must've had a fight."

"Just catching our breaths," my mother said, daintily lowering her cup to its saucer. "You think we don't deserve it? It won't last long." This was enough to set off a round of shouted laughter. Some of them had had a lot to drink since eating. My mother smiled at Sonny. "You got here a little late if you wanted a fuss made over you, Sonny. We're too pooped to say hello." She'd removed the cow-pie hat, but her hair was still flattened on top.

"What's Swampy Aalto's boy doing here?" Aunt Nora sat up rigid and cranky, thrashing about as though she would propel herself out of her chair and do something drastic. "He's not related to us!" But then she fell back and laughed, to let everyone know she'd been imitating herself for the sake of the shouts that rewarded her. She must have tossed back more than a few.

Sonny grimaced – he knew Nora. Caro crossed her eyes and dropped her jaw to suggest there were idiots in this company.

"Just don't tell the others where we are," my mother said.

"They'll come cramming in and spoil it, scared they're missing something."

"They aren't," said Grace, without looking up from her sewing. "Tongues are only going forty in here that went sixty miles an hour all day outside. We might run out of things to say any minute."

This was greeted with laughter too. Nobody could believe it.

"And some have been going ninety," said Kitty, perched on a roll of carpet at one end of the room, the toes of her cowgirl boots pointing at one another. She spoke in the direction of the bathroom door, which opened to the sound of a toilet flushing. I saw what she meant. Uncle Curtis's landlady stepped out, wiping her hands down her skirt. Mrs. Latour. She came to everything with Uncle Curtis – never brought her merchant-seaman husband – and acted as though she too had Macken blood in her veins. "Russell!" She hurried across to grab my face between damp hands and hauled me down to plant a fat wet kiss on my mouth. "Good to see you, lad." She patted Caro's shoulder before Caro could yank herself away. Then she headed for an empty chair, digging her thumbs beneath her heavy breasts.

They called her "Ma Kettle" behind her back. She liked to play up a resemblance to Marjorie Main. She wore her hair in a little twist on the top of her head, she let her heavy bust fall over her waist, she scratched at herself through her clothes. "Make y'self t'home," she would growl from one side of her mouth, before dropping her considerable weight onto a chair. Then she would answer herself: "Don't mind if I dew!" It was said that she let chickens roam her house, though no one had ever been down to Washington to see.

"By golly it's good to be back with the family!" she said. "Ain't it, Curtis, m' love?"

Smiling Uncle Curtis only nodded.

"I was mad as a coon in a trap when Curt's jalopy up and died in Ladysmith. Hoo-ee! Git this piece of junk of yers fixed, I told 'im, I don't wanta be late! Well, you seen how late we were!" She slapped one hand on her thigh.

When shy Curtis went off as a young man to find work across the line, he'd been grateful at first for his landlady's motherly attentions. He was grateful for her nighttime attentions as well, whenever the husband was at sea – no woman had ever given him a second look. She may have been older by thirty years and no raving beauty, but she was giving far more hospitality than he paid for.

He paid for it later. He was paying for it still. She'd decided to keep him for life. As hard as it was to imagine, they were a pair. She'd made it clear that if Uncle Curtis even thought about leaving she would tell the old boy what had gone on right under his roof. A man with a history of violence could be counted on for an imaginative revenge.

My father held Uncle Curtis up as one more warning for the country boy about to leave home. When I asked why he hadn't run, he explained that that was just the sort of person Curtis was. "He made his bed, he's got to lie in it." The same would be expected of me, I understood, if I were fool enough to get into that sort of mess.

It was more complicated than that, my mother explained. It wasn't just that Curtis was shy, or loyal. "When your grandfather got wind of her blackmail he went into a regular rage, he packed his bags and caught the bus. We thought he'd take the boots to the battleaxe for sure. But all he did was give Curtis a lecture on family honour. Mackens were never scoundrels. Curtis seemed to agree."

"I call these get-togethers family communions," said Mrs. Latour. "A person needs these to keep her soul in order, that's my way of lookin' at it. Being part of this family ain't nothin' you discard like a smelly old shoe!"

Caro slipped out to the porch. Sonny ducked out behind her, to smoke in the open air. I slid down the doorjamb and sat on the splintered sill. Whenever Mrs. Latour was speaking, Aunt Nora watched her with the uncomprehending and expressionless eyes of a sheep observing the antics of a flapping sheet. Nora had never directly addressed her in all the years she'd been attaching herself to the family.

"Well, there's something I've been waiting for a chance to say," Kitty said.

There was an amused catch of surprise in my mother's "What?" Perhaps a warning too. It would never do to have Curtis see you mocking his Mrs. Latour.

Kitty said, "I want to know how long this thing's been here I'm sitting on." She slapped her hands on the rolled-up carpet beneath her.

"That's been there for years," Aunt Nora said. "Toby brought it home but never laid it."

"All he had to do was unroll it," Kitty said.

"Goodness knows Glory hated this lino," my mother said, rubbing her toe at a patch where the pattern had worn away.

"Glory didn't like to get down on her knees and wax," Aunt Nora said.

"She hated stripes, is what I meant," my mother corrected her. "Did you catch her wearing any?" She turned her attention to me. "We've been all around Glory this afternoon, nearly broke our hearts before we quit!"

"And decided what?" I said.

"That we were just as much to blame as her," Buddy said.

Nora closed her eyes and kept her thoughts to herself for a change.

227

"Glory slipped away," Grace said. "We're in here hating ourselves for letting it happen!"

"Too busy!" said Mrs. Latour. She lifted a crochet hook from Grace's sewing basket and used it to scratch at her scalp. "You had yer own lives to live. I bawled these eyes right out when I heard what she'd done. I never done her a decent thing in my life – what's the matter with me anyway?"

"I'll tell you, Rusty, you wouldn't believe your ears," said Uncle Buddy. *Flick, flick*, went his tongue at his lips. "Before they were through, you'd think an angel had been amongst us for a while, instead of a poor, sad girl."

"Hold your horses here," my mother said, turning back a corner of the carpet Kitty sat on. "That's what I thought. Guess where this rug lived out its life before it died!"

"Don't tell me you recognize it!" Kitty cried.

"After walking on it for fourteen years you'd think Grace would know her front-room floor."

Grace placed her sewing on her chair and hurried across for a look. "Toby hauled this thing away three years ago, I thought he was taking it to the dump."

They were all speaking a little too loud, like amateur actors in a play.

"I hated this beige," Grace said, brushing a hand across the nap of the turned-back corner. "But it might've looked all right in this poky room."

"It would've hid the lino anyway," my mother said.

Mrs. Latour had observed all this with her intense gaze shifting from one speaker to another while she sucked on a yellow tooth. Now she slapped both hands on her heavy thighs, a warning that she was about to jump into the fray. "Well, by golly, let's unroll 'er then. Stretch 'er out and see what we've got. I once had a carpet turned the drabbest room into my favourite place in the house."

Then she told about the colour of this miraculous carpet, the time of day in which the sun came in the western window and gave it a golden glow. Its size, as well – "the size and shape of this here room right here." She stated the make of the carpet, and the name of the store where she'd bought it. She quoted a price, but abruptly changed her mind about that, "I wouldn'ta bought 'er if there hadn'ta bin a sale. Anyway, our dollar ain't worth but ninety-two cents of yers." Aunt Nora watched the rapidly moving lips and blinked.

Standing with her fists to her hips, my mother waited for the lips to stop. As soon as they did she gave orders. "Rusty, pick up Nora's chair and take it out to the kitchen. Sonny, take the other one. Somebody grab those end tables, will you? I'll kick 'er to get 'er started."

"Wait till I'm off it first!" Kitty screeched, leaping to her feet.

"With a little luck she'll flatten Latour and Nora both," Caro said through her teeth. "Get ready to stomp on the lumps!"

Nora padded off to the kitchen. "Frieda's always in such a rush!" She gathered up the china panther and the broken blackbird from the windowsill to take with her.

"Here goes the magazine rack," said Mrs. Latour. "Nothin' in it but beauty magazines – I looked."

"Watch out, this lamp's got to go." Buddy hitched his sagging pants up his skinny hips, then lifted the tri-light to his shoulder.

"Mice've been at that cord," Grace said. She ran it across her palm. "A wonder this shack never burned. Who's got electrician's tape?"

"Colin's kid!" Kitty held the photograph of Colin's baby high above her head while she checked the room. Helen and Avery weren't here. "Grandma Helen's newest treasure – catch!" She tossed the photo to Uncle Martin, who caught it as he came back from the kitchen. "I'll take the standing ashtray too," he said, "since it's mostly my butts that are in it."

Sonny and I lifted the shabby rose-coloured chesterfield and moved it outside to the porch. Uncle Curtis stood against the rail with a small apologetic smile on his face. He gave a quick little sideways jerk to his head, as though to suggest to me there were things he didn't need to say.

"Everybody stand back," my mother said. She parked her tongue in the corner of her mouth and held both arms out level like a football player driving in a goal. One barefoot kick was enough to start the carpet unrolling but it didn't go far. She kicked it again and again until it laid out its final curled-up edge less than a foot from the wall. Everyone cheered. Kitty demonstrated that her yodelling talents had not diminished. Uncle Martin put two fingers in his mouth and drove a long shrill whistle into our ears. My mother did a fake little tap-dance, and ended with a Shirley Temple type of frozen curtsey, holding the sides of her skirt.

Stout Grace stomped along the edges. "Now isn't that an improvement, Glory? I hope you're satisfied."

"Looks better here than it did in your house," Kitty said from the kitchen door. She ran her lipstick tube around her mouth as she spoke.

"Smaller room shows it off," my mother said. "You can come walk on it now – stomp the wrinkles out. Rusty can put his big feet to work."

"Never mind his feet," Kitty said. "Tell Cecil B to get his cameras rolling here! This oughta be in the movies!"

"Look out – they're bringing back the furniture!" Mrs. Latour skittered out of the way. "Land sakes, this excitement's made me hot!" She hauled her flowered blouse out of her skirt and flapped it as she might clear a tablecloth of crumbs.

"Don't bring that chair back till you've nailed its leg on

tight," Grace yelled, making herself sound bossy. "Just sitting on it makes me seasick."

"Somebody get out and find some stovepipe," said Uncle Buddy. "We'll hook this little wood-heater up to that hole in the chimney." Two little round patches had coloured up in his cheeks.

"Don't look far." My father said this from the front step. How long had he been watching? He crossed the carpet and reached behind the little brown heater. "It's right where it fell. Toby didn't know that all he had to do was pick it up and stuff it back where it was. There!" Two slaps finished the job – it was in there for good.

"Now look at your hands," my mother said. "Don't touch a thing till you've washed."

"Too bad Glory didn't have Eddie around," Grace said.

"Here!" Buddy placed an opened carton of Carlings on the rug. "Moving furniture can work up a thirst." He stood with an opener, snapping off caps for everyone who held out a bottle.

"You know what I'm goin' to do?" said Uncle Martin, as soon as he'd poured half the bottle down his throat and released a long melodic belch. "I've been looking at how that door frame's come away at the corner. One good nail would do it."

"Glory could've done that for herself," Nora said.

"Well, she didn't, did she!" Kitty said. "Toby would've yelled if he caught her. He didn't want a wife with calluses!"

"Calluses!" My mother showed us the palm of her own tough hand. "She'd get blisters first. You saw how soft they were."

"City girl hands," Nora said, flinching at each of Martin's hammer blows.

"Something else Glory could have done if Toby wouldn't have thrown a fit is paint these walls," my father said. "She hated that wallpaper, I heard her say it a dozen times."

Everyone glared at the guilty walls. Mrs. Latour ran fingers over the pattern. "They don't look like no flowers I ever seen – and I've lived my life in the garden!"

"Toby bought paint at a sale," Grace said, "but where did he hide it?"

Uncle Martin rolled one more turn on his shirtsleeves and gave both bulging muscles a slap. "This room needs our help. We might's well finish the job."

"I'm sitting," said Mrs. Latour, dropping onto the chesterfield. "No I'm not." She heaved to her feet again. "Somebody's liable to decide I need to be fixed!"

"Everybody *think*!" cried Grace. "Where would Toby leave a can of paint he was only pretending he'd use?"

Things might have stopped right there if my father had kept his thoughts to himself. "Dammit anyway," he said, when Uncle Martin had covered one wall with paint. "Toby coulda done this when Glory was here to enjoy it. It makes a person mad."

"We'll just have to enjoy it for her," said Kitty.

"I'm enjoying it already," called Grace, who sat with her feet on a padded footstool. "This chair is solid at last. I'm admiring the way that colour changes as the paint is drying out."

My father said, "You'd see things that wouldn't take ten minutes to fix, but you didn't like to offer in case it made Toby feel bad."

"Toby isn't here to feel bad now," Grace said.

"What did you want to fix most?" Kitty said. She held a little mirror up to her face and ran a black line where her eyebrows used to be.

"Back step," my mother guessed. "Eddie nearly broke his neck last week."

"Glory had to toss the dishwater out in the yard," my father said. "The goose-neck under the kitchen sink is plugged."

"Be our guest," said Grace. "If anybody's got the tools it's you. They're probably right in your car."

My father looked as though this was what he'd been waiting for. "By golly, I think I will. Rusty – go bring in my toolbox, will you?"

Nora sat forward abruptly. "What's Rusty know about tools?"

"You're not paying attention," my mother said.

Nora threw herself back in her chair and closed her eyes. My mother shook a fist and pulled a belligerent face. When others laughed, Nora's eyes flew open. Caught in the act, my mother sang out: "Just protecting my young!"

Nora snorted. "Just acting the fool." And closed her eyes again.

My mother was stung by this, and might have said more if Kitty hadn't interrupted. "Rusty don't have to use tools so long as he can aim a camera – he's going to make us all *stars*!" She struck a pose in the doorway and batted her eyes. "He's gonna let me play Annie Oakley – aren't you, kiddo. Betty Hutton will shrivel up and die."

My father said, "You think you'd recognize a toolbox if you seen one?"

"I'll shore try, Pa," I said. "I hope I don't pick up no doghouse by mistake."

Sonny followed me out the door. "Jesus, Macken, let's get out of here."

"He wants to stay," Caro said.

"I'll come," I said. "Just wait a minute. I'd better help with this."

"You won't come," Caro said. "You're as bad as the rest." She yanked at Sonny's hand. "Come on, let's see what's happening in town."

Sonny's parting look to me was a pleading one. Behind Caro's back he crossed his legs and crouched, cupping his hands as though to protect himself. Maybe he meant to suggest that he didn't have the strength for what lay ahead. But when he saw that I wasn't about to join them – that I only grinned at his antics – he dismissed me with a "what the hell" gesture and left.

Mrs. Latour came out onto the porch and jabbed a finger into Uncle Curtis's arm. If they didn't get out of there fast they'd be put to work, she said. "There's all them others wonderin' why we ain't been out to say Howdy. Tell yer feet to do what they were meant fer." Mrs. Latour held both hands against her breasts when she went down steps – afraid they'd start to bounce and throw her off balance, Kitty once said, and toss her onto her ear.

When I returned with my father's toolbox, people cleared a path to the kitchen. "Stand back!" cried Grace, throwing out an arm like a traffic cop. "Here comes one fixed sink!"

The kitchen was so narrow that to hand my father the tools as they were needed I stood in the doorway to the front room. Elvis was singing "Heartbreak Hotel" on the windowsill. Kitty interrupted her humming to say, "Eddie isn't happy unless he's improving the world."

Grace said, "He can come and improve my place any time he wants."

"I could do with some help myself," Nora said. "I didn't know a person had to die to get it."

"Don't you talk," my mother said. "You get enough out of him without dropping dead."

Nora's mouth fell open. "And you resent it!"

"You'd have him running up there every day if he'd go."

"Hoo!" said Uncle Martin, without turning away from the wall. He was up on his toes and slapping paint above the window.

Nora laughed. "Frieda Barclay's jealous – after all these years! My word!"

"My word yourself," my mother said. She didn't laugh. She emptied a beer into her glass and returned the bottle to the carton. She closed her eyes to savour the first taste. "You still think you own them, after all this time."

"Frieda," Kitty warned.

"Oh my," Aunt Nora said. "What have I gone and done to bring on this?"

My mother kept her eyes closed. "You'd take them all home to live with you if they'd go."

Aunt Nora looked as though she'd expected no less. "Put on a show about it, then! Barclays always loved the spotlight. Should we call the others so you'll have a bigger audience?"

"Hoo, hoo!" said Uncle Martin. He was coming up to the corner to start on his third wall, working his brush up and down at a furious rate.

"You missed a spot," Nora said. "Down in that corner."

"How long ago was grade four?" my mother said. "She did everything she could to keep him away."

"She was like that with us all," Kitty said. "She couldn't stand it when they started looking at girls."

"You've looked down your noses at me all your lives," Nora said. "All of you."

My mother sat forward, mad. "Don't you dare accuse us of that, after all we've put up with! Everybody always treated you with respect – had to!"

"I don't need to listen to this," Nora said. She hauled herself up out of her chair and padded across the carpet to the bathroom. "Frieda shouldn't drink." She slammed the door.

Grace, Kitty, and my mother all laughed. My mother had probably sipped her way through two bottles of beer at most through the course of the day. Kitty leaned forward and silently mouthed: "You oughta be shot!"

"Wanted to be the centre of their lives – still does!" my mother said, her eyes flashing towards the bathroom door. "She'd've kept them all at home for ever if she could."

"Now, now," cautioned Uncle Martin. He was down on his knees, slapping paint along the baseboard.

Grace blew smoke in all directions and sucked in more. "We won't forget the fuss when Buddy decided to marry his housekeeper! You'd think I was a one-legged killer with three glass eyes."

"I've got my own scars," Kitty said, "but this is not the time to show them."

"It never is," my mother said. "I've kept my mouth shut all my life." She turned her attention to me. "She'd do the same to everyone if she could. She made sure your father never finished school. He could've gone and got an education."

"Oh for Pete's sake, Frieda," Grace said. "What brought this on?"

"Eddie was in a hurry to make a living, don't forget," said Kitty. "He had his eye on getting married young."

My mother ignored this. "If he's ever killed in the woods you can blame her. *I* blame her for Vic and Tommy."

Vic and Tommy were only boys when they were sent off to work in the bush – dead before they were twenty.

Martin said, "It don't do any good to bring that up."

"That's right, we have to humour her," my mother said.

My mother recovered as quickly as she recovered from anything – the second she decided to. When Nora came out of the bathroom, my mother slapped her hands on her knees and stood up. "Well! I better go find something useful to do. Everybody seems to be working here but us."

Naturally people had crowded around the kitchen door while

my father fixed the pipes. You only had to look at faces watching him to know that he'd started something he couldn't walk out on now.

"Where's that sheet of arborite Toby brought home for the draining-board?" he said, with his head still under the sink.

"Under the step," said Reg, who stood wheezing outside the back door. "I'll get it."

"Get it if you want," said Grace. "I'm doing something about those walls – they're awful."

"Paint isn't what Glory wanted in her kitchen," my mother said. "Toby once took home two rolls of our leftover wallpaper."

"I saw it," said Grace. "Which cupboard was it in?" She started flinging open doors.

"Not *that* one!" my mother cried. Too late – the door came off in Grace's hand.

"Well, we can fix a hinge if we have to," said Buddy. "You got a screwdriver in that box?"

"Look what was under the step!" Reg stood in the doorway holding up a little cupboard with two doors. "Hinges are rusty but they'll work with a little oil."

"Don't just stand there with it," my mother said. "Grab a hammer and put it up – right above that table. Glory never had a decent place for her china."

Uncle Avery and Mr. Korhonen appeared in the door. George and Ethel Price were right behind, with their tribe of squint-eyed kids. "What's goin' on?"

"We got feeling bad about Glory," my mother called back. "George, you're the expert on windows – what do you think could be done with that broken pane?"

George Price removed the piece of stained cardboard and examined the hole. "I'll have that out in a jiffy, and put a new one in."

"He carries windows in his pocket?" Nora asked.

"He's got his business truck out there," my mother said. "You watch."

"Well, who's that other face in the door?" Nora said. "No relation of ours."

"That's Paul DeSoto," Grace said.

"Eddie tripped on that step the other day, Paul," my mother said. "Suppose you fix that board."

Big-bellied Paul DeSoto bounced. "Spike's nearly worked its way out." He reached for a brick to hammer it in.

"Those were for Glory's planter," said Ethel Price. "She wanted a little garden beside the step. You kids gather all the bricks you can find in the grass, we'll see what we can do."

"Maybe you can get them to grab a brush and do something about this door," Grace said to Ethel. "Ten years of that stupid dog wanting in and out has got it scratched right through. Thank God he finally died."

Kitty sighed. "Glory wanted to like that hound but it wouldn't look at her."

"Too many people in here," my father said. "If you think you've got everything under control I'm goin' up on the roof."

Things might have stopped there, too, if Mrs. Latour had not spread word that something was going on in Toby's shack. Volleyball came to an end. The horseshoe pitch was abandoned. Even fir-cone fights fell apart. People started to drift across the grass beneath the squawking crows, drawn by what my mother called a natural desire to be included and my father called an unnatural fear of being left out.

"Fixing it up for Glory," was all anyone needed to hear. Everyone wanted to help. Mr. Korhonen rustled around in the woodshed until he found a scythe, and started to use it on the matted grass around the house, uncut for nine or ten years. Two rakes were found for Billy Macken's boys to tidy up behind him. Colin, who'd stayed behind when Theresa took the baby home, dragged out a rusted lawn mower from the shed and oiled it.

Em Madill set out with Edna to gather up junk that lay where the hotel had been – bricks and bottles and battered pots, a wooden rowboat, a stack of windows, the drum from a washing machine. "You sure this isn't some goddam garbage dump we're into here?" Edna shouted. "I bet there's rats."

Some down-Island Mackens waded into the blackberry vines to make a stab at straightening up the salvaged lumber. Some carried two-by-sixes to Uncle Martin, who'd borrowed one of my father's saws and started to fix the front steps. Steve George and Morris Macken moved the green-slimed bathtub closer to the kitchen door where they discussed the possibility of building a lean-to just to house it. Rachel Macken (Billy's wife) climbed a stepladder to put the sagging eavestrough back where it belonged.

Of course none of this was done without a good deal of shouting and laughter – too much noise for the crows. Hundreds of them, perhaps thousands, lifted from the boughs of the firs, flapping black wings and squawking their protest at this human racket. They rose together as though responding to a single mind, acquiring a loose, wild shape that hovered a moment above the trees – a throbbing assembly of complaining beaks and beating wings that moved over the water and shifted abruptly back, to stroke frantically off across the bay and the inland stands of timber that stretched from here to the mountains.

14

Avery and Helen had put their boat in the water some time earlier, to go fishing with the Wintons. "Bring back enough for a midnight barbecue," was their mission. "If anyone lasts that long." Boats were black-pepper dots strung out along the straight-edge curve of the earth, between us and Cortez Island.

Colin made short jabs with the mower at grass the scythe had missed. "Look here!" He waded into the deepest tangle of vines to peer at something. "What in blazes did he think he would do with this?"

"What is it?" I said, and started over to see.

"Spiral staircase. Steel."

Others began to converge. "What's a spiral staircase?" Edna said.

"Take a look," said Colin. "Goes around a pole."

Some of those still working inside the house came out to investigate. The orange paint had peeled away, except for ragged patches. Steps were long triangles of tread-marked steel, radiating out like propeller blades from the centre pole. A narrow steel-pipe handrail formed a sort of cylindrical cage with its coils.

Buddy laughed. "Toby, he'd take anything free, then find out he'd wasted his time."

"A widow's walk!" Kitty said, putting both hands to her face. An idea had struck. "Glory always wanted a widow's walk on that roof, so she could climb up and take a look at her mainland."

"That makes me feel just terrible," said Grace.

"It makes me bloody *mad*," Edna said. "I bet Toby promised to build one. If he'd damn-well gone ahead and done it she might not've felt so lonely."

"Where is he?" Grace shook her fist at the trees.

"Don't waste your breath," said Buddy, using both hands to hitch up his pants.

"It's him that didn't do nothing for Glory while she could thank him," Grace said. She shook off a hug from Kitty. "Don't grab. I'll cry if I want, it makes me so blessed mad."

My father had been studying the staircase in silence. "Here, give us a hand to raise it."

Colin and I helped Shorty Madill lift one end from the grass. My father took the scythe from Mr. Korhonen and sliced away at the blackberry vines that stitched it to earth.

"Steady. Easy." He was the coach.

"What's that famous picture?" said Shorty Madill. His sticking-out ears were red. "Raising some flag in the war."

"Lift with your legs, not your back," my father reminded. "Don't let 'er drop on your feet."

"What do we do when she's up?" said Uncle Reg, his throat trembling with a low captured chuckle. "Turn 'er and *drill*?"

"Straight to China," my father said. "If we don't strike oil or hellfire first."

"Just shut up and take some of this weight!" said Shorty Madill, all of his face as red as his ears from the effort.

Once we'd got the end as high as our waists, others got under to raise it higher. "What will archaeologists make of this?" said Uncle Martin. "Fourteen Macken skeletons pinned under a giant corkscrew. And one puny Madill."

Aunt Nora stood frowning in the doorway to watch. No one offered an explanation.

When we'd got the staircase upright we leaned it against the eave. My father moved in with a pair of shovels and together we dug out a hole, inserted the bottom end of the pole. "I saw bags of cement around here somewhere," he said. "We'll strap it to that post to keep it plumb." He'd always got more pleasure out of doing things than talking.

"Looks like it come from somebody's castle," Grace said.

"There's plenty lumber to build your platform but do we think the roof will hold it?" Buddy called this out in his high thin voice. "Anyone have an opinion?"

Everyone did – a chorus of frogs would make more sense.

"Get up and try." My mother's voice sailed on when others' had faded away. "No, not Buddy. I mean Reg. He's the heavy one here. Go up and put your foot on the roof. If you fall through and break your neck we won't build it." She laughed.

Nora came far enough outside to look at the standing spiral. "You don't expect Reg to climb that!"

Reg was not crazy about climbing anything, but he put one cowboy boot on the bottom step and the other on the second step and bounced a little. Then he wound his way up the unsteady staircase while my father and I were still mixing cement into sand and gravel at its base. "Who used to plant a human sacrifice under buildings?" my father said. "Your horse'll miss you, Reg, but you're giving up your life for a pretty good cause."

Reg wiped the sweat from his neck with a red polka-dot handkerchief. Then he put a foot on the roof. "You people ought to know better than this," Nora said. "Reg broke more bones from falling than most of us even *have*!"

"When he was small," Kitty added.

"Reg was never small," Edna said. She was chewing gum again – Juicy Fruit, snapping air bubbles between her molars.

"Reg isn't Toby," said Grace. "Toby goes up like a squirrel."

We stood back to watch. "If they ever put a man on the moon you'll be the one that's not impressed," my father told me. "You've seen something more astounding – look."

"Get right up and jiggle," my mother called.

"Sssst!" said Nora, slapping at air in my mother's direction. My mother made a point of looking offended.

Reg pushed his handkerchief inside his shirt to wipe at his chest.

"Be careful, hon," Kitty cautioned.

Nora threw out her hands. "You people must be crazy, we'll never get him down. He's like a cat when he's high – scared to move."

Reg gingerly put one knee, and then the other, on the roof, and slowly climbed a short way up the slope.

"My God, look at that!" Edna shouted. "Reg, your arse end's the size of a barn!"

Reg placed an open hand in the middle of his rear and wriggled. Some people clapped, but Kitty scowled them into silence.

"Seems to be holding," said Reg. "I don't want to push my luck."

"That's good enough," Nora said. "Come down."

"Let's get that platform built," Grace said. "One side can rest on the roof, the other needs legs to the ground. It'll be a widow's walk and a porch roof all at once." She looked around for someone willing to take orders. "Haul some lumber over here quick. Time's flying!"

It took most of an hour to build the platform and erect a pretty railing around it out of spindles off a dismantled staircase found in the livery shed. When the final nail had been hammered home, Uncle Martin backed down the staircase and stood with us to admire it.

"You could train roses up those legs," my mother said.

Kitty closed her eyes. "Wouldn't Glory be pleased to see it!" She shivered.

Mrs. Latour and Uncle Curtis approached from across the grass, bringing others with them. All of them looked confused; they must have been too far down the beach to notice what had been going on.

"Don't you recognize anything?" Kitty yelled. "We *changed* it!"

Mrs. Latour leaned back with her hands on her rump and her elbows out, to look up at the leggy addition above the porch. "I'll be a cross-eyed hound!" she said. "Lookit that there – what is it? You turn that twisty thing to crank 'er up and down?"

"Something Glory wanted," Kitty said.

"I woulda put a sturdier railing on it," Ma Kettle said. "My mother's aunt in Lilliwaup had a railing like that give way. Third storey of her apartment building. Hoo-ee, she falls on her head, spends her life in an institution. She was a turnip after that." She bent to sort amongst some leftover lumber at her feet. "Someone take this up. Mr. Latour would have a crosspiece at a slant to keep things solid, this one should do the trick."

She was ignored.

Grace called out, "Who's goin' up to see what Glory'd see?"

"Not me," Kitty said, stepping back. "It'd only make me cry."

"Land sakes, I'd do it, only I'm worried about that railing," said Mrs. Latour. "If one of the men would nail this crosspiece on I'd be happy to do the honours. Deliver a short oration while I'm at it."

"It's got to be Frieda," Edna said, making "save us from Ma Kettle" faces all around. "Frieda was the closest one to Glory. Up you go and tell us what she'd think."

244

My mother was not surprised. Her face had already taken on a grim look, ready for the request. No one could carry off a solemn occasion better. The Queen Mother herself could not have gone up that staircase with more dignity. Blind Jane Wyman walking into the doctor's office in Zurich – tense with the expectation of good. Of course my mother knew her audience well enough not to overdo it – when she stepped onto the platform she looked down with a little smile. Applause rewarded her.

Then my mother raised her head as though she believed a hundred movie cameras were recording this moment – Movietone News. She acted the dignified person looking off towards the highway. She acted the dignified person looking off towards Mount Washington where my father and Uncle Buddy worked, and Forbidden Plateau and the glacier just beyond it. Then she acted the dignified person looking across the bay where the rotting hull and two sunken minesweepers had once protected log booms from storms. Finally she looked off across the Strait of Georgia towards the mainland Glory had left when she came here to live with Toby.

"Tell us what Glory would see."

"Could she see home?"

My mother did not remove her gaze from the mainland. "It wasn't 'home' she missed. What Glory missed is what nobody thought to give her when she needed it – a welcome that didn't think she ought to change."

"Oh, for heaven's sake!" said Nora, turning to go back inside. "Frieda knows better than anyone!"

I knew what the others were thinking. Maybe Glory had not been given the welcome she needed but she'd just been given *something*. Mackens were only doing what came second nature – taking advantage of an opportunity for excess. Glory's house had been transformed, just as she'd wanted it. The fact that it came too late was not the most important thing to think of now.

Still, it wasn't enough. My mother believed that it wasn't enough. At any rate, those who knew my mother best would recognize the face she turned to them now, high on that platform. She wasn't acting. Even in this twilight she was pale – she looked stricken. She put both hands on the rail.

"Get her down," Grace said, heading towards the steps.

My father got to the bottom first. "Be careful." He looked as though he thought she'd need to be caught.

My mother put a hand to her mouth and kept her face turned down while she allowed my father to guide her inside the house. Grace followed.

When my father came out a few minutes later, he said my mother was lying down. "She needs to catch her breath is all."

"She doesn't want to go home?"

"She'll be back on her feet before you turn around – you know her. Grace is with her. And Meg."

"Found good weatherboard in the shed," said Uncle Martin. "Enough to cover this tarpaper if we decide to."

"Why not?" my father said. "Might as well finish the job."

When I'd helped them carry the weatherboard siding up from the collapsing livery shed, I went inside to see how my mother was doing. Grace had gone out to help clean up the yard. Meg was at the kitchen table, drawing crayon pictures on grocery bags. Her cheeks were wet with tears.

"Tired?" I gave her a quick hug, and used the orange crayon to add the hint of a smile to the sorrowful mouth in her drawing.

"I don't like it here. I want to go home."

"She got herself overexcited playing hide-and-seek." My

mother's voice came from the bedroom. "I told her to take a blanket and curl up on the couch."

Nora was asleep on the chesterfield, a dropped magazine on Grace's old carpet beside her.

My mother sat propped up with pillows against the headboard of Toby and Glory's bed. One knee was pulled up, making a teepee of the satin quilt. She was smoking. My mother seldom smoked, never had cigarettes of her own. She must have bummed it from Grace.

"You okay?"

"Oh, for Pete's sake," she said. She tried to laugh, but hadn't the energy for it. "Nora will think I just wanted attention! 'Barclays love the spotlight – always did!'"

I lowered my voice. "If a bomb were dropped on your head she'd think you'd arranged it yourself, to be at centre stage!"

Her small laugh was hardly more than a hiccough. "I don't know what come over me, I must be getting crazy in the head." She rubbed a hand over the raised knee. "I'll just wait for my strength to come back. Rest my eyes while I'm at it."

Outside, a dozen hammers drove nails into weatherboard, some quickly (two quick blows and a final thump), some slowly, hitting wood more often than nail. There was no rhythm to it, just a cacophony of various sounds at different speeds, an army throwing tantrums against a house. Glass rattled behind the window blind.

The ash on her cigarette was long, bending from its own weight. I moved an ashtray across the bedside table, but she didn't seem to notice. The white ash fell to the quilt and broke apart, and sprinkled down the slope of her leg.

My mother had seldom been ill. It was enough to give you the shakes when she was, she looked so bad. Even the twenty-four hour flu could make her look as though she'd been brutalized. Pale. Her eyes dull, with dark bruises beneath them.

Worst of all was the grim set to her mouth, and the way her voice would weaken. It never failed to panic the rest of us.

I sat near the foot of the bed, on the white chenille, which was bald in patches. "You don't want me to drive you home?"

"You should've brought Lynette," she said, looking at the flowered wallpaper above the window. "She would get a laugh out of this! I was surprised she didn't come."

"You never liked Lynette that much," I said.

She raised her eyebrows with some indignation but didn't look at me. "When did I ever say that? I just didn't want you to get too serious, is all." She pulled her second knee up beside the first and rested her chin in the valley between them to study me. "You've been quiet today. Thinking about her? Or is it somebody else?"

"Who else would I be thinking about?"

She leaned back again and looked away, towards the yellowed window blind. Dark water stains fanned out from a bottom corner. "I just wondered." She sucked on the cigarette and immediately blew out the smoke – she didn't inhale. "I'm not sure you've been all that fair to Lynette."

"You think I've got somebody else stashed away?" I laughed. "Some Moonbeam McSwine in the mountains? Gloria Swanson up for a rendezvous with her teenaged gigolo!"

"My gosh," she said. "I hope not." She smiled weakly towards the window. "I've had this strange feeling for a while, is all." She closed her eyes.

It could scare you half to death when my mother got one of her "feelings." It meant she could read your mind. "Someone say something to you?"

"Not exactly, no. But I could imagine. I could tell there was something she wanted to talk about but was scared to. I'm afraid I didn't encourage her. Maybe I should've."

She was not talking about Lynette. As she spoke, I felt the

heat rush to my face. Mercifully, my mother had spoken towards the window wall.

"It was worrying me sick, Rusty," she said. "But I couldn't think of what to say. I was hoping you'd talk to your dad. But now –"

Instead of finishing whatever she was about to say, she sighed. Hammers continued their assault on the walls. I could think of nothing to say to her. My heart raced so fast that I would not have been able to say anything without trembling. I watched her hands, which rested on the satin quilt at her knees. Her engagement ring flashed weak light off three small diamonds. Nineteen thirty-seven.

"Watching you these past few days my heart would nearly break. But I just couldn't think what to say."

"You're making things up, just to have something to worry about," I said. "Maybe I'm thinking about moving away. I'd better go give them a hand."

"Heathens hammering like crazy for the glory of God."

"What?"

"Don't tell them!" She laughed. "There's so many out there they must be tripping over one another by now."

"Still –"

I stood, but she put her hand over mine. "I don't think you've been worried about moving away. That's exactly what you've been waiting for. It's something else. I wish you would *say*."

"I guess it's just the funeral," I said.

"I guess it is, then," she said. She pulled her knees up tighter to her chest and jabbed her cigarette butt in the ashtray. "Go on and help them. I'll stay here a while and rest."

My mother knew too much, or thought she did. She'd always known too much. You couldn't get away with a thing. We

249

sometimes accused her of being psychic. But she would say it was just that she could see in your eyes what you thought, even what you felt. She couldn't help it. "That's just the way I am." I'd have had to move out of the house if I'd wanted to keep her from guessing what I'd been through the past while. I could hardly be surprised now.

Rushing out through the front door, I bumped into Uncle Reg coming in. "Sorry there, Rusty." He reached inside and flicked a switch. "Getting dark."

Light streamed down from several spotlamps up in the trees. Glory's little house with its repaired steps and painted window frames, its newly hammered-on wallboard and brand new widow's walk, was brighter than day in a world surrounded by night.

I hurried away from this harsh light and crossed beneath the firs to the beach, then walked along the gravel to the farthest end of the property, my neck an aching stem of rigid chords, my throat so tight I thought I might stop breathing. The wide black wings of some nameless horror swept at the air around me.

What more might Glory have said if I hadn't left when I did? That she was giving me a chance to save her life? What if I'd just, for a minute, thought of *her*?

Far out on the Strait, fish boats had stayed out too long. Some were racing shoreward now – bows slapping at waves, lights bouncing, Evinrudes roaring full throttle.

Even from far along the beach Glory's shack had become a lit-up stage. It was probably this, the sense of everything becoming theatre, that prevented me from leaving. To hurry back inside that lighted circle was more attractive than dealing with my thoughts.

Even before I'd stepped into the light I heard Uncle Buddy complaining. "You mean that's it?" Clearly disappointed.

"Listen," Kitty said. "Somebody doesn't agree."

Somewhere behind the shack, a couple of hammers were slamming away at nails where we couldn't see.

I joined the others hurrying around the bedroom end of Glory's shack to see who didn't know when to quit. Uncle Martin. Uncle Curtis. They were so busy they didn't notice us. They didn't seem to notice what they were doing, either – they set down a two-by-four stud and drove in spikes that held it in place and bent for another stud without seeming to think. A dozen empty beer bottles stood along the sill. Joists and angled shiplap flooring were already in place beneath them. A row of studs had been raised, a skeletal wall that went out from one corner of the shack to follow the outside foundation of the old hotel. It had reached a corner, and would now have to turn and enclose the great old tilted kitchen stove, still warm and faintly smoking from the long day's use.

They bent, and together raised a new section of wall and nailed it upright in place. They didn't seem to notice we were watching.

"Just like Marty to start something and go off on a tangent," said Uncle Buddy.

"Hey there!" my father shouted. "If all you wanted was to build a sundeck you didn't need to make the railings so high."

Martin and Curtis looked confused. "What're ya saying?" said Uncle Martin. "What else was the lumber for? This is the entrance hall, where you 'n' your sweetie sign in."

At that moment Paul DeSoto came around the corner carrying a pair of sawhorses. "Found them behind the old shed," he said, and set them on the new floor.

"How much you boys been drinkin' anyway?" said Uncle Reg. "The rest of us decided it was time to stop – the job's been done."

"It don't look done to me," said Uncle Martin. He hammered

another nail. "Can't leave 'er like this, she'll look like hell. Hopper's down the back there cuttin' joists for the second floor."

"Shoot!" said Uncle Reg. "It's late. Don't get carried away."

But they were right. My mother was right. It wasn't enough. What if we could know what it was like to be somebody else? I grabbed up Uncle Martin's measuring tape and spun it out along one of the two-by-fours that Paul DeSoto had rested across the sawhorses. Drew a line with a nail. Uncle Curtis handed me a crosscut saw, and I set its teeth against my mark and started with quick little strokes. It was better than standing by to watch, it was better than having to think.

"This old stuff won't last us very long," I said.

"That's how we'll know when it's time to stop!" said Edna.

"Somebody phone Albert Storch," I said. "Order a load of new. Toby's truck is gone."

Kitty frowned. "Storch's lumber on MACKEN LUMBER land?"

"He can bring Toby's lumber," Reg said. "Pick it up at the mill."

"Some of us can meet him there and load it," I said.

"Eddie, your boy been into the sauce?" This was Shorty Madill.

"He's bin hanging around the rest of yous too long," said Mrs. Latour.

The scrap end fell from the two-by-four. Uncle Martin took the stud away and started nailing. I laid the measuring tape along another.

I could sense my father watching me. Nobody said anything while I sawed through a second stud, and a third. "Looks like Rusty can handle that saw all right," he said. "I'll go carry Hopper's joists."

Uncle Buddy stepped forward then and held my two-by-four in place. "I suppose it's the natural thing to do. Keep on till the job is done. We might as well rebuild the goldarn thing."

252

Roars greeted this. They might have been roars of derision or approval. People just liked to roar.

"We still got over a hundred people here," my father said. He turned to Shorty Madill. "You call Storch? Colin, you follow the foundation around – set up a marker wherever it's crumbled. Where's Korhonen? Tuomo's got a better eye than anyone – we've gotta make sure these walls are braced up straight!"

"Send up more nails!" called Uncle Martin. He sat with his feet dangling from the top sill of a raised wall.

"I'm goin' for windows." Paul DeSoto. "There's some stored in my own garage."

Kitty sang while we worked. She would spend her "lafftime," she sang, "Luh-uhvin yeeou. Making belee-eeve."

We worked harder, faster, with her singing. Uncle Curtis brought out a bottle of Scotch and started it on its rounds – each person tipped back a gulp and passed it on. Uncle Reg did a little two-step dance as he brought me the two by fours. He did another bit of fancy footwork when he whisked them away. Uncle Buddy took them and ran, pill bottle leaping in his shirt pocket. "Here! Bring 'em here!" yelled Shorty Madill somewhere across the rising structure. "Don't let my hammer stop or it might never start again!"

Kitty set off into "I Forgot More Than You'll Ever Know" but when Grace brought Kitty her fiddle, she stopped singing and started her own kind of sawing, faster than mine. I increased my speed to match hers. Grace set out a chair on the subfloor and started hemming her piece of embroidered cloth.

"You been wasting your life on that pole vault," said Reg at my elbow. "That arm was made for a saw."

"Maybe Rusty's gonna build his own scenery," said Uncle Buddy, who'd settled to see if he could rig up a set of electric door chimes out of a broken clock. "False-front saloons and Egyptian pyramids. Show them fellas how it's done."

253

"He'll be back," Reg said. "A taste of the city'll cure him."

"Hookers on every corner, tryin' to give him diseases," Uncle Buddy said.

"Strangers buying him lunch and picking his pocket clean of cash," said Reg. He shuddered. "He'll be glad to come home and saw boards."

Kitty interrupted her song. "Pick-pockets and dope addicts're nothin' to the kind of people he'd be mixin' with in the picture-show business," she said. "Big-time crooks and sleazy glamour-pusses – one fat snake-pit full of slimy critters."

When I rested briefly, panting hard, Colin poured a mason jar of cold water over my head. "Once you got it out of your system over there, I'll hire you to help with my house."

Work paused when Uncle Avery and Helen and four of the Winton brothers came up from the beach with their catch. Each held a salmon so large it rested across both outstretched arms, scales flashing silver and blue-green in this light. "And there's plenty more in the boats!" Helen said. "Not one of them under thirty pounds."

Uncle Avery bulged out his eyes, a child. "Every damn tyee in the chuck was trying to get into our boats. We couldn't pull them in fast enough!"

"Wintons caught so many they started to sink," Helen said. "We figured they'd never make it to shore."

The Winton brothers said nothing, only grinned.

"We stood up in the boats," said Uncle Avery, "so we wouldn't take up space we needed for fish."

Uncle Reg hooked his fingers into the gills of Helen's salmon and held it as high as he could, to admire it from every side. It reached from shoulder to knees. Uncle Avery handed his over to Colin. "Imagine hundreds just like him trying to get into your boat. I didn't know whether to shout for joy or run!"

Noisy admiration was all the reward they were going to get

for now. "Suppose you stir up the barbecue coals," my father suggested. "We'll keep working up our appetites till you come and tell us they're done."

At that moment, the bedroom window sash slid up and my mother leaned out. "My gosh, I thought you'd quit or died. Do I have to get up and *boss*?"

"There's plenty already doing that!" cried Kitty.

"Well, they can't be doing a very good job," my mother said. "Shouldn't someone be over there building that chimney? Curtis, you used to know about bricks." She held Glory's kitchen funnel to her mouth and exaggerated the way she imagined bosses acted – important – deepening her voice and pointing with great authority at the broken chimney. "First you'll have to put a floor under that stove to level it, this end's sunk bad as before."

Then she added, "Here, Rusty, you're the one should have this. Sit on the windowsill and holler orders." She lifted the funnel to her mouth to show me what she meant. "Lights! Camera! Action! Let's get this show on the road!"

15

By two in the morning all the walls were up and braced. Uncle Curtis and his crew had begun to put on the outside sheathing. Martin and Buddy split cedar shakes for the roof. Rafters were up and battens were being cut. It would be possible now to visit the thirteen bedrooms on the second floor – rooms that had once provided my imagination space to try out various lives. Prison warden. Fireman. Archaeologist. Movie director. Ambassador to Peru. But within their naked studs they resembled cages more than remembered rooms, more skeletal even than the rotted hull in the bay.

Work paused when the baked salmon was pronounced "done." The surrounding world, black as the underside of a stove lid from within the floodlit circle, turned out to be nearly light as day. A three-quarters moon shone down through the firs. We might have been flooded by a thick, silvery band of ocean water – trees and their shadows were eelgrass and coral, anchored to ocean floor.

In the barbecue pit, coals glowed crimson from inside white jackets of ash. We leaned against trees, sat on the ground, ate till there was nothing left but bones. We praised the grinning

Wintons, told Avery and Helen we hoped they hadn't left the Strait stripped clean of its fish.

"We could still be out there hauling them in," said Uncle Avery, glad for the chance to tell about it at last. "Thousands of them, fighting to be next at the hook."

"I was scared they'd start jumping into the boat," Aunt Helen said. Her wandering eye roamed the shadowy trunks of trees. Fish might come swimming out from behind them. "I'd have to throw Avery overboard to make room!"

Edna said it wasn't too late to toss Avery back and hope for something better, she planned to toss Martin back herself one day. "Catch Spencer Tracy instead." She opened her third beer since we'd halted work, and held the bottle aloft. "Anybody want to say I haven't earned this? I'm not the kind that likes to brag but I could drink that whole damn case and holler for more."

We laughed, and again made exclamations of gratitude to the fishermen, but kept close watch on the hotel that hadn't been there a few hours before, in case it disappeared.

"Listen," someone said. A sound like snorting horses brought us all to our feet. It might have been an entire herd, somewhere out on the water.

"Blackfish."

Killer whales. They went rolling past on the moonlit Strait, not a hundred yards from shore. We climbed the tangled heap of driftwood to watch. Great black animals came up out of the cellophane-surfaced water, gleaming, and rolled under again, their tall dorsals like arms on a great turning wheel. You could see their nearer eye, or imagine you could. Sometimes you could see the white on their throats. Families – ten, twelve, more of them. Some calves, stitching along beside mothers.

"Salmon knew they were coming," Uncle Buddy said.

"Trusted Avery to save them." He made a show of licking his fingers.

"Oh lord, Rusty," said Uncle Reg beside me. "This makes my heart just ache." He placed a hand on his chest and hummed a single trembling note for a while as we watched. Fifteen, sixteen. Jets of air cleared water from their blowholes. "I'd give up everything – music, horses, my ranch – to be one of those creatures for a year or two. I bet you never thought I'd say a thing like that." His belly rose and fell with his heavy breath. "I saw them first when I was a boy, dreamed of them ever since. In the dreams, I'm a long skinny circus performer riding their backs." He looked at me and chuckled, the little motor rumbling in his throat. "Like being king in a never-ending parade."

He pressed a fist to my arm and winked. He'd know I would understand. Tired as I was at that moment, I wouldn't have traded him or any of the uncles for all that movies or college might have in store. I was, for all intents and purposes, one of the Macken brothers tonight, one of the crew.

When the telephone rang, more than a few cried "Toby!" At the same time Mrs. Latour called, "I'll get it!" from inside the shack. She'd probably been asleep beside Nora on the couch. When she came to the door she called, "Where's Rusty?"

It was Toby's friend Cal. "You got your car? I think you better get over here. My place. Don't tell the others where."

"Is Toby all right?"

"We'll see."

I ran out the door calling "Tell you later!" to those who wanted to know what was up, but did not get past my dad.

"Toby?" he said.

I told him Cal – something was wrong.

"You want me to go with you?" He took three-inch spikes from his mouth to say it.

258

I shook my head, though I was not at all sure that I wouldn't be glad to have him with me. I had no idea what I was going to. Toby hanging from some crossbeam maybe. Toby down a well. Toby in jail again, this time for something that mattered. "I'll be all right."

"Drive careful, then," he said, as he said every time I stepped into my car.

Gerry kep the engine running smoothly for me – changed the oil and checked the spark plugs, reminding me every time that I would sooner or later have to let him borrow the car.

By the time I'd passed the Experimental Farm the Meteor was already doing seventy. I nearly lost control at the first sharp bend. I slowed a little. Who did they think they were that they could snap their fingers and expect me to risk my neck?

I should have brought Colin along, despite what Cal had said. I would have brought Sonny if he wasn't somewhere being Caro's slave. I might have brought Gordie along if he hadn't deserted me long ago. I couldn't even imagine Gordie with me now, I could not imagine him on the seat beside me – Gordie had remained a kid.

Gordie may not have changed but it seemed that I had. Why should I be racing down this road to see what sort of mess Toby was in this time? I wasn't his little "sidekick" any more. I wasn't so eager to do whatever might please him.

At the Store, I cranked the steering-wheel knob and turned off the highway, then started down a narrow road leading inland. Some of these roads had once been railroad grades. Corners were long and slow. All this area had been dense with timber once, a centre for logging operations, with a series of railroad spur lines taking logs to the main line and down to the booming grounds in the bay. Iron tributaries to an iron river. After that the area had been carved into the small farms and stump ranches by the Returned Soldiers from the First

World War. Now it was tidy countryside. Fences. Pastures. Barns. Pale houses back from the road. Nameless streams leading crookedly to Portuguese Creek.

The route to Cal's place, zigzagging from one back road to another, would take me past the end of the lane that led to Lynette's. Someone else could have been doing this – one of Toby's brothers. I should be going to see Lynette. "I'm not sure you've been all that fair to Lynette," my mother had said. She was right. Lynette must have known, must have guessed, and yet had not let it make any difference until Glory died.

Never complained. Never refused to park. Kissed hard and long. Kissed with mouth open and tongue teasing tongue. Slid her hand up your thigh and licked your ears, and groaned, and wrapped her limbs around you as though she would climb you. Let you open the zipper of her dress just a little and slip your hand inside, though not for very long. Panted, and held you off, licked your neck and kissed you until you were begging and she said No, No, I'm sorry, we should've stopped before, this is terrible, what are we going to do.

While she knew that it was someone else you wanted.

Shame was what I felt. My neck burned, the heat moved into my face. My mother had thought of this. It wasn't that I'd imagined Glory while I was with Lynette. But it had been a temporary sort of thing. I was only making do. Lynette must surely have known.

I could telephone from Lynette's, tell one of the others to get Toby. He expected too much, he expected too much from us all.

She would be sleeping. I would sneak across the junky yard and tap on her window. Not far from Toby's mill I crossed a bridge and turned to set off up the gravel towards the mountains. "Que sera, sera," sang Doris Day. I turned the dial until I picked up Tony Martin, already starting to surrender to that kiss of fire.

260

She might invite me in when I tapped on her window; more likely she wouldn't. She would open the window and scold me: who did I think I was? But when I'd explained why I'd come she would say, "Just a minute," and put on some clothes and come out. While we sat in my car I'd make it clear that I understood how badly she had been treated, that I was sorry.

Fifty yards up the rutted driveway I parked on a narrow grade through an alder grove. Any closer, I'd be heard by her parents. I took the flashlight from my glove compartment – moonlight barely penetrated these woods.

Though the house was dark, light flared out from the opened doors of a shed. Mr. Macleod came out from behind a red Ford truck and shouted: "Who's there?"

I turned off my flashlight but didn't run. He'd have a shotgun nearby. "Rusty."

His gum boots were covered with grease. So were the knees of his loose green cotton pants. He held a crescent wrench in one hand – no doubt he'd been dismantling a wrecked truck for its parts. The hood of the Ford was up, like the hungry jaw of a crimson crocodile. Behind the shed, slender alder saplings stood amongst glinting car bodies in a silver field.

"You're working late," I said.

"Couldn't sleep." A large drop of moisture hung from the tip of his bony nose. He rubbed it off, but a new one formed immediately. "You must be lost." He stepped up close enough to breathe onion on me. "Car break down?"

"Just hoping to find Lynette still up."

"You see any lights in the house?"

"Nossir."

He let me think about that for a moment.

"She's out?"

"That's what I meant."

"I don't suppose you know when she'll be back?"

261

"I don't suppose I do. I suppose it depends. This guy looks like the kind would take her off to Vancouver or somewheres and think of the consequences later."

"She never mentioned anyone else to me."

"This one's got a name but damned if I remember it. A cop! He's been comin' round for a few weeks now. Lynette, she's pretty crazy about him. Not as crazy as she used to be about you, but she tells me that cooled off a while ago."

"I guess I didn't notice soon enough," I said.

"Well, what can we do?" He put his greasy hand on my shoulder and gave me a shake. "A Mountie, for crying out loud! What does she want with a damn Mountie?"

"You think she's serious?"

"*He* is. He'd marry her tomorrow if I let him."

"He'll take her away – Mounties are always on the move." I tried to make light of this. "They'll get posted to Quebec. You'll have grandchildren speaking *français*."

He slipped the wrench into a back pocket of his pants and hauled out a rag – somebody's underpants – to wipe his hands. "Shoot," he said. He pulled back to spit on the ground between his feet. "I had hopes for you, son. Don't mind telling you. The boys don't like this fella much. They're a couple of hellions, them two, but they liked the idea of having a high jumper in the family."

"She could've waited till I was gone."

"You already left, is her way of seeing it. She wants to get on with her life."

I could hear old long-eared Max whining inside the house, wanting to get out and jump all over me. "Well, I better go."

"Not gonna wait and beat the crap outa him?" His dark little eyes twinkled.

"I guess not."

"Yer uncle would."

"I guess he would," I said. Toby would beat that fellow's face to a pulp, cop or no cop. He would break windows, tear boards off the walls, release all the animals from their pens. He wouldn't just turn around and leave.

"But I'm not him."

"You make sure you come again, okay?" he said. "Just because she's fallen for that cop don't mean the rest of us don't want to see you. There's always Cassie. Cass don't say too much but she's kinda sweet on you too."

Cassie had stolen Student Council money to have her hair bleached white like Marilyn Monroe's.

When I turned to leave he laid his arm across my shoulder. "Yer uncle, there, you tell him I'm sorry about his wife. Tell him I'll forget the steer. He's got enough trouble already, he don't need any more."

"I'll tell him that," I said.

"Come see us any time – okay? Come and see Cass and the boys."

Anger, humiliation, relief. This confusion of contradictory emotions waited until I had closed the car door and started the engine. Idiot! I drove down the lane, then set off up the old logging road. Fool! I crossed the railroad tracks and a narrow plank bridge. What had been the matter with me, to expect anything else? I accelerated up the gravel – pushed the speedometer beyond sixty, seventy, eighty, something I'd never done on the highway. Potholes jarred, washboard shuddered through the frame, patches of new gravel sent me fishtailing through the night. Roadside elderberries and pink fireweed slapped at my windows. Headlights swept through a countryside of blackened stumps, an entanglement of fallen slash, blackberries, and new alder growing up to reclaim the logged-off land.

The deer leapt into my vision from the right – a two-spike, wide-eyed and long necked, a sudden explosion from the brush. I slammed on the brakes and felt the car slide in the loose gravel. The engine stalled. The deer bounded off, its white tail flashing, through the crackly moonlit bush. A sickening weakness swept through my entire body. With head to the steering wheel, I felt waves of something cold drive through me. Shame. Relief. Shame. Had I believed that things could be so easily repaired?

Cal came out of his house and led me by the arm towards his Piper Super Cub, which sat in the hayfield he used for a landing strip. "I'll tell you while we're flying."

"He's not here?"

"We have to get him."

"I don't think so," I said. "You shouldn't have waited for me. He thinks he only has to snap his fingers and I'll jump, then he gives me hell anyway. Let him get out of this one himself."

"He didn't ask for you," Cal said, ducking beneath the wing to open the door. The surface of the wing was some kind of fabric, painted yellow. "I didn't know what else to do – he wouldn't listen to me."

"He won't listen to me, either. He pushed me off a roof this afternoon. Where's he at?"

"Up there." He nodded west.

"In the mountains?"

"On the top of the goddam Comox Glacier! Get in!"

Before I could ask for an explanation, Cal pushed me towards the door of his plane. "In!"

I'd seen the Piper Cub before, sometimes in the air, sometimes sitting in Cal's field. It looked like my first model airplane, except for the oversized Beaver tires he'd added so that he could land in fields, on beaches, on alpine meadows. He flew charters. Government Mines and Forestry officials hired him, and timber cruisers, Fisheries people, geologists, anyone who needed to get into the mountains. He hadn't, so far as I knew, ever crashed

When I'd climbed in – first time in any plane – Cal pushed a button that brought little round dials to life. The propeller appeared to be going in both directions at once, then settled into a steady transparent blur. "I would've come and got ya if I knew you'd take so long." The cockpit smelled of oil.

Once the engine was running at full throttle, he released the brake and we shot ahead – bouncing down his moonlit hayfield. Then we left the ground and roared up over the neighbour's barbed-wire fence and roof and above the trees. The plane tilted, shifted, as though it might have been swinging from cables, controlled from above. We dropped abruptly, then rose again.

"He showed up at Harry's this afternoon," Cal said. Shouted. "He'd already been drinking. We had quite a lot to drink ourselves after that, just sitting around and bullshitting out on Harry's dock." He scratched at the dark whiskers of his bony chin. "We kept saying we ought to get in Harry's boat and go fishing but we never did. Then Toby said he knew what he wanted to do, it'd come to him when he was on the bridge."

"Not fishing, I bet."

"He wanted to dance on the glacier. It didn't seem such a stupid idea after we'd been drinking for a couple more hours. He kept bringing it up, bringing it up, until he talked me into taking him. He wasn't interested in climbing the mountain, he just wanted to dance on the goddam glacier. He said I could take a picture of him and then we'd come down. But he didn't want to wait till morning, he wanted to do it right away."

"In the dark."

265

"Even in this moonlight I'm risking my licence, but Toby don't care. We drove out to my place and put on some winter clothes. Harry, he wouldn't come with us, he was scared. He also didn't want to be crammed in there behind you."

Behind me was space meant for gear and supplies. A man would have to pull his knees up to his chin.

The lights of town were off to our left, where two rivers met not far from the head of the long narrow bay. Our shadow slid over silvery farms and followed one of the rivers towards a lake that wedged itself between mountains.

"He got out and did his little dance on the ice and I took a picture. But then the dumb prick wouldn't leave! I tried to talk some sense into his head but he might as well be deaf. So I figured I better get someone he might listen to."

We were rising up the face of the mountain now. Scrub timber, lumpy outcroppings of black rock. And then the slanting grey and white wall, the giant world of ice.

To the Indians the glacier may have looked from below like a whale left high and dry by the receding Flood, but as we approached there was nothing of the whale's smooth hide about the surface ahead of us. It rippled – a startling white and dark grey foreign landscape, shadows and light, the contours of a windswept desert. This would be more like landing on sand dunes than on the tilted skating rink I had expected.

"See if you can spot him," Cal said. We flew closer to the surface than I liked, a few miles in a southerly direction, then tilted and turned and flew back. Nothing down there looked human. A frozen ocean, a glistening desert.

We passed up and down the length of the glacier a second time, then Cal cut the throttle and we started to descend. "I think this is the spot about here. Thank Christ the moon's still shining!"

The plane bounced, and shuddered, and tilted, then moved

quickly across the surface, and threatened not to stop at all until Cal ran it up a slope towards a crooked pinnacle of rock. He cut the engine, and we looked out over the slanted world of ice while the propeller spun.

"He must've moved. I just hope he didn't fall into some crack. There's a bloody lake below us."

You stupid bugger, Toby, I thought. You'd better be alive, and you'd better be sorry, and you'd better be grateful. I didn't even want to get out of the plane.

Once the propeller had stopped spinning, Cal opened his door and hollered. "Macken? You out there?" He didn't want to get out either.

We listened. Nothing. A steady chill wind flew from the west. Beyond the level horizon of ice, the moon shone down on the snow peaks and rocky slopes of other mountains, a terrifying jagged world that went all the way to the Pacific. White peaks, black jagged stone, silence.

"Take this flashlight," Cal said. "He must be in a dip somewhere. Don't take a step without looking first. Some glaciers you could fall a hundred feet down a hole and go chuting through an underground stream, they'll find you in sixty million years and wonder what the hell you're supposed to be."

The surface was wet and slippery, but surprisingly soft. My feet made the same sort of shallow footprint as they did in damp beach sand. Almost immediately, I felt the cold through the soles of my shoes. And up my legs. I wasn't dressed for this.

"Go out a hundred yards in that direction," Cal said, waving towards the horizon. "I'll do the same over here. Then we'll circle the plane. Don't let it out of your sight. He can't have gone very far."

He hollered again for Toby. I hollered as well. There was nothing here to send back echoes. Our voices were absorbed in silence.

It was not as bad as Cal had suggested. The surface was ribbed with long curved wind-rows, like the sand in the bay at low tide. I might have been walking across the ridged white surface of a frozen dome, spanning many acres. I found no holes, no sudden wells. Still, I kept my eyes on the surface ahead, and took every step with care.

He may have disappeared, like those Indian women and children who were supposed to have been taken to Forbidden Plateau out of the way of invading northern tribes. He would become a part of legend. He'd slipped down into some underground stream. He'd gone over some cliff that waited ahead for me to go over as well. He'd been mauled and eaten by some monstrous polar bear come south from Bering Strait. Waiting somewhere for me.

The dark figure ahead – twenty, twenty-five vertical feet of black jagged stone – may have been the tilted hull of some old ship, a stony prow slicing up from beneath the ice. Marooned long ago by the Flood, it might have been just surfacing now, or slipping under. Easing myself around to the backside, I held to a jagged corner against the pull of a sharp downhill slant. Here was a crater the size you might see where a large cedar stump had been pulled from the ground.

"Aw, shit," Toby said, and looked away. He sat cradled in the rounded bottom of the hole. One eye was swollen, crusted probably with blood. Dark streaks ran down his face.

"This wasn't my idea," I said.

"You just happened to be in the neighbourhood."

"I just happened to be called by Cal. He figures you're crazy." Moonlight glinted off a wad of ice in one ear. There was white ice caked in the hollow of his throat. "What are you doing here?"

"Lost my footing and fell – what does it look like?" He said this as though I were an idiot not to have figured it out.

268

"I mean up here at all."

He shrugged. "I must be frost-bit from my ass right up to my neck. I tried to crawl out myself but the pain in this arm's so bad I think I passed out. Must've broke the sonofabitch when I fell." Toby could never believe that anyone was genuinely mad at him, which may be why no one stayed mad at him for long.

I moved around to the far side of the hole, and sat on my heels. The smell of Scotch was so strong I turned away. "Sheeee!"

"Broke the bottle," Toby said. "My clothes are soaked."

At least he'd put on a tuque and quilted winter jacket before flying up here. Even drunk, he'd had that much sense. I wished Cal had warned me in advance how cold it would be.

White flesh gleamed through a tear in his pant leg. When I moved the flashlight beam up the black stone wall behind him, I found a fragment of cloth snagged on a jagged wedge. A triangular piece of his wedding suit.

"You were up on the top of that?"

He kept his face turned away. "You getting me out of here or not?"

"You're lucky you weren't killed." I moved the pale circle of light over the rock, though it was impossible to know what was frozen blood and what was only ice.

"God damn you," he said.

He wasn't just swearing, he meant this as a genuine curse. I understood. "She never loved anybody but you," I said. "God knows why."

He looked at me quickly, then away. He knew resentment when he heard it. His breathing was heavy, noisy, as though the inside of his nose was swollen.

Wanting to get on with this, I offered my arm. "Grab hold."

"This place is a bloody disappointment," Toby said,

ignoring my arm and knocking a fist against the ice. "I figured it'd be high enough but it isn't. There isn't any high enough – not here."

It was high enough for me. To lose my grip on the ice would be to fall out of this world. Here was the feeling again that I'd had all summer, the paratrooper about to step out into air. Below us – past the stony prow and the field of ice – light from the lopsided moon threw the entire flattened-out shelf of populated land into spooky relief, and you could see the dark ragged coastline from the town running up past the scattered Macken farms towards Toby's shack. A colourless map, splashed with lakes and etched with creeks and spiked with stands of timber. Down-Island a lighthouse flashed, and flashed again. All of this, everything laid out below us along the base of Forbidden Plateau, was the entire extent of my world. The only world I knew well enough to love. Across the Strait and far to the south, unseen beneath the pale pink glow in the sky, was the city I would be moving to at the end of summer. And all the rest of the world beyond it.

"Move your light over here," Toby said.

At first I thought the butterfly was on the surface, just now alighted and weighted with moisture. But looking closer, I saw that it was suspended, a tiny, half-opened fan, just beneath the surface of ice. A pressed poppy bloom.

I bent closer. Orange, and maybe brown. You had to wonder how it had got here, how long it had been here in its transparent coffin. Was it working its way towards air, or would it one day be buried even deeper than it was now?

"That'd be me if you'd taken another hour to get here," Toby said. He laughed. A cruel laugh, I thought. I couldn't tell whether he meant that I'd come too soon or that I'd almost come too late.

I felt a rush of cruelty myself. "It could still be you," I said.

270

"We haven't got you out of here yet." I gouged a hole with one heel and then the other and braced my feet while Toby grabbed my hand and attempted to hoist his weight.

"Can't!" His hand slipped free.

I leaned closer and moved my hand up his forearm to grip behind his elbow. He clamped his hand behind mine. This time, though he shouted in pain, he managed to get to his feet. "*Careful!* That hurts! Let go!"

"I won't let go!" I yelled. "Keep coming!"

"*Let go!* You goddam stupid –"

"Go to hell then!" I released my grip, letting him fall back against the opposite wall of the crater. "I didn't ask for this."

"I sure as blazes didn't ask for you, either!" He sat back on the ice, panting, glaring at me out of his one good eye. Somewhere far away, Cal was calling. Toby said, "So why don't you leave?" Mocking, I thought. He knew I couldn't.

"You'd like that!"

"I might."

"Then you'd have someone to blame!"

He wouldn't look at me. "What do you care who I blame?"

"You could sit here thinking you're some tragic figure. The first person in history ever had something bad happen to them."

"Just bugger off, willya! Don't start lecturing me or I'll drag you down here and kick your head in."

If I'd laughed he would have laughed too, and then it would be over. But tears had come to my eyes – already freezing along the lower lids. Muscles in my throat had tightened. "Maybe it's about time you bloody-well grew up!"

He looked at me now, probably surprised by the childish break in my voice. Then he closed his mouth against whatever he was about to say.

Cal yelled again in the distance. Not just "Macken" now,

but "Rusty" too. Cursing as well. He thought he'd lost us both.

Toby shouted, "Over here!"

"You ready to try again?" I said.

Toby knocked my hand away. "I'll wait. Maybe Cal can haul me out of here without wrenching my arm from its socket, or splashing my brains all over the bloody snow."

16

By the time we were free to drive north from the hospital the sun had risen high above the mainland mountain peaks – another cloudless day. Sven Dahlberg's cattle were filing out of his barn and plunging through barnyard muck. Uncle Dennis hoed beans in his garden. There was no sign of the family car in our yard but I honked anyway, in case Gerry had come home in the night thinking the funeral was over.

For most of the way, Toby leaned his head against the window and said nothing. This was fine with me. I didn't need to hear any more of his voice. Once in a while he fingered the white dressing that covered part of the sunset-coloured swelling above one eye. It wasn't until we were approaching his shack that he had anything to say – a growl. "I'll just crawl into bed and conk out. I'm dead."

"Not until you've given me back my clothes."

He was wearing my jeans turned up at the ankles, and my tartan shirt with one sleeve hanging empty over the cast on his arm, in its sling. One pocket bulged with his makings. He seemed shrunken, somehow, inside them. The hospital had offered to burn his torn and smelly clothing, everything but Cal's winter jacket and Toby's shoes. Though we'd beaten out most of the sand from my clothes they were still a little damp. He wasn't likely to grow possessive.

The hotel was almost as much surprise to me as it was to him. With all we'd been through in the night I'd forgotten what I'd left behind. When I slowed to approach Toby's gate, he hissed between his teeth like a tire leaking air, and eventually found his word: "Sonofabitch." Annoyed or disbelieving – I couldn't tell which.

The little hotel had been completely rebuilt against Toby's shack, which stood where the dining-room wing had once been. The new verandah across the hotel's front entrance extended across the front of Toby's shack as well, tying it all together. Siding had been painted green, window shutters white. On either side of the wide front door were narrow stained-glass windows, amber and green. Windowboxes were filled with red geraniums outside each upstairs room. On the roof, Uncle Martin and Shorty Madill still had a few last shakes to nail. My mother and Kitty painted verandah posts in the yellow morning light, their hair wrapped up in Aunt Jemima rags.

"You knew about this?" Toby's face had coloured up with marbled patches of red.

I grinned despite myself. As though some sort of joke had been played. "Shoemaker's elves – caught in the act." This was the little hotel we'd played in long ago, resurrected out of memory and gleaming with new paint! It wasn't hard to imagine the tangle of roses growing over it again, or even to remember their scent.

When he saw I was about to turn in at the gate, he shouted, "Keep driving, for chrissake! I'm not going in." And grabbed at the steering wheel.

He steered us into a leaning gatepost, so loose that it toppled to the ground. When I'd yanked the wheel free, I

274

made the decision for us – accelerated down the potholed drive. Toby cursed, and opened his door as though he would jump and run.

He might have run when we'd come to a stop in front of the hotel, if we hadn't been immediately surrounded by family. Someone must have seen us coming and set up a cry. People poured out through the new front door.

Uncle Buddy leaned in and took hold of Toby's good arm. "Come on out of there. Goodness gracious, let's get a look at you!"

Toby threw me a murderous scowl before he got out. He wouldn't forgive me soon.

"What's he got to say about our long night's work?" Aunt Edna shouted. Her eyes were a little wild, her face too pink. "It damn-well better be good!" Puffed-up and belligerent with booze, she would think of herself as a "character."

Faces could not have looked more pleased with themselves. Or with the returning Toby. Though Edna may not have been the only one into the sauce, the rest were giddy with their success, and ready for more. When Toby stepped out of my car the noise that greeted him might have been meant for a conquering hero. The fact that he had come back alive was enough for them to assume he'd come back triumphant.

But Toby did not immediately have something to say. Hissing again in his teeth, he studied this building that stood where nothing had stood before but a tilted stove in weeds.

"He's stunned," said Uncle Reg. He meant he hoped so. Reg looked like a child so pleased with himself he could only grin. His blue silk cowboy shirt was stained with patches of sweat.

"He's wondering if he's Rip Van Winkle," cried Mrs. Latour, coming down the shack's porch step with both hands clamped to her heaving breasts, purse swinging from her arm. "Slept through years while everything changed!"

She'd probably slept through most of it herself. She dropped her jaw and waited for someone to fill her in.

No one did. Edna jabbed an elbow into Em. Both snorted, and clapped hands to their mouths. Kitty said, "Shush! He's got to let it sink in!"

There was silence while Toby let it sink in. Eyes watched his face for signs of appreciation. Some made a show of biting their bottom lips.

Toby shook his head like someone who couldn't believe his eyes. He planted his feet apart. Whatever else he said, there was only one way he could start. Anyone here except Buddy could have said it for him. "Jesus Christ!" he said. "Some people just don't know when to quit!"

This met with a roar of approval. Not knowing when to quit was what they were proudest of.

"We figured you don't have enough to do," Avery said, bugging out his eyes. "You can nursemaid weary travellers in your spare time!"

"Think of the parties you can throw!" shouted Uncle Martin, climbing down the ladder from the roof.

Toby glanced at me, and away. What did he think I ought to be doing? He was too tired, he probably didn't know if he could handle this. Yet he shook his head, and tried to look pleased, ready to give them more of what they wanted.

"A bunch of bloody thieves here too," he said. "Which beer parlour did you steal the windows from?"

"Nobody's!" Buddy was proud to answer. "Found them out behind that little Comox church – they're doing renovations."

"Ask us where we found the curtains," Edna said.

Toby removed his makings from my pocket and laid them out on the Meteor's hood. "What makes you think I won't open a gambling casino here and turn you away at the door? Or a cathouse for the rich and famous." With his free hand he tapped shreds of tobacco into the sharp fold of paper in his other palm.

"Because you wouldn't dare," my mother called from the verandah. "We'd take it down again one board at a time and make you eat it. Leave you with less than what you had before!"

Someone had used binder twine to attach the old rosebushes to the newly painted posts.

"You probably thought we were home in our beds and snoring," Kitty said. Not enough praise had been heard.

"Busy beavers!" Toby shouted, keeping his eyes on what he was trying to do with his hands. "Whipping up a goddam miracle here."

Grace's voice was the first that wasn't loud. "We didn't think nothing of it at first, but then we went and got carried away. We did it for Glory."

"Yes," someone murmured. Silence fell. Eyes watched Toby. Faces got ready to look sad. The morning smell of kelp and tide-washed rocks came in on the breeze, and the metallic scent of dry sand. Glory's narrow tea towel still flapped and twisted on her clothesline, along with a dozen others.

"Yeah," Toby said. His eyes could find nowhere to settle. "I figured." He was trapped in this silent crowd. More came outside every minute that he stood here. Voices were quickly hushed. He looked down at the cigarette he was trying to roll. His hand trembled. He wiped the back of it across his jaw.

"Glory loved that old hotel," Reg said.

Grace added, "We didn't do nothin' here she wouldn't've liked."

"Who's this we?" said Edna, between clenched teeth. "Grace spent most of the night on that tablecloth!" She laughed. Others laughed as well. Grace, who was pulling a needle through the cloth even now, did a few dainty dance steps on her sturdy legs and stuck out her tongue.

Toby put a hand to his forehead. Then he looked at his fingers. Did he think he was bleeding again? It was sweat. He wiped it off on his sleeve, my sleeve, and looked around like someone needing escape.

My mother stepped down from the verandah to rescue him, still holding her paintbrush. "What we want to know is what you've been up to all night long."

Reg said, "Building a little hotel's not going to look like much beside it, I'll bet."

"I'm waiting to hear what happened to that arm," said Uncle Avery.

Toby's gaze darted to me. I didn't know what that meant, it could have meant anything – hatred.

"Just try not telling us!" Kitty cried. "What do you think we've been waiting for?"

Toby's fine ginger hair was damp, his eyes inflamed. His hands were so shaky that shreds of tobacco dropped to the ground as he carried the half-made cigarette through the crowd towards me. "Give me your keys, willya. I've got to get out of here."

"Where to? Where is there left to go?"

He flung the tobacco and paper aside. "Come on, kid, give me the goddam keys!"

"I'll drive you somewhere then, let's go."

I thought for a moment that he intended to hit me, but he turned away. "To hell with it. I'm going to bed." He raised his voice for the others: "Party's over! Go home and let this useless bastard get some sleep."

Em Madill was outraged. "We're not going to let you talk like that! You're spoiling it!"

"Spoiling what?" Toby said. "What's left that I haven't spoiled?"

As he started across the scythed and tidied yellow grass

278

towards his shack, I caught up and walked beside him. He was shivering like someone caught in a polar wind. Hugging himself. He paused for a moment, and bent over with his hand against a tree trunk, and made vomiting noises. His stomach heaved, but nothing came. It was a terrible thing to see — Toby's face gone red and ugly, his bottom lip stretched wide. He wiped a sleeve across his mouth and tried to keep his face turned away. But there were relatives everywhere.

He waved me away, waved everyone away, and stood up to walk unsteadily towards the door of his shack. "Anybody in there better get out, the model husband's returning to his bed."

Once he'd slammed the door there was silence. Uneasy glances were exchanged. The first words after that weren't loud.

"Did he have to go and snap at us like that?" This was Helen, sounding hurt.

Kitty tossed her curls. "Rusty won't fill us in, I can tell by the look on his face. I'm going to decide that Toby was just around that corner all night, watching us."

"Cops did it," Uncle Martin said.

Buddy placed a hand on his heart. "The arm?"

"He made fools of them at the bridge is why," said Uncle Martin. "I hate them Mounties. Provincials used to *know* us!"

My mother came up to stand beside me. "I guess we should've killed the fatted calf." She swiped the brush back and forth in front of my face to show that she'd be glad to paint it.

I snatched at the brush to let her know I'd be glad to return the favour. She yelped and ducked away, holding the brush as far out of reach as she could. I grabbed her arm to wrestle for it. "Help! Help!" she cried, a movie heroine. "Would you do a thing like that to your poor old mom?"

I would and did — just a dab of white to her nose once I'd wrenched the brush free. Then wiped it off myself with a finger.

"Look at that," I said. "What a mess. Soon we won't be able to take you anywhere." Then I returned the brush.

"Carousing?" my mother said, as I started away. "Hiding down the road to avoid a little work?" Whether she meant me or Toby she didn't say. I didn't answer. "What turned you into such a grouch since we saw you last?"

"Nothing," I said, though of course something had. I could have bitten off heads.

"I know why you're cranky," she said. She waited a moment, in case I wanted to be told. "You could hardly wait to get away from us – and now *this*!"

"This what?" I turned to see what she meant.

She used the paintbrush to indicate something – maybe the hotel, or maybe the people inside still building it. "You've seen how much fun you'll miss."

"Ha!" was the best I could do. Of course she could have been right, as usual. This sort of thing would still go on while I stuffed my brain for exams on photosynthesis.

When she'd gone back to her verandah posts and most of the others had gone inside, I sat on the ground against the thick rough bark of a fir, and pulled up my knees so that I could rest my forehead on them. My father crouched on his heels beside me. "What's Toby doing in your clothes?" He was ready to be amused by any answer.

"Hospital's burning his," I said, and pinched my nose to show what I meant. "High!"

My dad laughed. "And the cast?"

"We found him up on the glacier, broke his arm."

He gave me a suspicious sideways look, in case I'd like to reconsider.

"He decided he had to dance on the top of the world. It took Cal's plane and a lot of talk to get him down. Somebody should be with him in there now," I said. "He's not in very good shape."

"Don't worry, the women'll keep an eye on him." My father grinned the sort of grin that acknowledged the world was still as crazy as he'd thought. "If you weren't already itching to hightail it out of here, I guess Toby's done it for sure."

"I guess so."

He raised his eyebrows – he'd expected more enthusiasm than this. "I wouldn't move to a city for a million bucks myself, but that's what you wanted, isn't it?" He put a hand on the tree to shift weight so he could lower himself to the ground. "I could've swore you took that scholarship so you'd get out without a fuss, then turn around and become another Whatsisname, DeMille. You won't make any movies staying here, I'll tell you that for sure."

A pain shot up my chest, a long hot wire up through my jaw and skull. The useless Bell & Howell hadn't been in my jacket pocket when I'd got Toby my clothes from the trunk. It had probably fallen out in the hull, while I lay on my stupid back in the tide. Buried in sand by now, with all the disappeared treasures off the sailing ship. Yet I'd felt no real dismay at its loss. Somehow it didn't matter.

Somewhere along the way I'd stopped believing. When I thought I was lying to Glory – only pretending that I'd lost interest – I hadn't really been lying to her at all. "It was never going to happen, you knew that. The others played along, they even encouraged me, but they never really believed it either."

"You sure of that?"

"What they really think is that I'll come home and work at Toby's mill for ever, and pretend that I *might* have gone off to make movies if something hadn't stopped me. Just waiting for me to smarten up – one more stupid dreamer amongst millions, most of them under twelve."

He frowned his Gary Cooper frown at me for a moment, then looked away, considering what I'd said. "What have you been talking about for years, then? What else have you been reading about, with your nose always stuck in a book?"

"Photoplays? *The Book of Knowledge*? Our set is dated 1946! What do I know about anything?" I hadn't thought of this before. My own voice said these things aloud, telling me what I knew. "If I mentioned this to anyone over there, they'd laugh in my face."

I was making this up. The truth was, I couldn't see myself doing what I had always wanted to do, it was as simple as that. I still wanted it but I could no longer *imagine* it, as I once had done. And that, it seemed to me, was something I couldn't ignore.

My father frowned in the direction of the hotel. "Well, I guess you've gone and finally run up against the facts of your life," he said. "The fun will be to see what you can do with them." He looked at me aslant from beneath the brim of his hat, daring me to say, *It isn't fair.* "Anybody raised around *this* bunch shouldn't find it hard to throw a simple movie together."

He couldn't help but see people as slightly absurd, including himself. You could count on him to keep you aware of how human you were. Who else had taught me to notice when I was getting above myself? That it had taken so long in this case was not his fault.

"Too bad your old man's not some filthy-rich lawyer in Montreal," he said. "Or better still, in a country where they do the kinds of things you care about. Instead you got stuck with us – bush monkeys grubbing for a living on this island. You'll have to made do with what you got, like the rest of us."

"Looking after seedlings for the Forest Service?"

He shrugged. "Who knows what you'll find out about yourself over there. Don't go making decisions when you're upset." He put a hand on my shoulder to help himself get to his feet.

"Only a damn fool tells his horse to stop when his wheels are still deep in the muck."

What was he saying? Was the one who'd tried hardest to keep my feet on the ground now saying I'd heard him wrong? If so, he may have left it too late. The doubt was already loose, encouraging the same imagination that had fed the dream to turn against me now. Anyone who could conjure movie plots could devise elaborately detailed scenes of his own humiliation. I could sense them coming. Only a small step led from the imagined laughter of city-raised fellow students to the public disgrace of a failed movie, with thousands of dollars wasted, critics howling at flaws I wasn't smart enough to have seen, the movie world turning its back in scorn when I'd barely started. The wonder was that I hadn't thought of this before.

"Foot's gone to sleep," my father said, and stomped it back to life. "You coming inside for a look? It's a long way from being finished but it's starting to look pretty good."

Maybe he knew what the empty upstairs rooms had meant to me once. Had I really believed that I'd been conceived in every one of those rooms, that as many versions of myself were waiting to be discovered? I suppose I believed it still. So long as I put off submitting to a single fate I could hope for many, or for one that included the rest. It seemed that growing up would mean this would have to stop.

My father may not have thought so. At any rate, he thought seeing those reconstructed rooms would have some meaning for me. But before we got inside, a pickup turned in at the gate and rattled down the drive, a black 1940 Ford with its spare wheel mounted on the side and a chrome stripe down its pointed nose. Two old men stood in the back, leaning against an upright piano. One of them was Stokes.

When it pulled up by the hotel's front door, several people came out to meet it. Two old men got out of the cab – Howie

Twist and Sandy Roberts, both hunch-shouldered and bearded. The man in the back with Stokes was someone I didn't know. Maybe the Prince of Wales, or whatever he called himself now.

"How could four old guys get a piano onto a truck?" I said.

My dad shook his head. "Same way kids get cookstoves onto wagons, I guess."

Twenty, twenty-five, thirty Mackens gathered outside to watch this in silence. Maybe they were wondering if they should put a stop to it. Nora would.

But Nora was not amongst them. Either she was still asleep inside or someone had driven her home. Some of the men moved in and looked as though they would slide the piano off the truck. Uncle Reg. Uncle Avery. Mr. Korhonen. Colin unhooked the tailgate and let it drop open. But this was not what the old men had in mind. Sandy Roberts waved his hands as though to send everyone back. "Don't stop! We heard what was going on here – brought you some music for while you work!" Stokes sat on the piano bench. The second man lifted the lid from the keys and stood by. Sandy Roberts and Howie Twist rested their arms along the side of the box.

A few chords announced Stokes's intention. Then a run up the scale and back. A single clear note was struck repeatedly, as though he were listening hard for a sound within the sound. My mother and Kitty went back to slapping their brushes up and down the verandah of the hotel. Somewhere inside, hammering started again.

At first I couldn't tell what he played in the bed of that truck. Something clear and light, something that sounded like a single plaintive voice busy at narrative. A simple pretty melody sailed forward a while, then suddenly turned back on itself and became something else more frightening and complex before breaking free to soar again. It raised gooseflesh along my arms. He'd lifted this from the air: the song of wind in the rotting hull.

"Smoke," my father said. He said it as though its implica-
tion hadn't hit him yet – he was only naming what he saw.
Smoke leaked out through the opened window of Glory's
bedroom. Pale grey shreds of it streamed from the window, followed by darker billows that twisted up through the boughs of
a Douglas fir. Above the porch, Toby rested his elbows on the
railing of the new widow's walk, studying the two old men on
the back of the truck.

Of course they forgave him for it, once they'd beaten out the
flames and soaked down the bedroom with pots of water
from the kitchen tap. Furniture was scorched, walls charred,
blankets fell apart in ashy flakes. But the flames hadn't spread
far, and the smoke had done little damage to other parts of
the shack.

Still, if it had been ignored the fire would have burned down
everything they'd done in the night. Kitty stomped one cowgirl
boot in the debris and clenched a fist. "Shoot me if you want
but now I'm going to say it. He's finally made me mad."

"Couldn't stand seeing what we done here," Buddy said. "He
should've done it himself, long ago – he knows it."

"Well, I guess he had to give it a *try*." Helen exhaled loudly.
"Maybe now he can settle."

They were certain this hadn't been a hostile gesture. I wasn't
so sure, but they didn't want to hear. Neither did they want
my help. "You're in the way – go on, we've got everything under
control." So I climbed the spiral staircase to lean on the railing
with Toby, who seemed unaware of the commotion he'd caused.
He was still watching the men on the truck.

"You'd think the old bugger would've slit his own throat years
ago, wouldn't you," he said, "having to live his whole life
knowing what he did."

I watched Stokes sway over the keyboard. The same simple phrase had taken on added colour, more complication. He was improvising with it, playing around.

"But he didn't," I said.

"Playing a damn piano on the back of a truck. Maybe you have to be a little crazy to stand the things that happen."

"He doesn't look so crazy to me," I said. "No more than some others I could name."

He didn't look at me. He said this off towards the cars parked in the old golf-course grass. "I guess I give you a pretty hard time, don't I?" He was still wearing my clothes. He'd probably decided to keep them on to annoy me.

"I'll be out of here pretty soon anyway," I said. "You'll have to find someone else to chase you over glaciers."

"You think so, eh. We'll just see how far you get. You think I never tried?"

"Not hard enough, you didn't. You shouldn't have brought her here – not to stay."

He didn't respond right away. He shifted his weight from one foot to the other and drove fingers through his wild hair. "I didn't mean to stay. You don't need to think you're the only one with plans."

"What plans did you ever have?"

"Always wanted to be one of those road builders. I never told anyone this. An engineer. I couldn't go to college but I got myself into the vocational school over there, even started some courses. I was pretty good at them too, for a week."

"So why didn't you stay?"

"Whaddaya think? We come over here, for Glory to meet the family. Once I got here I couldn't see myself going back to school."

Kitty came out into the yard. Buddy came out as well, and my father and Reg and Uncle Martin. Their faces were smudged, and their clothes were decorated with long black streaks where they'd wiped their hands. Kitty shaded her eyes and looked up towards us. "We've taken a vote and decided to quit," she said.

"We'll finish the hotel some other day," Martin said. "Right now we need some sleep. You can clean up the rest of this mess by yourself."

"Nobody's going anywhere!" Edna yelled. She and Em Madill had come out of the old livery stable and were crossing the grass towards us, dragging something – rope.

"What have you got there?" Kitty said. "Grace?"

Grace had come out of the shed a little behind the others, rolling her tablecloth around what looked like the handle from a rake or old hoe. Mrs. Latour came last, her Ma Kettle hair-knot undone, her purse slapping against her thigh. She looked uncertain about what was going on but didn't want to miss it.

"We're not going any-bloody-where until we've raised a flag!" Edna said. It was Toby's climbing belt she had over one shoulder, with the rope attached. Em carried his spurs.

"What flag?" Toby said, though of course we could see what was coming. Grace stepped up and showed it off: her tablecloth unfurled from the rake handle. The pale green cloth was patterned with dark twisting vines – white flowers with red-green leaves. Loops of string down the length of one side attached it to the handle, whose tapered end was the colour of rust.

"Get out of here with that," Toby shouted down. "We don't need no flag, this isn't a goddam courthouse."

"We're not going until it's up," Edna said. She stood firm, or tried to, with her hands on her hips, but tilted a little into Mrs. Latour's thick shoulder.

"I was making it for your kitchen table," Grace explained, "but these two lushes talked me into letting them fly it. Just for a while."

"Edna's doing the climbing," Em announced, rolling her eyes for Edna's sake. Both of them laughed. Mrs. Latour put her hands to either side of her face, apparently horrified.

"The hell she is," Toby said. "You put that back where it come from."

"Edna's not going anywhere but to bed," Martin said. He tried to remove the climbing belt and rope from her shoulder but she moved back a step and cursed him.

"Maybe Toby would like to do it himself," Kitty said, taking the rake handle from Grace and offering it up to Toby.

Toby shook his head. "Forget it."

Edna's smile was cruel. "Let Rusty do it, then." She tossed the gear to the ground. She was still chewing on that Juicy Fruit.

"Not me," I said. "I don't climb."

"He *jumps*," Em said. She seemed to think we should find this hilarious. "Where's his jumping pole?"

"Sure you do," Martin said. "You've done it."

It was true that I'd once asked Toby to show me how to climb the pole. He'd strapped me into his climbing gear and let me work my way up. It had taken me most of an hour to get to the top, almost as long to get down. Once I'd been up and down a dozen times I was only beginning to get the hang of it.

"Start from the roof and you're halfway there already," said Uncle Martin. The pole was only a couple of feet from the gable end of the hotel.

"Let's not lose our heads here now," my father said. "Rusty hasn't had any more sleep than Toby has, or the rest of us. Just nail the flag to the roof. Hang it on the clothesline's good enough. Let's go home!"

Martin went into the shack and came back with a clawhammer and a pair of two-inch nails.

"We can't let Toby do this," Buddy said. "He'll break his

goldarn neck." His tongue flickered across his lips. "If Toby goes up in the condition he's in, we might as well call the hearse."

"Toss them up," I said. Kitty handed up the rake handle, which I jammed inside the back of my shirt and down through my belt. Martin lifted the rope and climbing belt from the grass, and took the spurs from Em, and brought them up the steps. He squeezed my arm, but not as hard as usual. Had I passed some kind of test? I pocketed the nails, hung the clawhammer through a belt loop, slung the gear across my shoulders, and started up the slope towards Toby, who'd gone ahead to sit on the peak.

"Just nail the damn thing to the ridgepole," my father said. When I looked back, he'd come up the stairs to stand by Uncle Martin. "If you haven't slept you got no business even thinking about anything else."

Why not? I'd tried drowning. At least I'd imagined what it would be like to drown. I might as well try climbing air. It was not too late to salute what had happened here tonight. Whatever it was that I felt – admiration, love, regret that I was sending myself into exile – it should be enough to drive me up that pole. Even to dance, if necessary, on the top.

My father was capable of stopping me, even by force. He would not mind looking foolish if it meant saving one of his children from his own stupidity. Anybody smart enough to go to university ought to have the brains not to risk his own neck, he would say. If we can't trust you not to do idiotic things at home, how can we trust you not to do worse in the city?

It was part of who Eddie Macken was, to put wife and children before pride or anyone else's idea of what ought to be done. It wasn't easy having a father who was the most sensible man in a crowd. But he knew what I was asking of him: even Eddie Macken would have to let go. For a moment we eyed one another across that space between us. Macken faces

289

looked at one another – same nose, same ears. There was no cascade of falling bricks between us this time but there was something else more damaging: years in which I'd been watching the wrong man for my cues. I saw it now – this late.

Below, Stokes sat back from the piano with his hands in his lap. My mother stood amongst the growing crowd, looking up. She'd removed the Aunt Jemima kerchief from her head. "What are you thinking?" she called. Even at this distance she could guess your thoughts. "Come down and we'll get you some breakfast."

Toby went up the wooden extension ladder to the hotel roof, and stood holding the top of it steady with his one good hand while I climbed. Then I followed him at an angle up the low-pitch slope, his cast-arm oaring like a broken wing ahead of me as he headed for the end nearest the pole.

I didn't have to look down to know that some Macken faces would be grinning but most would not. Rusty Macken didn't do this sort of thing. Rusty was not another Toby. Without a vaulting pole in his hands, he kept his feet on the ground. People who'd looked with amazement and joy at Toby's dancing would be looking at me with dismay. They expected to see me fall into the pattern of their belief: Rusty was never much good with his hands, he turned out to be worse with his feet.

Broken bones were not the worst that could happen. Not even a track-meet sawdust pit or landing pad could have helped me here. Falls of this nature could result in paralysis. Was that too high a price to pay? It depended on what the price you were paying was for.

For being born. That is, for being born a Macken. Who had ever escaped? Gordie, maybe – but who knew how? Uncle Curtis had gained some distance but had hardly broken free. Even those who'd moved down-Island came home every chance they could. Gerry might have been getting ready for flight but could just as easily be practising up for centre stage. If Toby could be said to have survived, it had been only through fancy footwork that he'd done it, dancing in high narrow places. He had never dared to stand still, or remain on the earth like the others.

Somehow my father had survived on his own terms, or at least on terms he had made his own. But by keeping my eye on Toby's precarious dance, I'd failed to notice how he'd done it. I'd been looking in the wrong direction all my life. At seventeen, I hoped it was not too late.

Toby sat on the ridge with his feet apart while he rolled a cigarette. His hands were steadier now. "Just put 'er down, you'll only break your neck if you go up there."

I sat beside him, and draped the gear over the peak. "I can't go back without doing it."

"Who says?"

"Look at them. They want their flag on that pole."

My mother's expression was grim. Even from this height I could see the set to her jaw. My father had gone down to stand beside her. Frieda Macken, Eddie, trusting in something – I didn't know what.

"They'll get their flag," Toby said. "I'll do 'er in a minute."

"No you won't. You're lopsided and full of pills. They'd kill me if I let you."

"I can't fall," he said. "When I'm up there I just imagine that if I ever started to fall I'd only fly!"

Could Toby not imagine failing even now? For the first time since I'd joined him I met his gaze. There was something different in his eyes. He held them too steady on mine, like someone waiting for you to guess what they'd never say for themselves. This was not like Toby at all. But I may have been the only one here who knew how hard he had to work at being Toby, how ashamed he was that he'd fallen short. The

291

only one – he knew this – who might be tempted any minute now to pity him. I'd seen this sort of look in Gordie's eyes, when older boys were tormenting him – when he was frantic for your help but just as frantically wishing you hadn't been there to see.

Maybe Toby was afraid of missing one more chance in the spotlight. Maybe he was scared I might like it up there or even make a success of it and decide to follow in his footsteps. I doubted he was thinking clearly enough for that. Judging by what I saw in his eyes, he might have caught me trying to steal.

"Anyway." I said the obvious. Why hadn't he thought of this himself? "You need two good arms to climb."

Toby put the cigarette between his lips and stood, then flung the climbing belt out off the edge of the roof. The rope snaked like a living tail behind it. He tossed the spurs down as well, to plough up the grass. "Go bring me the ladder."

When I hesitated, he shouted. "Go bring up the ladder, dammit!"

I crab-walked down the hotel roof to the eave and dragged up the extension ladder, then carried it up to Toby, who directed me to rest it against the pole. One leg on either side of the ridge. By pulling the cord I was able to raise the last rung to almost the top of the pole.

He shouldered me aside and put one foot on the bottom rung to test it. He raised the second foot. Then, with the rake-handle shoved down inside the back of my loose shirt and Grace's tablecloth flapping behind his head, he went up, using just the one hand, while I kept the legs in place with my weight. When his shoes had risen to eye level I stopped him while I turned another roll on the cuffs of my jeans, which were hanging over his heels.

At the top rung, where he was meant to nail the rake-handle in place, he hesitated only a moment before climbing awkwardly up to sit on the top of the pole, letting his legs dangle free. He grinned. Something had been accomplished. For a moment he raised a bare fist over his head. Then he removed their tablecloth-flag from behind his neck and held it aloft by the rake-handle's rusted end. You couldn't tell if he would nail the flag in place, or if he intended only to catch his breath before standing up to dance, but you could see that he was claiming this one high narrow place in the world as his own.

"What can you see?" voices below shouted up.

Toby didn't answer. The tablecloth slapped and fell limp, and then fluttered again.

What did he see up there? People had always asked this when Toby was up a pole. What did that crazy man see? This time I could see for myself, from the roof. Across the Strait the mountains were watery pale beneath the risen sun. Glory's mainland. Over there was something that had never released its grip on her heart, a secret. (Something that waited for me.) Maybe Toby, from the tops of poles, had tried to see what it was. Perhaps thinking he might see it by rising higher was what had made it possible to lift his feet and dance.

I may have begun to understand what Toby's dancing had meant. What else did dancing ever mean? A powerful instinctive desire to take off – to leave this world – was locked in conflict with an instinct to keep to the earth. He had performed a desperate balancing act all his life. What looked from the ground like a dance was really a battle. The wonder was that he was still alive.

What any of this suggested for me I didn't know. That I was leaving in the nick of time? That I was a fool to leave at all? I didn't know yet what it suggested but I would find out soon enough, I supposed, once this summer was behind us and I'd taken that first brave step into air.

This would have to be a helicopter shot, this ending. The camera would rise above Toby's renovated shack, above the hotel with the giant woodstove at its centre and its empty upstairs rooms, above the man on the pole, even above the firs. Like the ending of *Picnic*. We would see crowds of Mackens looking up from the old golf course, and younger Mackens waking up amongst driftwood along the beach, Caro and Sonny crawling out from behind a wall of logs, and cars still parked on the grass – my '50 Meteor ready to leave. Rising higher, we would see down the curving coastline, fold after fold of soft blue peninsulas and furry slopes of trees and crawling grey waves, and of course the long dark ribbon of highway leading away from the hotel site, down through the creek-veined stumpy district of our childhoods and the little town beneath the enduring glacier, and down along the coastline leading south eventually to the steamship terminal and out into the world.

OTHER TITLES FROM
DOUGLAS GIBSON BOOKS

PUBLISHED BY McCLELLAND & STEWART INC.

A PASSION FOR NARRATIVE: A Guide for Writing Fiction *by* Jack Hodgins
"One excellent path from original to marketable manuscript. . . . It would take
a beginning writer years to work her way through all the goodies Hodgins
offers." *Globe and Mail*
                Non-fiction/Writing guide, 5¼ × 8½, 216 pages, trade paperback

OVER FORTY IN BROKEN HILL: Unusual Encounters in the Australian
Outback *by* Jack Hodgins
"Australia described with wit, wonder and affection by a bemused visitor
with Canadian sensibilities." *Canadian Press* "Damned fine writing." *Books
in Canada*   *Travel, 5½ × 8½, 216 pages, trade paperback*

THE HONORARY PATRON: A novel *by* Jack Hodgins
The Governor General's Award-winner's thoughtful and satisfying third
novel of a celebrity's return home to Vancouver Island mixes comedy and
wisdom "and it's magic." *Ottawa Citizen*
                Fiction, 4¼ × 7, 336 pages, paperback

INNOCENT CITIES: A novel *by* Jack Hodgins
Victorian in time and place, this delightful new novel by the author of *The
Invention of the World* proves once again that "as a writer, Hodgins is unique
among his Canadian contemporaries." *Globe and Mail*
                Fiction, 4¼ × 7, 416 pages, paperback

OPEN SECRETS: Stories *by* Alice Munro
Eight marvellous stories, ranging in time from 1850 to the present and from
Albania to "Alice Munro Country". "There may not be a better collection
of stories until her next one." *Chicago Tribune*
                Fiction, 6 × 9, 304 pages, hardcover

THE CUNNING MAN: A novel *by* Robertson Davies
This "sparkling history of the erudite and amusing Dr. Hullah who knows
the souls of his patients as well as he knows their bodies" *London Free Press*
is "wise, humane and constantly entertaining." *The New York Times*
                Fiction, 6 × 9, 480 pages, hardcover

CONFESSIONS OF AN IGLOO DWELLER *by* James Houston
Building snow houses, eating raw seal meat - the man who brought Inuit
art to the outside world tells about his Arctic adventures between 1948 and
1962, a time when the North changed for ever.
                Non-fiction, 6 × 9, 320 pages, maps, drawings, hardcover

PADDLE TO THE ARCTIC: The Incredible Story of a Kayak Quest Across the Roof of the World *by* Don Starkell
By kayak across frigid waters, dragging a sled over the Arctic ice, Don Starkell (author of *Paddle to the Amazon*) fought his way 3,000 miles through the Northwest Passage in an epic of survival.
Adventure, 6 × 9, 320 pages, maps, photos, hardcover

WHO HAS SEEN THE WIND *by* W.O. Mitchell *illustrated by* William Kurelek
For the first time since 1947, this well-loved Canadian classic of childhood on the prairies is presented in its full, unexpurgated edition, and is "gorgeously illustrated." *Calgary Herald*
Fiction, 8½ × 10, 320 pages, numerous colour and black-and-white illustrations, hardcover

THE BLACK BONSPIEL OF WILLIE MACCRIMMON *by* W.O. Mitchell *illustrated by* Wesley W. Bates
A devil of a good tale about curling – W.O. Mitchell's most successful comic play now appears as a story, fully illustrated, for the first time, and it is "a true Canadian classic." *Western Report*
Fiction, 4⅝ × 7½, 144 pages with 10 wood engravings, hardcover

ACCORDING TO JAKE AND THE KID: A Collection of New Stories *by* W.O. Mitchell
"This one's classic Mitchell. Humorous, gentle, wistful, it's 16 new short stories about life through the eyes of Jake, a farmhand, and the kid, whose mom owns the farm." *Saskatoon Star-Phoenix*
Fiction, 5 × 7¾, 280 pages, trade paperback

ACROSS THE BRIDGE: Stories *by* Mavis Gallant
These eleven stories, set mostly in Montreal or in Paris, were described as "Vintage Gallant – urbane, witty, absorbing." *Winnipeg Free Press* "We come away from it both thoughtful and enriched." *Globe and Mail*
Fiction, 6 × 9, 208 pages, trade paperback

THE ASTOUNDING LONG-LOST LETTERS OF DICKENS OF THE MOUNTED *edited by* Eric Nicol
The "letters" from Charles Dickens's son, a Mountie from 1874 to 1886, are "a glorious hoax . . . so cleverly crafted, so subtly hilarious." *Vancouver Sun*
Fiction, 4¼ × 7, 296 pages, paperback

HUGH MACLENNAN'S BEST: An anthology *selected by* Douglas Gibson
This selection from all of the works of the witty essayist and famous novelist is "wonderful . . . It's refreshing to discover again MacLennan's formative influence on our national character." *Edmonton Journal*
Anthology, 6 × 9, 352 pages, trade paperback